WE GON EAT

This book is a work of fiction. Names, character, places, and incidents are the product of the author's imagination and used fictitiously. Any resemblance to actual person, living or dead,

SO REAL PUBLISHING, INC

Business establishments, event and locales are entirely coincidental.

We Gon Eat is a So Real Publishing book published by arrangement with the author.

Printing   History
First   Printing
11/1/2011

Cover Design and production by Melissa Talbot for Okane media

For information www.sorealproductions.com
Authormikiellos@gmail.com
ISBN: 978-0-9840216-1-1

Printed in the United States of America

Acknowledgements

First and foremost to God, the author, the creator, and the governor of the world I give my loyalty, undying appreciation, and faithfulness. Thank you for blessing my life with tribulation, education through trial, for my successes and my failures, and mostly for blessing me with the gift of verbal art because I am only what the creator allows me to be.

To my family, my So Real Family! Hutch, to the top with this So Real shit! I appreciate your friendship and loyalty, family. To my lil bro, B Riley, bruh I admire the type of man you've become over the years. A great father to my God daughter and a great friend. Stay true to yourself and your craft and the world is gonna keep blessing you. To my guy from the ave, Dave, congratulations on the new store. You're a great man, and now the world is gonna see what I knew long ago. Get that paper, bruh. To Christoper Lindsey and A. Roy Milligan, the newest members of So Real, do yall thang my guys!!

To the ladies of EyeCU!! What up doe?!! You all are a classy bunch of women. A picture of what I'd like to see in my daughter as an adult woman. God blessed the world with the creation of you all!!

To the Queen of Hood Books, Michel Moore, I appreciate all the advice and authentic love even when it was the tough kind! You kept it a hundred from day one and nothing has changed. Much love, mami. And to your question, IT MEANS EVERYTHING TO ME!

And last but not least I wanna dedicate this book to my hood niggaz worldwide who are faced with the penalties for their transgressions! I been there and that's where this shit started so enjoy and know that one of your comrades is doing their thing!! So Real to the top.

SO REAL PUBLISHING, INC

PRELUDE

GUCCI

I blew through the dark Detroit streets, letting the cool fall air hit my face. The Vance & Hines pipes, on my Hayabusa, purred like a ferocious jungle kitten. The dark streets were reminiscent of an "I Am Legend" scene, you know the movie that Will Smith starred in alone. All that was missing were the animals because the hypes were out, scouting the deserted streets, looking for a street soldier to cop from. I slid up St. Jean, taking a quick glance at the Eleventh Precinct, before hooking a right on Jefferson. A few hoopties cluttered the parking curbs that aligned the streets in front of the abandoned mom and pop spots. 'This shit is getting real!' I thought, seeing the scene in a haze as I passed by. At a hundred miles an hour, everything seemed small. My bag sat snugly inside of my seat net. My tinted helmet visor hid the content of my eyes. I'd just blown a Swisher of the Kush which left my body numb and emotionless.

"Slow up before we swing the corner." My mans, Drake's voice, came through my chatter box. I peeked into my side rearview mirror and saw a set of lights whip behind me. Right on time. My crew was always on point. We had a rule: show time or no time, and we all respected the game. Me, Drake, and Tutsi.

The set of lights separated becoming singles and I heard the roar of Drake's CBR blazing up on me. I slowed, letting him pass me. Tutsi's Ducati closed in siding parallel with me.

Tutsi looked over to me and nodded his helmet. "You ready, Gucci?" he asked. Without hesitation I answered, "Hell yeah, nigga!" I watched as Drake hit the corner. He eased his Mac 10 out of his jacket. His shoulder strap fluttered in the wind. Me and Tutsi reached for our steel. The club was just letting out and niggaz were doing their thing – parking lot pimping to the fullest.

Some of the illest whips were out front. Jags, Benzes, and an inked up H2 Hummer sitting on 30 inch DUB sploaters, those rims that spin and float at the same time. The H2 was wet as a water moccasin. It was a custom joint. That couldn't be mistaken, which made it an easy target for the team. 'Yeah, nigga!', I thought, holding my finger snug on the trigger as I whipped the corner behind Drake leaning hard, nearly letting my knee scrape the gravel. 'We gon eat!'s
Blah..tah..tah..tah..tah!
The sound of Drake's mac spitting was music to my ears. I held the handlebars of my bike and let off. Brack..cah..cah..cah..cah! Fire spit from my calico. Drake had already riddled Trey Pack's body with slugs, but me and Tutsi's job wasn't done. We were the clean up team. Drake hit them with the gas and we hit them with the flame. The automatic lead from the calico melted the glass on the police cars, slumping one of the officers who sat inside. The other officer knelt beside the squad car and bust off a few rounds from his service revolver.

"I thought they used automatics nowadays?" Tutsi's voice spoke into my ear causing me to chuckle. Suddenly I heard what should be the show stopper. Tutsi had thrown two grenades into the crowd, finishing what we'd started – a muthafucking war!

We all zipped off into the night, splitting up, just in case. You never knew where the law would ambush a nigga, especially after taking out one of theirs.

DRAKE
I pulled the throttle back, letting the pipes on my CBR purr as I sped through the desolate Detroit city streets. There weren't any cars out driving and the crack fiend zombies had died off to a bare minimum. The game wasn't dead, though, because base heads didn't die, they multiplied. We'd done it. Me, Tutsi, and my main

nigga, Gucci, had pulled off the coldest hit that the Motor City has ever seen. The prince of the city was a dead muhfucka.

"Huh," I grunted arrogantly. 'And it was all from the slugs that I spit!' I thought, nodding my head as I pulled up to the garage of our meet up spot. I didn't see any trail marks from the bike tires in the gravel, so I was sure that I was the first to get back as usual.

I lift the garage door and pushed the CBR inside. It was a good ride, but it would never see the streets again. "Sorry, baby girl." I rubbed the side of my bike. We'd been through a lot together, but this was the end of the road. I flipped the kick stand down and went for the tool box. It was time to strip her down. We'd planned to skin all of our bikes after the hit went down. It was the only right thing to do. Ain't no way I could still comfortable on this muhfucka! I slipped the socket onto my ratchet and started stripping the fiberglass off. The pop of wheels rolling across gravel startled me. I looked up nervously before remembering that the squad was meeting me. That must be Gucc? I was almost certain because Tutsi was the worst rider of us all.

Tutsi was a nigga who Gucci brought into the fold. A triple black muhfucka with purplish lips. Not from smoking because the nigga wouldn't touch the ganja. He was from Sierra Leone, an African country where the blood thirsty diamond trade had caused the death of a civilization. After the cease fire agreement of 1999, he was granted temporary citizenship for his work with UNICEF. He'd helped them navigate through the heavily violent and war-torn terrain of Zimi and other parts of Sierra Leone. What they didn't know is that he'd been part of the problem. Tutsi was a young warrior, born and bred to destroy shit. He would tell me and Gucci about a team back home that he was a part of called the "Kill Man No Blood Unit" or "KMNBU" describing brutality in a way that I'd never imagined. They were a team that went into villages assassinating people without causing bloodshed. The shit was so gruesome that I didn't believe him.

I walked to the door and chuckled. "Ain't this some shit," I said while watching Tutsi rolling his bike up the gravel toward the garage door. I pulled the door up to let Tutsi in. I'd been waiting on Gucci so I could gloat about being the first to arrive once again, but Tutsi's black ass would do. He solemnly shook his head while pushing his bike into the garage, letting me know something was wrong. I looked around and behind him and pulled him the rest of the way inside.

"What the fuck happened?" I asked bluntly, not wanting to waste any time. 'Come on nigga!' I thought, staring at him while rage swelled in me. I was sure that whatever it was, it would cut me deep.

"Bro'tah," Tutsi began, his deep hardened voice without excitement. "I saw the law get behind Gucc and his bike went down." Tutsi shook his head, giving me the impression that Gucci's last breath was blown while he lay dead across the cool blacktop of the Detroit streets. 'Hell nah!' I thought, wanting to blame Tutsi, but knowing that it was no one's fault.

"Fuck it!" I spat, tapping Tutsi's back for him to follow me. We walked toward the entrance of the garage. "I got heat in the truck!" It was parked out back. We were supposed to use it to disappear with the bike scraps, but we had another problem. Gucci was our man a hundred grand so we couldn't leave him. It was against the code of the team. "We goin to get him."

Tutsi looked over to me. 'Say it, bitch ass nigga!' I thought, warranting a cowardly response. I still had my four fif tucked handily in my waist and wouldn't hesitate to use it. Gucci was my mans, but Tutsi was just a nigga I met along the way which made him expendable. Shockingly, something that almost never happened with Tutsi happened. The nigga smiled, flashing all thirty-two of those gold rocks that aligned his mouth.

"I was waiting on that call, but it had to come from the head," Tutsi replied and pulled his heat from his back. Cocking the gun caused the heavy click clack sound of metal grinding together. He looked at me and nodded, gesturing for me to lead the way. I'd known Tutsi for a while, but at the moment I realized I had three mans: Gucci, Tutsi and Quan.

"If one eat, we all eat. And if one bleed, we all bleed," I said as me and my mans, Tutsi, hopped into the Tahoe and peeled out of the alley. We were on a mission. No man left behind.

SO REAL PUBLISHING, INC

CHAPTER 1

TREY PACK: How it all started

I sat out back waiting on my team to arrive. We were supposed to be moving an hour ago. Everything was set and we were late as usual. 'This shit is gettin too sloppy!' I thought al I walked back into the house after hearing the doorbell. It was a long trip, but I'd made it to the top of this game and wasn't willing to crumble because of the niggaz around me.

Detroit had changed, but the game remained the same. If a nigga wanted to eat, he had to muscle his way into the hustle. It was the unspoken rule of the game. There was a time when I was selling three dollar pieces of crack in the hood. I was moving that shit with precision back then. Slinging out of after-hours joints, moving out front of corner stores and doing hand to hands at the parks. It was a hard grind, but I stayed persistent. Now, I AM the streets. 'Yeah,' I thought, looking at the diamond bezel around the face of my Rolex. Shit has definitely changed.

I peeked through the window blind and saw Rocsi. I watched as she popped those thick as legs backed like she does. "Um um um!" I hummed to myself, lustfully eyeing her sexy stance. Rocsi was the type of woman that could make any man drool. She was light and cute in the face, thin in the waist, and had a nasty walk. Her ass was round and plump, but it wasn't donkey. It was one of those manageably tight asses with wide hips that made it look bigger than what it really was. Her eyes were light brown and had that Chinese slant, but her lips are what brought hood niggaz to their knees. She kept her lips heavily glossed, making them look like they were always puckered. I've wanted to fuck since the first day we met, but I stood down out of respect for my nigga. Rocs was mans, Ship's, cousin and he asked me for that much. Otherwise, I would have slid this hammer up in her a long time ago. I opened the door, glancing at my watch at the same time. I wanted her to know that I realized how late she was.

"Damn, Roc," I said in an agitated tone. "I'm glad you could make it." She walked in and I closed the door behind her. I could tell she had an attitude and I wondered why especially since she was the one who was late.

"My watch says 11:45," Rocsi replied nastily. 'Bitch!' I thought, wanting to slap the shit out of her. If she was anyone else on this planet, breathing the same air as me, she wouldn't have been able to recycle that shit anymore. But, she was Ship's family.

"So, by my time, I'm fifteen minutes early, pimp," she finished and plopped onto my couch like she was running this show. I looked at my watch again. Although the face was cluttered with premium stones, I knew how to tell time and the time was 12:46.

"You need to upgrade your shit because it's a quarter to one," I retorted, shaking my head at the way she'd bounced into my spot all high and mighty. Simple minded ass young bitch. That was the problem with pretty women – they always felt like the world was aligned with them. I glanced at her once again, noticing the French pedicure on her toenails. Shit! Although I was upset about the blatant disrespect to the game and the crew, her beauty was undeniable.

"Nah, Trey." She shook her head, laughing while looking at the Cartier watch that was strapped snugly to her wrist. "I'm upgraded just fine, but you should have set your watch back for daylight savings, pimp." I looked at the Rolex. SHIT! I'd slipped on that shit. She smirked after seeing the embarrassment on my face. I knew that I'd made a fool out of myself, but I wouldn't admit it. I looked at my watch.

"Imma slap the shit out of NaShell's ass," I said, changing the time on my watch. I wasn't lying, though, because my girl,

NaShell usually took care of shit like that. I took care of everything else, so handling domestic shit was the least she could do.

"Yeah," Rocsi said, giving me the same nasty smirk from earlier. I was sure that she was laughing at me, and that I'd be hearing about this later, once Ship got here because she was a snide type of broad.

"You bring the print?" I asked. Rocsi pursed her lips. It was one of those 'Nigga! What you think' looks. She dug deep into her bra and came out with a box.

"Quit doubting a bitch," she replied and tossed the box to me. I didn't doubt her because I knew she could work the best of them, but I doubted myself. 'Doubting if I could keep from choking her smart mouth ass' I thought as I opened the box and stared at success.

"Imma let that smart ass mouth slide since you handled up, but sooner or later, Imma slap the shit out of you," I said calmly, staring up at her with a quick assuring glance. Try me if you want to.

"I thought we were crew and we kicked it like that?" she asked with a nonchalant shrug of her shoulders. I could tell that she didn't respect the clique and it was irritating me. I'd brought her in because Ship trusted her. But, fine or not, she was just as replaceable as any other broad. When Ship introduced us, she was green as grass and as fresh to the game as fish on a hook, but her attitude was the same – fucked up.

I was at that barber shop getting my locs twisted when Ship called me. I heard that Jay-Z joint "You Must Love Me" from the Carter album beating from inside my pocked, so reached in for my cell. I loved that song because it told my story, which wasn't too different from a lot of niggaz around the way.

"Speak to me," I said after putting the phone to my ear. It was my street phone so I kept it hood whenever I answered. Just like a nigga couldn't bring the streets to the boardroom, a nigga couldn't bring the boardroom to the streets. That kind of shit would get a hustler misjudged and plotted on.

"Hey brother," a mild mannered and polite voice spoke into my ear. Instantly, I knew it was Ship. If I wouldn't have grown up with him, I wouldn't believe his ghetto status. His hood stats were probably unmatched. His appearance didn't reflect who he really was because Ship was a certified gangster by any measure.

"What's good, Ship?" I asked after hearing his humble voice. I would usually take a crack at him because of his timid sound, especially knowing that he stood six foot three, two hundred and sixty pounds, and had a George Foreman knockout punch. But, for some reason, I let him slide this day.

"I'm trying to get my little cousin some work," Ship's reply was flat and straight to the point. 'Some work?' I thought, sure that Ship could make shit happen for his lil cousin just like he'd done for me, but I played along. I would never turn my back on Ship because he'd helped me change the game.

"It's done, what's the name?"

"Roc. You should be getting a call at noon. Thanks, brother." Ship hung up leaving me wondering about this cousin.

Later on that day, around noontime, I was at the C-Note Lounge over on Van Dyke listening to some local niggaz battle rapping when I got the call from Roc. I usually stopped by C-Note to scout out talent for my exit plan out of the game. I'd been funneling bread through a phantom record label for a few years. When the time came, my retirement was in music.

"Speak to me," I answered.

"Hey," a sassy voice spoke into my ear. It was unrecognizable, but certainly a hood bitch. "This is Roc."

"Who?" I asked, knowing Ship wasn't trying to play me. 'This nigga sound homo as fuck!' I thought, pissed off while waiting on a response from the nigga on the other end of my phone.

"Rocsi, Ship's people," she said and my anger eased. Oh! I chuckled, relieved that Ship hadn't thrown a lifetime friendship away playing homo-thug games.

"Oh, you're a female?" I asked just to make sure. I'd already mistaken her for a him, so a nigga wanted to put a gender with the name and voice.

"All woman, pimp," she grunted, letting me know that she was all woman with an attitude.

"Right, so what can you do?" I asked, making small talk because there was no way that I was bringing a groupie into my circle. 'This nigga trippin!' I thought. Ship had to know I wasn't a equal opportunity employer. A muhfucka had to be street to run the streets with me.

"Whatever the hood calls for," she grunted again, but this time her grunt wasn't annoying. Instead, it was interesting. 'Damn,' I thought, 'this hoe might like the bitch off New Jack City!' Her swag was street and Ship had shot her to me, so I said fuck it and brought her in. She fumbled a few times along the way, but eventually she took to game and innovated that shit, but that didn't mean she could disrespect the squad.

SHIP

I hopped out of the car, into a full sprint, rushing towards Trey's house. I was always late when we had a meeting, but it was warranted. I had a nine to five unlike him and Rocsi. I knocked on the door and saw Trey peek through the window blinds. 'I don't know why he does that shit,' I thought, knowing that I could have surprised him with a slug when he peeped out at me. Trey was a creature of habit, which made him an easy target, and I'd warned him plenty of times, but he swore that he was untouchable.

"What up doe?" Trey said after opening the door, letting me into the house.

"Nothing. I'm good," I replied, bending my head around the hallway wall, looking around for my cousin. "What's up with you? I saw Rocsi's car out front. Where is she?" I walked deeper into the house, still searching for her. I watched the way Trey eyeballed Rocsi and didn't like it. I'd warned him about trying to push up on my family, and hoped he wouldn't violate what was asked of him. We were down until the end, and the end could be close depending on how much he respected my request.

I bent the corner to the kitchen and saw her sitting out back in Trey's four season sunroom. Little Rocsi had grown up, but in my eyes she was still my little cousin.

"What's good, Roc?" I asked, walking into the sunroom. She saw me and lit up. Her chinky brown eyes were beaming.

"Cuzz!" She leaped up and rushed over to me. I hugged her while glancing over to Trey. He was standing near the doorway watching us. I could feel the curiosity in his stare and made a mental note to check him about what he was thinking.

"Did you get the print?" I asked anxiously and she smiled while nodding, assuring me that she had. Trey grunted, pulled a box from his shirt pocket, and threw it to me.

"I did it just like you asked me to," she said excitedly and quickly glanced over to Trey. I didn't know what they had going on between them, but I was going to watch them a little closer. Either way, we all were about to blow up from this lick. I took the printout and looked at it. 'Damn!' I thought, holding a seven figure come up in my palm. Rocsi had managed her end of the play. The rest was up to me.

CHAPTER 2

ROCSI

I walked out of Trey's house twisting my ass because I was sure that he was watching. Trey had a habit of peeking through the blinds of the window. I'd heard Ship tell him on a few occasions to quit taking peeks out of the blinds, but he wouldn't take heed. Ship was a gunman who would spill blood in any street for the right price so he was a nigga who I'd be listening to. I guess in a way, I always have.

Growing up, I used to skip school a lot and always found myself around Ship and his crew. He was always a boss and I admired that shit. I used to take his swag and prance around my hood like I was the female version of him. It had gotten my ass whipped a few times, but the females around my way clung to me. I couldn't say or do anything wrong and they were willing to ride at any cost. Life changed after that hoe karma caught up with us.
***

I was nineteen and one of the finest pieces of ass in the city. I'm not just saying either. I'm talking about statistical facts. Niggaz was coming at me daily offering trips, cars, cash, or whatever I desired. It wasn't about fucking either because some of those clowns just wanted to taste this sweet young thing. I wasn't having it though. I wasn't a virgin by no means, but I wasn't a prostitute either. Bitches killed me thinking they could sell pussy at will, but not be classified as a prostitute. They may not walk the streets soliciting niggaz to fuck for money, but selling pussy was selling pussy no matter where or how a bitch performed it.

My girls, Aries and Queenie, were the bomb too. Aries was a redbone with deep dimples and a slim curvy build. She had an exotic look that made want to cash out off appearance alone. I'm all woman and strickly dickly, but Aries was fine. Queenie was cute too. She was caramel complexioned with thick silky hair.

Her hips and ass were rap video worthy and she had a sensual sway that was hypnotic. I used to watch her stroll intently until I crafted a similar one of my own. My walk wasn't as sexual as hers, but it was good enough to make a nigga want to come off some change and Quan wasn't an exception.

It was a Friday night in the D when I met Quan. We were at Skateland, a local roller skating rink on the east side, and it was jumping. We were too young to hit the clubs up, so this is where we canvassed the scene for our come ups. Quan was a young, fly, and flashy nigga off the east side. He was tall with clear chocolate skin. Not to mention, but the nigga had a 430 Lexus with the wettest paint in the hood. I wasn't a groupie, but the sound of 'Blood Raw' pounding out of Quan's trunk drew me to him.

Quan whipped into the parking lot with his trunk thumping like a jackhammer. The TV's in his Lexus lit the inside of his ride up like a Christmas tree. 'Damn!' I thought, watching as all of the attention turned to him. He was the man at Skateland. Niggaz envied him and females adored him, including me and my crew. Queenie tapped my shoulder, startling me.

"Bitch, you see this nigga?" she asked and I rolled my eyes at her. 'I'm trying to!' I thought, turning back towards him.

"Yeah, I see him," I replied, still checking him out. I wanted to see if he noticed me because there was no way that I was making the first move. I had a reputation to uphold and I planned on doing just that. I turned and walked into the rink, not wanting to be like the other females out front dick-handling. I had my own following and refused to bow down to him.

"So what's the plan?" Aries asked, after we sat at the concession area, certain that I was up to something. I smiled connivingly.

"I don't know. Plus, I ain't feeling Quan like that," I lied, knowing damn well I was feeling the shit out of him. My girls laughed causing me to look around. I wanted to know what was funny until I realized they were laughing at me.

"I'm amusing, huh, hoes?" I giggled knowing the joke was on me.

"We didn't say shit about Quan," Queenie quipped and Aries laughed. "Ain't nothing, though, because we all feel that nigga." We all laughed. Queenie was right too. Us and every other female in the rink felt Quan. 'Um!' I thought, smiling after glancing over to him as he strolled into the rink followed by his entourage. His clique held him down like a prince too, letting the scene know that he was a hustler. Quan's platinum chain swing low and was anchored down by an iced out Q. The cut and clarity on the diamonds that were inlaid in the Q flickered like a strobe light showing their quality and I was impressed. I wasn't about to let him know that I was either.

After getting our skates on, me and my girls slid out to the floor to stunt. My hips rotated like sploaters, moving from side to side and spinning as I hit the corners of the rink. 'I know these bitches is hating and these niggaz is jocking!' I thought, taking a peek at Quan from my peripheral. "I knew it," I whispered to myself, after seeing Quan gawking at me. I slid up the middle of the floor and giggled before really putting on. My glow stick gave my body a slick silhouette and the glitter on my clavicle shimmered. I was the main attraction and I knew it. When I came around the DJ hollered couples only and guess who whistled out to the floor – Quan! He grabbed my hand while skating backwards. 'Who does this nigga think he is?' I wondered, wanting to pull my hand away, but it was useless because this nigga had me at the entrance. I just let loose seeing if he could keep up with me. 'Come on now, pimp,' I laughed knowing he wasn't used to having anyone take the lead on him. He liked being in control, but it was clear that I was the better skater. We tore it up, though, and then he rode with me back to the concession area. This was what I wanted all along, but I couldn't let him know that. I would have seemed desperate if I would have, and I was far from being desperate. We sat down, both breathing hard and smiling, and he pulled his chain back out of his shirt. I guess he'd tucked it in so it wouldn't swing around while we were on the skating floor doing our thing.

"So what's up?" Quan asked, still breathing heavily and smiling just as heavy. 'He must think I'm a groupie,' I thought, wanting to act up but his brown eyes calmed me. Quan was a smooth looking nigga. He wasn't the finest puppy in the litter, but he was unquestionably the flyest. Quan had a gem rarer than the ones in Jacob's wristwatch and platinum piece. He had that thug nature that groupies adored so much, and I was falling in with them.

"Nothing," I replied, shrugging my shoulders and popping a fresh piece of Juicy Fruit into my mouth. I liked to chew gum around niggaz because it drove them wild for some reason. Maybe it was the way I did it? "So what's up with you?" I smiled, letting know that I didn't only peep game, but I had a little of my own. I'm a real product of the D so good game was in my DNA.

"Nothing. I'm tryna make sure you're good though. You feel me?" his smile was mesmerizing, but I had to stick to my script – hard to knock.

"Oh, so you care that much, huh?" I giggled, glancing off to my left, seeing my girls leaning on the rail near the restroom. They were always on guard because they knew how flip my tongue could get at times.

"Yeah," Quan replied, still smiling. 'This nigga think he's toying with a little girl' I thought, giving him a judgmental once over.

"Boy, you don't even know my name so stop gaming, pimp," I giggled girlishly and leaned over, loosening my skates. They were smoking hot too. We'd gotten it on so heavy on the skating floor that my skates were smoldering inside from the friction.

Quan giggled before replying, "Nah, it ain't even like that, Rocsi." I looked up from tying my skates, embarrassed that I didn't have a comeback for him. Usually I was witty as hell, but he'd caught me off guard knowing my name. Everyone in the rink knew who he was, but I didn't know my rank was that high.

"Yeah," Quan continued with an arrogant nod, "I did my homework on you." He was still smiling.

"Oh, okay," I replied, smiling because I was impressed that he actually knew my name. He was the first youngster to step to me correctly. Most of the times an old nigga would come proper, but I wasn't with riding shotgun on a power scooter. "So what's your name?" I asked, pretending not to know, and sure that he was on to me. He chuckled and rubbed his nose. Later on, I found out that rubbing his nose was a habit of his. I guess he thought it made him look suave or something.

"Quan, but everybody calls me Q," he said, pointing at the uppercase cursive Q smothered in diamonds. 'Good trick, wrong bitch!' I thought, knowing I was supposed to be impressed by his jewels. I'd learned from the best – Ship – and he'd warned me about being impressed with what a nigga has. He told me that bitches should be more impressed with what a nigga was willing to part with.

"Right," I said with a sarcastic chuckle. I wanted him to get the hint that I wasn't as impressed as he would have liked me to be. And to my surprise, Quan nodded, letting me know that he acknowledged my statement. That was rare from a young cat, but I guess that's what separated young niggaz and Quan.

After that day, me and Quan started kicking it strong. We hadn't said it, but it was known to the city that I was his bitch. Him and his niggaz, Gucci and Drake, were young in the game but they were on their way to the top. Bringing so much money in from slinging dope that they couldn't fold their bankrolls; they had to stack them. The streets were watching and the snitches were ear hustling, so pretty soon the word got back to the law. I was at Quan's apartment when the raid happened.

We had just got back from Loraine, a small town in Ohio, where we were moving rocks. Gucci held down shit in the city and Drake used to move up in Minneapolis. Although I wasn't officially part of their crew, I was trusted because I was Quan's girl. I didn't have to move any product, but I always did shit to earn my keep. It was just an unspoken rule for a real gangster bitch.

We'd ordered a pizza and were waiting on the delivery when something flew through the window, smoking the front room up. Quan pushed me on the floor and upped his strap. He rushed to the window.

"Aw shit!" Quan yelled, throwing his burner under the couch. "They raiding!" He'd already given me the drill, just in case we ever ran into the law, so I knew how to react. I stayed on the floor and he ran back and dove beside me. I thought we were clean that day.

Although there weren't any drugs in the house, Quan was arrested on federal drug trafficking violations and sentenced to seven years federal time. I was convicted of complicity to traffic cocaine and sentenced to eighteen months. Me and Quan wrote each other throughout my stint, bringing us closer than ever. Once I paroled, Ship put me into position with Trey. Ship had made his transition out of the streets and changed clothes by then, but he wanted me to be safe so he gave me a nest with his mans.
***
I hopped into my 3 series BMW and purred off, seeing the blinds riffle after Trey took his stalking eyes off of me. I knew he wanted me, and I teased him often, but there was no way he was getting

inside of my goodie bag. Trey wasn't' the type of nigga a bitch like me would fuck with. He was a grimy ass nigga with a stifled integrity that was as short as his dick. I hadn't seen it, but he fit the category of a nigga with a shorty.

Trey kept the hottest shit. From his whip game, pushing 600's with letters behind them, to his flamboyant jewelry collection, rose gold and platinum pieces that swung low and wrapped his wrists. Those are the type of things that niggaz hid their lame dick with, and I was almost certain that Trey was no different. He used to try and stunt in front of me when I first started hustling with him, but I wasn't falling for game. I'd just cracked the pavement after a year and a half stretch, and had picked up nationwide game from bitches who'd done it all, so I was airtight with my shit. Of course, after being on the streets for four years, I wasn't as focused as I was when I first hit the rock, but a bitch was still about her business.

I pulled up to Khalid's Harbortown condo and called up. I smiled after pressing send on my cell. Khalid was a hustler's dream. He had it all – money, credit, clout, prestige and a bitch like me wanted it all. It wasn't solely my call; it was a team effort and we always got our mark. Ship wouldn't have it any other way because he was on his way to the top of the food chain in Detroit and was taking me and that grimy ass nigga Trey with him. Joi was another issue. Joi was Ship's woman and my biggest competition, but I was sure that she wouldn't be around too long because she was a snobbish tramp. Ship usually kept them moving anyways.

"Hey, Boo!" I cooed into the telephone when Khalid answered. He sounded sleepy, but he perked up immediately after hearing my voice.

"Baby boo," Khalid replied, sounding as corny as ever. "I was just thinking about you." He lied without hesitation, but niggas like him did that kind of shit for a living. I'm sure that he wouldn't let his personal life interfere with his supreme lying ability. 'Phony ass clown,' I thought with a snicker, while holding the phone to muffle the sound of my giggling.

"That's good because I'm downstairs without any panties on, waiting for you to invite me up." I lied because my panties were pressed snugly against my body.

"Oh, I see you!" he replied with excitement. I looked up and saw him staring from his balcony, waving me inside. "Come on up, baby boo."

"Okay, boo," I said and hung up. Got this clown! I laughed and parked before snatching my panties off. I had to make it look good, and I was sure that it would take more game to get out of his condo unfucked than it did to get inside of it. But I would manage somehow. Even if I had to slap-box those huge balls of his. I giggled and walked up to the building.

CHAPTER 3

GUCCI

I walked down my driveway and quickly snatched the mail out of the box. The suburbs was a place that seemed fit for a fly young nigga, but it just wasn't my lane. I looked around, just as I'd done each morning since I'd been out, knowing this is where every hustler in the hood wants to be. I thought so at one time too, but now that I'd shifted gears, it was time for me to change lanes. I'm a rugged nigga with a couture name, but ain't shit upper echelon about Gucci. 'I'm a name brand nigga with a lot of nameless victims,' I thought with a faint grunt. I glanced through the pile of letters and was surprised with something that I'd been looking forward to for the last two years.

"Hell yeah!" I yelled and jumped into the air throwing a fist. I was staring at my freedom – an early parole release. No more muhfuckin reporting to these crackers! I darted back up the driveway, nearly losing my slippers while rushing through the sliding side patio doors. I saw April standing in the kitchen wearing a sexy lavender negligee. It fell right below her pussy showing those pale bony ass white legs that I'd grown to despise over the last couple of years. Her blond hair that swung over her shoulders was her best quality. She had some nice titties, but I'm a street nigga and wasn't into that type of shit. I like ass and hips! April smiled showing her coffee stained teeth.

"Hi, babe!" she spoke in a high pitch that made me want to slap the shit out of her. The only time I liked to see her mouth open was when my dick was sliding out of that muhfucka, which was often because I couldn't salute to a hoe with an ass flat as a piece of plywood.

***

Me and April met while I was in prison. I was sixteen months in on a four year stretch and all out of resources. I was nineteen and all hood when I went in, so you know my funds was low. Don't get it twisted, me and my mans Drake and Quan were eating, but we stunted harder than we hustled. We were copping a couple of ki's to split, but balling out like we had major distribution. I had that drop Vette, Drake had an Infinity truck squatting on deuces, and Quan had a 430 Lexus with the wettest paint in the city. It wasn't much, but for a few niggaz coming out of the Parkside housing projects, that was balling hard. Anyway, with no money I had to get it in how I had to get it in.

I hooked up with Shane, this young hippie looking nigga who locked a few cells down from me at the Michigan Reformatory. The reformatory was gladiator school. A nigga couldn't be weak or a lone in that muhfucka because that would make you prey for the wolves. Niggaz used to say, "Don't feed me, feed the bear," which meant they liked to be hungry for the taste of blood. He was mixed and had long ass dreads that fell across his back like a cape. Niggaz was at him and I knew it. He was in for manslaughter, but that didn't mean he was a killer. One of his friends had died during a drunk driving accident. His guy was white and he was drunk, which landed him a seven to a quarter. I had a little clout on J5 by the time he got there. I'd busted a few heads and put iron through an old school nigga out of Saginaw. I wasn't feared, but I was respected which was a lot in a community of killers. I immediately embraced Shane, calling him Skateboard P, the name that Pharrel from N.E.R.D. went by. They kind of looked alike and had the same swag. I figured the least I could do was eat off the chump for a while until someone thought about a nigga and slid some bread through. But whatever it was, everyone knew that Skateboard P was rolling with Gucci, so they stood down.

I was standing by the door of my cell on mail call one afternoon. I was expecting something from the house for my birthday. The CO, an old bitch ass white boy named Smitty, floated across the range with the mail bag. He smiled and tapped my cell door antagonizing me. He'd seen me looking out for mail throughout the week and knew that this was the last call until Monday. He chuckled and walked up to Shane's door.

"Step back," he demanded arrogantly. He was an egotistical honky that made niggaz feel like less than men by antagonizing them. 'I hate this bitch!' I thought, staring at him cold as he slid Skateboard P his mail. It was a heavy stack and I was sure that it was laced with a few ends, because P kept us full.

"I guess the white side of your family hollered?" Smitty said in a mocking way. He was a deep rooted racist muhfucka who wasn't ashamed to show it. He looked back toward me and snickered, "More than I can say for the full blooded niggers around here." He walked off.

"You racist ass bitch!" I screamed, blood boiling and ready to spill some of his. He'd deliberately called me out, disrespecting my people. 'Imma kill this honky!' I thought, still fuming when Smitty threw his middle finger into the air. His back was turned to me, not acknowledging what I'd said so I thought it was over. He passed out the rest of the mail, but later on he came back with a few of his goons and they beat the shit out of me. I fought back, but being caught asleep by four horsemen with billy clubs was a no-win situation.

The next day at rec, Shane walked up staring at the Flintstone knot on my forehead. I was sure that he'd heard the scuffle the night before because the range was sounding off; letting those guards know that they were on some hoe shit. Shane shook his head.

"My guy," Shane said, still shaking his head causing his dreads to swing from left to right. "Was it worth it? On the real, fam?" He nodded toward the knot.

"Hell yeah, muhfucka!" I replied, pissed that he'd even had the courage to ask me some shit like that. "Damn straight it was worth it! I'm tired of these honkys dogging a nigga!" I was serious too. Smitty and his goons had put a good one on me, but the last laugh would be mines because I'd copped me a hawk earlier and it was going down.

"So what's up, bro?" Shane shook his head disappointedly. "You're just gonna wild out like fuck freedom, huh?"

"Freedom?" I asked, knowing he was mistaking my situation for his. The only niggaz on earth that would show me love were behind bars too, so I didn't have shit to look forward to on the streets. "Freedom don't mean shit to a nigga who ain't got nobody, brah!" I chuckled sinisterly. "My peoples is locked the fuck up, nigga!"

"So who gon feed them if you're doing life, bro?" Shane stared at me with curiosity. 'Damn!' I thought because I wasn't ready for that question. Who would feed my nigga, indeed. I couldn't even answer that question without making a fool of myself. P had settled my anger, but the fact remained that I was leaving the confines of prison without anything to look forward to.

"Yeah, bro," Shane said although I never answered him. He already knew what it was because he was a smart nigga. He just nodded knowing that he'd made me take a look at myself. "I got something for you though, pimping." He tried to sound hood although he was the furthest from it. He slid me a folded sheet of paper.

"What the fuck is this, nigga?" I asked while unfolding it. It was an address with a name. "April Young." I read the name on the paper.

27

"That's my neighbor and she loves hood niggaz." He nodded like he'd given me the key to the world. I started writing April thinking there was no way she'd fuck with me. I was halfway through a four year stint and she was a successful white bitch from the suburbs, so what would she see in me? To my surprise, she saw a lot in me. Not only did I get visits and fat ass money orders, April let me parole to her crib. She wasn't the finest hoe by no measure, but she was what I had to work with so I rolled with it.

***

I felt April's hands wrap around my waist and reach into my shorts. I'd been lost in thought while staring at the release papers.

"So are you going to speak back?" she asked while stroking my dick. 'Shit!' I thought, enjoying the feel of her soft hands pulling on my piece. She massaged me, bringing my hammer into a thick erection. I wanted to pull back but her stroke was the truth.

"Wha.....what's up?" I finally answered. April was putting something special on me and as reluctant as I was, I was accepting it. Her lips slurped and semen streams were pulling from her tongue with every pull. She was a certified head doctor.

"Shit! Goddamn!" I groaned while exploding into her mouth. Giving her a taste of my DNA was the least I could do for the bitch. After all, she'd given me a place to stay while I stacked my chips.

I pulled my dick out of her mouth and tucked it back into my shorts while walking away. She stood staring at me throwing daggers from her eyes. 'Bitch don't make me do this,' I thought, ignoring her cold stare because I didn't want to leave with ill feelings between us.

"Gucci?" April called, causing my body to tense up. Her voice was annoying as hell. 'Just leave it alone, hoe,' I thought and turned, giving her w warning glance.

"Gucci?" she called again, hustling up behind me looking upset. 'Why you gon make a nigga do this?' I thought still walking toward the bedroom. She was following close behind me, so I gave up.

"What?" I asked with an agitated tone. Although April was a white bitch, she was aware of when to back off of a nigga. I'd gone upside here head before and swore that I was going back to prison. But for some reason the bitch accepted it. I was a fucking king in her household, but there was just something missing – the hood.

"Bitch! I'm outta here," I chuckled while packing my shit. She stared at me like she didn't understand what I was saying so I made it clear. "It was a nice ride. A nigga appreciate the way you looked out, but it's a wrap! Sheeeeit, yo people fucked over mines for four hundred years!" That was something that the Muslim cats used to say all the time in prison. I hadn't researched it myself but those muhfuckaz were scholars so I just took their words for it. Tears poured into April's eyes, but she didn't say anything. She sat on the bed looking pitiful, so I tossed her a suitcase.

"Put my shit that's in the drawers in here. Imma need that shit." I tried to be as cold as possible because I wanted that broad to move on. She'd been too good to me to just stick pipe in her all the way. She'd dressed me and nested me, and for that I owed the hoe some leniency.

April packed my sit and walked me to the door, just as she'd done every day since I'd gotten out of prison. But this time would be her last because I wasn't coming back. Bitch! I'm a muhfuckin G and I need a gangster bitch to hold me down! I walked out and slammed the door. I could hear April's whimpers as I walked off the porch, but they weren't the type of cries I expected. This hoe knew it was a matter of time. I was sure that she'd woken up plenty of days wondering why a nigga like me was still in her bed. I hadn't had the opportunity until now, but I looked down at my paperwork and shouted, "Today is my muthafuckin day!" I hopped into my '86 Monte Carlo SS and peeled off letting the tires leave tracks in front of April's house.

Niggaz were scattered around the courtyard of the apartments when I pulled up. 'This shit bout to change,' I thought, jumping out of my whip and giving a few niggaz hood head nods. They didn't mean shit to me because they weren't part of my team, so being fake was warranted with them. I didn't have any loyalties to them just because they hustled in the same streets that I did. I walked through the corridor and up the fire escape to the kitchen window of me and Tutsi's trap house.

I climbed in and Tutsi damn near broke his wrist upping pipe on me. "Hold up, nigga!" I said, throwing my hands clear into the air and laughing. Tutsi was a real gangster from the Congo of Africa. He'd killed more niggaz than the Hussein brothers. He was my mans and I trusted him thoroughly.

"My brotha," he replied, easing up and tucking his steel back into his pants. I have him dap and walked through the kitchen, seeing who else was inside of the house. Tutsi was too gullible for bitches at times so I liked to creep up on him. Me, I know how hoes are so I treat them accordingly, but my guy was another story. He wanted to house every piece of pussy he ran across – tramps and all.

"Who else in this muhfucka?" I asked and peeked my head into the front of the apartment. Cheese and Omar were in the living room playing a video game. Cheese leaped up excitedly when he saw me.

"What up doe, Gucci?" he asked and walked over to me giving me a pound. Omar kept his eyes on the video game. It was written that I didn't like him and he didn't like me. I stayed in neutral because he was Drake's cousin. He was little bit older than us and as soft as they came, but he had a loyal following from the fiends. Omar was a west side nigga with clientele from Vernor to Telegraph. 'Bitch ass nigga,' I thought, staring at him, but he wouldn't make eye contact with me. It was possible that Drake had warned him about my gangster, or maybe he was just too soft to test me, but it was official that he didn't want any problems.

"What up, Omar?" I asked just to incite something in him, but it didn't work. He stayed idle, only throwing me the deuces. I could have jump all over that, but let his coward ass slide.

"What's up, my brotha?" Tutsi's voice was full of bass and hardened like he'd been living for a thousand years. He rarely showed emotion and kept his tool tucked and cocked. "You just came by to see what's up? I know you can't be around here for too long." Tutsi was always worried about me. I was the head of what we had going, but our shit was petty anti-hustling. We were barely copping a brick and our paper hadn't even touched six figures. Tutsi knew that, but he was loyal to a fault, even though we were just on a come up.

"I'm good, brotha," I replied, mocking the way he said brother. His accent was thick, but he swore that all he spoke was English. He said that he was Mende, a southern speaking nigga out of his region.

"Naaaah!" Tutsi shook his head defiantly and walked to the door. He was ready to put me out of my own shit. "Come on, brotha." He gave me a head nod to leave. Tutsi thought I was still on parole.

"It's good, Tutsi," I was chuckling and waving my hands. "I'm off papers, my nigga." I threw him the envelope and gave Cheese dap while Tutsi looked over the papers.

"You 'bout to be deep in the streets now, huh nigga?" cheese asked, seeming overjoyed for me. 'I gotta start keeping an eye on this nigga,' I thought, wondering why he was so fond of me. If this nigga a homo…! I glanced over to him knowing that he'd be a memory if I found out some shit like that.

"Ahhh! My brotha!" Tutsi rushed his cocky ass over to me and hugged me. It was a rare form of affection that I'd only seen a few times since I met him. We sent Cheese and Omar marching before counting our paper and making plans for the future. I was off of parole and hungry as a jungle animal, and the streets were my prey. 'I'm gon eat!' I thought, still flipping through the thin paper stacks that we were counting.

CHAPTER 4

SHIP

I crept around the back of the house. We were about to hit The Made Men, a team of youngsters of the Brewster projects. They'd migrated into the West Outer Drive area and Trey couldn't stomach it. Trey was a supreme hustler, but he'd get gritty whenever he felt violated. Moving in on his territory was a serious infraction. I've known Trey since we were kids, and I knew what he was capable of because he'd shown me as much throughout our dealings. He was my guy and I didn't trust him, so the streets had a better wear a helmet when dealing with Trey because he was brutal. He'd been turning me on to drug robberies for a while. I wouldn't commit any other capers because it was too risky, but dope boys were social outcasts and weren't protected by the same laws that sent them to prison for life. Before the robberies, we'd committed a few murder for hires and shook a couple of gambling spots down, but it was never on the scale of what we were doing nowadays. Moving on The Made Men set is a hustle of opportunity and necessity and had fell into our laps by chance.
***

I was at the Bounce, a little whore house in River Rouge, when Trey called me. He wasn't his usual arrogant and upbeat self. He had an excitement in his tone, unlike his usual swag.

"What's up?" I answered, knowing that it was Trey because I'd seen his number on the caller ID. Otherwise, I would have let that son of a bitch keep ringing because Sweets, the thick redbone whose head bounced up and down on my dick, was devouring me. I'd already had my way with all of the broads at the Bounce, but Sweets was my particular favorite. She had that natural rosy red blush on her skin and would always get naked although she knew I only wanted head. I'd fucked her too, but her head was what kept bringing me back.

"Ship?" Trey replied anxiously. "Brah, I gotta holla. On some real shit."

"Is everything alright?" I asked, eyes closed and knees shaking from what Sweets was putting down. Her lips were the Holy Grail of head.

"Yeah, brah. It's the muscle, not the hustle, my nigga." Although Trey's tone warned me something wasn't right, he tried to calm my concern. 'What the hell this nigga done got into?' I wondered, knowing that anything was possible when it involved Trey. He'd caused so much beef in the city over the years that I was even nervous to roam the streets without my team. Trey was wild like that. He'd calmed over time, but once a gunner always a gunner.

"Alright, bro. I'm on my way up to the cafe," I said keying him that I'd meet him at our usual spot and hung up the phone. Me and Trey were on two different sides of the game. He was the hustle and I was the muscle, so we tried to keep our distance from one another as much as possible, although we really coexisted. I dropped my load off in Sweets mouth and slapped that fat ass of hers – WHACK – before leaving. There was something about seeing my palm print on that mountain that made me feel ownership over it.

"Thanks, babe," I said and threw a couple of fifties on the dresser while she wiped my pole off with a wet towel. I didn't have to pay, but Sweets was my boo and we kept what I tipped her between us. I hollered at Marge before I left and rushed out to my care. I had to get to Trey because there was something telling me that bad blood was brewing. I'd been around him long enough to know and when I got there, my suspicion was confirmed.

I walked into the apartment and saw Rocsi sitting on the couch looking all grown up. 'Damn,' I thought, looking at how firm her thighs were. 'Little cuzz has grown up.' I'd never really taken the time to notice because I was always trying to protect her from the world, but Rocsi had become a woman – and a fine one too. I looked around for Trey, but didn't see him.

"What's up, foxy Rocsi?" I asked with a slight chuckle. That was a name that I used to tease her with when she was younger. She looked over to me smiling and threw me the middle finger.

"Fuck you, cuzz," she giggled and went back to watching television. 'Why is she here?' I wondered, still looking around for Trey when he walked out of the bedroom. I looked back down to Rocsi and back up to Trey. If this nigga is fucking my little cousin, I'm gonna bust his shit open. I wondered why he was coming out of the bedroom all gaily and shit. He looked like a nigga who had just gotten a piece of ass and I hoped it wasn't Rocsi's. I didn't request much from Trey because I knew that he was incapable of certain shit, but keeping his dick out of my cousin was something that I expected him to honor.

"Ship," Trey said, walking over and giving me dap. He was smiling and had that same excitement in his voice that he'd had while we were on the telephone earlier. "My nigga, we gotta move on these clowns off Six Mile and Outer Drive." He nodded his head like I was supposed to fall in without knowing what he was talking about. Sometimes I didn't know why we were even friends because Trey's expectations of himself were so low.

"What niggaz?" I asked and Trey ran it down. The Made Men clique had moved in on what we'd claimed years ago and precedence had to be set immediately. Trey wanted to go in with the usual plan, sending Rocsi in as a decoy, but I wasn't with it. We'd ran that play too much and soon the hustlers would put two and two together and come for her ass. That was where most ski mask niggaz made their mistakes – they kept running the same

35

play against the same defense and before they knew it, the opposition was ready for them. I knew we had to do something because a s team of gorillas couldn't move in on a team of gorillas without some type of repercussions. All hustlers lived by hood rules and The Made men had violated ours.

"So you got something better, nigga?" Trey asked after I slammed his plan. 'Damn straight, my nigga,' I thought, casually nodding my head, letting him know that I was two steps ahead of the game. I wanted to go in head first because they weren't expecting it.

"Yeah, we're going to move on them. Fuck the playtime, bro. We just go in head first and see if these cats are the real deal." I was ready to have a showdown in the middle of McNichols. I wanted to see if Trey would back me, like I'd done for him so many times before.

"It's on then," Trey replied without hesitation and gave me dap. 'That's my nigga there!' I thought, smiling at his brisk response. I didn't expect Trey to be so willing to go my route, but he had and I was surprised. He'd usually try to take the helm, but this was my show that I'd produced and would be starring in too.

As we crept around the back of the house, I reached into my ankle holster and pulled my alley revolver out tucking it into the waist of my fatigues. I lived for the excitement of kicking in dope boy's doors and seeing their faces before I took their lives. Ship was like the Boogieman, but I usually caught my victims sleeping while they were awake.

I waved Mikey, a short dark skinned cat who was on my team, over to me and ordered him to take the side windows. We'd already staked the hose out throughout the last week, so we were aware of their movement, but I didn't want anyone escaping through the window. The shit that would be happening inside of The Made Men's stash house couldn't leak out because it would bet me and my team life prison sentences. I saw Mikey slide around and post up beneath the window on the left side of the house in the neighbor's driveway. The rest of the team had surrounded the house in their perspective locations throughout the property and I was posted by the back door. I grabbed my radio from the pocket of my vest. "Go! Go! Go!" I ordered everyone to rush the house. Big Reggie hit the front door with the force of ten men sending it flying off its hinges. I hit the back door, followed by Chico, a Hispanic cat who I'd met during summer training.

"Police!" We all yelled in unison. I saw a young Rastafarian looking motherfucker with nasty looking dreads reach for his heat. 'Right on time motherfucker!' I thought swinging my semi-automatic mini 14 submachine gun toward him.

Blah..tah..tah! I spit out a three round burst hitting him with all three shots. Two peeled his chest plate open and one hit him in his eye socket, killing him instantly. I heard shooting from the front of the house and knew that the rest of my squad was taking care of their business.

I saw Ace, the head nigga out of The Made men, and swung my pistol towards him causing him to throw his hands into the air. I'd seen him before, but couldn't put my hand on where I knew him from. I moved on him, taking short quick steps, still holding my .40 caliber police issue pointed at his dome. I was ready and willing to kill him if he made me, but I was more interested in talking to him. 'Do it nigga!' I thought, still moving down the hallway and closer to him. I'm the law nigga! I got a license to kill! I was sure that he knew it by now because I was close enough to him where he could see my badge hanging from my chest.

"Lay down, motherfucker!" I yelled, taking my free hand and reaching for my cuffs. WHACK! I slapped him over his head sending him to the floor. I didn't like repeating myself, especially to chumps like him.

"Ace, right?" I asked while cuffing him. He was still awake, after the blow that I gave him to the head, but blood was trickling down his face. 'Don't get scared now, nigga!' I thought, seeing the fear swell within him. It was in his eyes and at that moment I was sure that he was ready to give it all up.

"Yeah, that's me," he finally replied in a cowardice whisper. I could feel his body trembling beneath the knee that I had pressed against his back. I should slap this clown with my pistol again. I couldn't stand a nigga who played gangster, but bowed down when the drama came into play.

Mikey walked into the room where I'd cuffed up Ace, nodding. That was his way of letting me know that everything had been accomplished. They'd laid everyone in the house down and were searching for the dope and money. Mikey and Chico were the only guys on the raid team that I trusted. Big Reggie was a sensitive motherfucker, who would always question what had happened when there was a shooting, even when it was him who had done it.

"Where is it at, baby bubba?" I asked, taunting some type of reaction from him, but he didn't comply to my patronizing. He just put it all on the table.

"Man, if I ain't gotta do no time, I'll give y'all the safe too," Ace replied serious about everything he'd said. I stared at him with disbelief. 'This clown is making our jobs easier than I'd originally thought it was going to be,' I thought, before snatching him up by his cuffs.

"Ah, shit!' Ace screamed after feeling the metal tearing against the thin skin around his wrists. Blood was leaking from his head and his wrists at that point. I was about to make it clear that it could be leaking from his heart if he was bluffing or pulling a stunt move on me.

"Come on, baby bubba," I demanded while pulling him by the cuffs, making the pain in his wrist wounds intensify. I'd been doing this for a while and knew how to create fear, panic and pain whenever it was called for. I drug him through the house pointing at his team who lay against walls and were sprawled across floors and couches. One was slumped in the refrigerator with the door swung open.

"Ah, man!" Ace whined again, as I yanked the cuffs pulling him toward his mans who was slumped in the refrigerator.

"See this nigga?" I asked while pointing at the hole that was in the back of his cranium oozing thick clots of blood and brain matter. "This is what your shit is going to look like if you bullshit me, baby bubba." I chuckled and patted Ace on his back.

"Man, I ain't tryna die out here in these streets, brah," Ace's voice had squirmed into a high pitch that made me want to murder him right then. 'This nigga ain't even in the streets!' I thought, and pushed him in his back roughly. I was becoming more and more angry about how this clown was playing the game by each statement he'd made. That is, until he made one that I was up to hearing.

We were walking upstairs to the room where he'd hid the bricks and the money, when Ace said something in a faint whisper. I could barely hear him, although, I was certain that I was supposed to. He was trying to give something extra up. Something that he thought would be valuable to me.

"What did you say, baby bubba?" I asked, putting my ear close to his face. 'Now say something ignorant, nigga,' I thought, wanting him to give me another reason to slap him with my heat again. I wanted to punish this clown before I ended his life because he was a disgrace to real street soldiers like my mans Trey.

"I said I got something else that should spare my life, man," Ace reiterated with a sniffle. I know this fool ain't crying! I glanced over to him, making sure he wasn't tearing up because that would have done it. I couldn't tolerate being in the presence of a grown man weeping. Fuck that!

"Coward ass bitch! Hurry up and kick this wall in!" I demanded, pressing my throttle snugly against his temple He'd brought me to that point and I thought there was no return.

Ace obeyed and kicked the wall causing the drywall to crumble. It was thin and the plaster hadn't dried on it. 'Damn!' I thought, after seeing what looked like ten or twenty ki's, while still pressing the pistol into the side of Ace's head. Ace kicked the wall again and again until it was all punctured with foot holes.

"Ay dios mios!" Chico said with his heavy Hispanic accent. At times, the sound of Chico's on again off again accent bothered me, but this wasn't one of those times. The wall that Ace had kicked down was loaded with at least fifty to sixty kilos of powder cocaine. I stood in amazement while staring at the wall of ghetto riches. 'Oh Shit!' I thought when it finally hit me. He'd said something earlier.

WHACK! I slapped him across the back of his neck. "Where's the rest at nigga?" I held my cannon up, letting him know that its next motion would be toward his head. I had to have it all, especially if the rest was in a bundle as big as this one.

"That's what I'm sayin man," Ace replied, trying to tuck his head behind my back, shielding it from another blow of my iron. "I wanna do more, but I wanna live too! I know where and when the pipeline sails in. I wanna give that to you, but I gotta live."

'Why is living that important to a nigga who had lived like a coward?' I wondered, knowing that there was something to what he was requesting. I looked up and saw Big Reggie's punk ass standing in the doorway watching. Bitch motherfucker is going to try to cock block!

"Reggie, come take this nigga out to the van," I ordered and pushed Ace onto the floor as Big Reggie walked over. Big Reggie leaned over, grabbing Ace by the cuffs just like we'd always done. While he was bent over, I pulled the alleyway .38 from my waist and offed him.

BLAH! I sent a single shot to the back of Reggie's head and emptied out the rest of the shells.

"Grab it nigga!" I demanded and pressed the handle of the throwaway against his fingers. "I'm not asking again, bro." This time Ace unballed his fist and wrapped his fingers around the handle and trigger of the revolver.

"Come on, baby bubba," I said and drug him out the back door and through the alley to my car. I tossed him in the back seat and called Rocsi to come pick it up. I tossed him in the back seat and called Rocsi to come pick it up. After Rocsi came, I rushed back into the house and radioed for backup and emergency units. The .38 with Ace's fingerprints on it was my insurance policy that he'd follow through with his offer to give me the motherload. What was supposed to be a light come up ended in a forty-two kilo bust, which me and Chico took thirty of them before the rest of the squad arrived. Big Reggie was an expendable part of our operation. Killing him was a bonus because I didn't trust or like him too much. This game had its own holy trinity – LOYALTY, TRUST AND HONOR. Of those three, Big Reggie held one and he did with it – he died with honor.

CHAPTER 5

ROCSI
I walked into the visitation room looking as fly as ever. Quan made it clear that he wanted to see me looking my best whenever I came to visit him. 'I know y'all looking,' I thought with a polite and seductive grin while walking past a few inmates that were lined along the wall eyeing me. I made sure I swung my little onion shaped ass erotically because it had probably been a while since they'd gotten any love. My boo knows I'm a trooper, though, because I've been holding him down tightly since I got on. My paper wasn't as heavy as Ship or Trey, but the paydays I was seeing were far larger than most of the so-called hustlers in the city. The Jimmy Choo sandals that I scuffed the waxy prison floors with were out of reach for some of the niggaz who were trying to get into my panties.

That's part of the reason I'd been so loyal to Quan. Whoever I've fucked since he's been in prison has been out of necessity, not pleasure. Quan isn't just my man, he's my nigga! I smiled watching him sail out to the dance floor. That's prison lingo for the visitation room. Quan's swagger was unmatched even with prison browns on. He was creased up like he was going to the club. He kept a pair of butter soft wheat Timberlands on his feet. He said a few words to the CO before walking over to our table.

"Hi, baby!" I cooed before falling into my man's arms. He'd put on some weight and I was feeling it too. Quan had gone into the joint as a teenager, but was coming out a full grown man. All of the inmates in the room watched as Quan got a handful of ass and a mouthful of tongue. 'Damn!' I thought, rubbing my thighs together after feeling the moisture in my panties.

"How's everything been going?" Quan asked while still holding a palmful of my butt in his hand. I guess he had to get all that he could while he could because prison was relentless with taking an inmate's liberties, especially a black one's.

"Yes, baby," I nodded letting him know that everything was good. "I've been fine, but I'm here to check on you. To make sure everything is good with you." I smiled and reached across the table grabbing his hand. Although he hated holding hands, he'd do it for me. Quan always made sacrifices for me and I showed him how much I appreciated them.

"That's real. I'm cool, though," Quan looked at the way I stroked his hand and chuckled. Although I considered myself to be a thoroughbred gangster bitch, I could get real intimate when I was with Quan. He brought that maternal shit out of a bitch, but it was all good.

"I'm amusing, huh nigga?" I asked giggling myself. 'Damn,' I thought, still smiling and giggling, 'I love this nigga!' After all of the time that we were away from one another, I still held on to that. Ship was my cousin and the only family that I dealt with, but my love for Quan still trumped the love that I had for him. Every time I looked at Quan, I remembered the day we met at the skating rink, when he knew my name. I was so fucking embarrassed.

"What's up, ma? You keep looking down and smiling. What? You got something good to tell me?" Quan stared at me, wanting me to share my thoughts with him. I wanted to, but I hated feeling vulnerable, even to him because at some point a man would always try to exploit a bitch's love for him. Quan was my boo, but he was still a man so I expected nothing less than what his nature bred.

"No, I was just thinking about how soon it'll be here," I lied about what I was thinking, but the smile that wisped across my face from knowing that Quan was 4 months from being a free man was as authentic as they came.

"Yeah, that's wild, right?" he chuckled while shaking his head. I was sure that he couldn't believe that the time had flown so fast either, but it had and I'd stayed down like I promised. I kept Quan's commissary account huge. His prison account was larger than an average working family's savings because I stacked him monthly for the last couple of years. It wasn't necessary but I wanted to show him how much I believed in us. I knew that there were two times in a man's life when he needed his woman the most: when he was sick or incarcerated. And Quan was sick and tired of being incarcerated.

"I've been doing this shit like a boss, though, baby girl," Quan looked around the visiting room and snickered. "All these clowns out here, caking with these raggedy ass white bitches and look at me." He gave me a lewd once over, assuring me of what I already knew – that I was the baddest bitch in the room. Good game, baby. I smiled while nodding my head, accepting his compliment. There was only one day of the month that I wasn't my own woman – the day that I visited Quan, because that day I was his woman and at some point during the visit, he would always make me acknowledge that truth.

"Yeah, look at you," I reiterated, smiling at him with my eyes.

"Right, I'm holding the coldest bitch in the city down. Feel me?" He stared at me. Giving a cold look that sent a chill through my body, but I liked it.

"Yes, baby," I nodded, agreeing with him. "I can definitely feel you." I smiled and reached underneath the table, running my hand softly across his mounding dick. He always responded to my touch, whether it was a kiss or a rub of my hand; he'd always rise to the occasion.

"This shit is over, but I'll be calling you soon," Quan said and stood up. I didn't want our day to end but time flies when you're with someone you love. And I definitely loved my man.

***

After making it back to Detroit, I took a nap and slipped into my hood apparel: Dereon jeans and Prada sneaks. 'A bitch needs traction!' I thought chuckling because there was no telling when the law would get behind what me, Trey and Ship was into. We'd been scouting out and robbing hustlers throughout the city for a couple of years and I was certain that heat would be set beneath our asses eventually. That's the way the game went. When a team balled, they usually balled until they'd fall. Me, I was just trying to grind until Quan got release. He was like a mad scientist – always trying to devise some type of get rich scheme and I believed in him. I believed in Ship too but the shit that Ship was working on would be the decider of his fate. Either he was going to blow up or he was going to "blow up!" Whichever it was, he was retiring from jacking and I was retiring right along with him.

Big cousin had given me the game uncut and raw as an opium plant. When I got out, he gave me an option. Either I could get paid quick and illegally or stay out of the way until he paved the way legally for me. And me, being the gangster bitch that I am, I chose to get how I'd lived my whole life – illegally. I had to check on the youngster, Ace, who I'd taken away from Ship's hit yesterday. His head was leaking blood like a water faucet and I was sure he would die overnight from the nasty wound, but Ship didn't want me to clean it up for him. I'd cleaned Ship's bullet wounds up on several occasions, so I didn't understand why he didn't trust me to take care of the youngster. He got pissed when I insisted.

"Nah, Ship," I said, grabbing a towel from the linen closet and attempted to walk back into the small living room of the apartment. "Imma clean him up because that wound's going to get infected." Ship stood in the center of the hallway, blocking me from going any further.

"I said no!" he screamed, shocking me because big cousin didn't talk to me like that. 'I know this lick ain't corrupting big cousin!' I thought, staring at him with my hands on my hips.

"Let the motherfucker bleed! I don't give a fuck if he bleeds to death because the truth is he's going to die anyway. I'm just draining him for all the information I need before I blow his fucking head off." I stared at Ship and dropped the towel in the middle of the hallway after realizing he was serious. I didn't understand. If he was going to torture the guy, he should have tortured him. Whatever he was trying to do was confusing and not only to me, because Chico was with me. We wanted to keep him living long enough to get what we needed and that would require cleaning up his head wound.

'Fuck it, though,' I thought, shrugging my shoulders while walking into the apartment. Today's a new day. Trey was in the front room watching Ace who sat in the corner, still cuffed from the day before. He wasn't as confident as he'd been while floating through the city in his tinted out platinum Range Rover. I'd been following him for weeks prior to the hit because Trey wanted me to ease in on him. After Ship cancelled that, he kept me following him because he wanted to know where and who he made moves with. That was Ship's way of setting up our next caper, because one would always bring two.

Ace was a trick ass strip club junkie, though. He didn't make too many moves unless he was doing it through the bitches he fucked because his nights ended at a different strip club daily. He'd always leave with a piece of new pussy too. I was sure that he was paying because his bankroll was thicker than the watered down game he spit. I knew because he'd slung it at me. I thought he was making moves with some Arabs around the way, so I followed him into a store that he was frequenting. Before I could get inside, he was already coming out. He saw me and smiled.

"What it do, lil mamma?" Ace asked and grabbed my hand. I wanted to snatch my shit back and slap him across his face with my snub nose tramp five seven, but I kept my cool and smiled back.

"Nothing, but I'm married boo," I lied, although the feeling that I had for Quan were a deep enough commitment to be matrimonial.

"Word?" he said, staring at me with a lame smile while still clasping my hand. "That's real and whoever he is, he's a lucky man." Ace let my hand go and walked back to his whip. I looked back while holding the door and he called out.

"Lil mamma," he said, standing with his truck door open, one foot inside and one planted on the ground. I guess he was trying to impress me with his ride. Some females would have jumped at the chance to ride shotgun with a major cheddar getter, but I had a 3 series drop and an Infinity truck that I drove daily, not to mention they're both paid for in full too.

"If you ever wanna cheat on the nigga, though." He smiled and held his arm out with a piece of paper in his hand. I was certain that it was his number, but I passed. 'This clown is a lame,' I thought and smiled back while shaking my head no.

"Not in this lifetime," I replied and walked into the store. He didn't realize it then but I was part of a group that was going to decide his expiration date and from the looks of his wound, it would be coming any time now.

"Sup, Rocsi?" Trey asked, greeting me with a quick glance before shooting his eyes back to the television. Although he was supposed to be on watch for Ace, he was the least bit attentive to the nigga. Ace could have been pulling a courageous escape or something and Trey wouldn't have seen it coming. 'Ignorant ass motherfucking nigga,' I thought, shaking my head and walking over to Ace, checking his cuffs and head wound. The crease that

Ship's pistol had put across his head was deep and caked up with blood.

"Y'all ain't clean his wound up?" I asked, upset that they'd be so careless. I wanted to get at the shipment, but it was evident that I was alone because they were going to let Ace die before we could get the information we needed.

"Fuck that nigga," Trey replied with a nonchalant grunt. He wasn't interested in what I was talking about. 'I'm tired of these niggaz!' I thought while walking back into the room. I was going to clean Ace's wound whether Ship wanted me to or not. It was about the lick and could care less about Ship's fragile male ego. I cleaned his gash, wiping the thick clots of pus and blood away from the wound. I was sure that another day would have caused the infection to set in and there was no way that we'd be able to get the plot from a vegetable.

CHAPTER 6

DRAKE

'Ooooh, shit!' I thought, pounding Lexie from the back. Lexie was fine. She had a fantasy body with an ass like a quarter-horse and hips to match. Her face was babydoll cute with caramel skin and light grey eyes. I'd met her through Antoine, a nigga used to run for back in the day. He was a little older than me, but we shared the same taste in women – freaks.

"Geh..geh..get this pussy, bally!" Lexie cooed an erotic request that stroked my ego. I stiffened my trust sending pipe crashing into her slippery pussy. She was wet enough to drive a car inside of her. Shit! Sweat poured down my face, dripping onto her glistening body. She had a natural tan that made her skin look unreal.

"Goddamn this pussy is good," I said in a winded pant. "Aaagghh, sheeeit!" My ass tightened, my legs shook, and I exploded inside of her. I pulled out and sprawled across the bed tired and sweating from an hour of getting it in.

"Are you serious?" Lexie asked and leaned upright onto her elbows. She looked offended and I'm thinking 'Bitch! You ain't satisfied with that??' She shook her head and rolled off the bed, grabbing her panties.

"What's up, Lex?" I asked getting up and walking around to her. This wasn't her first time complaining either. She'd complained about a nigga's quick count before and it was understood. But this bitch is on some bullshit this time! I stood in front of her, still breathing heavily from the pounding that I'd put on her. And I was sure that she'd came at least twice. What more can the hoe ask for?

"You keep playin me like one of these groupie bitches, Drake!" Lexie spat while sliding into her panties. She was visibly upset although I'd broken her off.

"Nah," I shook my head, grabbing her before she slipped into her pants. She looked at my hand and it off of her shoulder. I knew what type of shit she was capable of and I didn't want to have to kill the bitch. "I'ont think you no shorty! Where is that shit coming from?"

"From you, nigga! You fuckin me like Imma muhfuckin little ass girl. I wanna get fucked, Drake." She shook her head knowing that I didn't get it. 'This hoe must be a nymphomaniac!' I thought, staring at her, still wondering why she was flipping out on a nigga.

"Bitch!" I was mad as hell. I'd just given her the business and she was still ungrateful. "I'm a man, bitch! I'ont give a fuck where you come from, but when you in here, hoe! You my muthafuckin bitch!" I wanted to slap the hoe because she'd tried to emasculate a nigga. I've never been talked to like that, by a female, and wasn't about to let Lexie be the first. She reached for her pants and grunted.

"Nigga……..fuck you," she said boldly. 'This hoe done did it!' I though and slapped the shit out of her.

"You's a simple ass bitch!" I grabbed her bra and slung it, slapping her across the face with it. At that point, I was ready for her to bounce before I really acted up, but she wasn't ready yet. Lexie leaped up and rushed me, kissing me wildly and gripping my body like I was her hoe or something. 'What kind of shit is this bitch into?' I wondered as she fell to her knees pulling on my dick with her mouth like a vacuum. Dayum! I looked down at the top of her head bobbing up and down, bringing my piece into a throbbing erection. Oh shit! It finally hit me. This bitch wanna get gorilla fucked!

"Bitch! I ain't tell you to put yo muhfuckin mouth on me!" WHACK! I slapped the hoe across the side of her head sending her to the floor. She held the side of her face while looking up at me. It was lewd, knowing look that gave me the thumbs up. I calmly walked over to her and snatched her panties off while she crawled toward the bed.

"Um!" she moaned and slid her fingers into her box, causing slushing sounds as she masturbated. 'This shit is wild!' I thought, watching as she lay her face into the bed, bending over doggie style and massaging her pussy. My dick was pulsating to an erotic rhythm because she'd turned me on. I straddled her from behind and shoved my pole into her, pushing as deep as her walls would allow me to.

"Ah...ooooh! Oh, sh...shit, Drake. Baby, oooh!" She cooed and maoned while I paddled that ass something vicious.

"This what you were lookin for, bitch? Huh, tramp ass bitch?" I asked nastily while plunging deeper into her womanhood. It was dripping wet and hot as an oven, but she wasn't as loose as most sluts. She had an elastic grip on my dick that contracted with each pull. She rolled her hips as I ground inside of her. This bitch is a real tramp! My piece was numb from stroking her, but she wanted more. She was like a wild animal.

"Yeah, bitch, you wanna play?"

"No, daddy," her voice was silky and she pushed backwards meeting my every stroke. I'd been with a lot of women, but Lexie was showing me another side of erotica. 'I got this hoe!' I thought, pulling my dick out and ramming it straight into her ass.

"Ah! Ooooh....shit, Drake!" Her pitch rose into a shrill pant, but she wasn't backing down because her hips were still grinding into my pelvic area. I pounded and pounded and she panted.

"Oooooooh! Drah...Drake....oh...shit, Drake!" She screamed and grabbed her pussy, roughly massaging until she poured her juices onto my sheets. Now, she crawled away from me, causing a slushing sound when my dick slid out of her ass, which had been just as wet and warm as her pussy. Lexie was sprawled across the bed, laying in her own moisture and breathing heavily. 'Yeah, hoe,' I thought, bragging to myself because I'd finally tapped the bitch out. If I would have known she wanted to get fucked like that, I would have done it a long time ago – like the day we met.

I lay back, putting my hands behind my head, feeling more confident in my fuck game than ever. I'd put in a two hour session that broke the best of them. And got to go upside the hoe's head for poppin her lips at a nigga! Lexie crawled over and laid her head in my lap. I'd tamed her and she was ready to do whatever I requested.

***

I walked in on Gucci and Tutsi. They were counting their trap money. 'Look at this nigga,' I thought with a faint chuckle after seeing Gucci tuck the stack of cash that was sitting in front of him into a paper bag. Gucci was secretive like that. Although I was his mans and hadn't given him a reason to question that, he was still cautious around me when it came to his bread. We had a code not to eat off of each other's plate. We only broke bread with the big licks. Besides, I had a crack spot that pounded like an ape's chest and there was no way that I'd be splitting that take three ways. Hell nah!

"What, nigga?" I said staring at Gucci with a cold haze in my eyes. "You think a nigga gon rob you, playtime?" Playtime was an insult to a hustler's character, because everyone who ran the streets knew that there was no time for play when the rest of the hood wasn't eating. Either you were on top of your grind or you were in the way – playtime.

"Playtime?" Gucci asked nastily and stood up. He was about an inch taller than me and had a more muscular build, but he knew that I'd mop the floor with his ass. 'Make a move, nigga,' I thought, walking in circles as he approached me because he'd always go for my legs. Instead, he seen a no-win for him and bowed out.

"I should bust yo head, nigga," he said, giving me a pound and bringing me into his embrace. We'd usually throw a few before we chilled, but today Gucci wasn't having it; at least, not while his cash was out in the open. He swept the rest of his money into the paper bag and took it into the bedroom.

"What up, Tutsi baby?" I asked, giving Tutsi dap. I liked Tutsi, but there was only room for two in my heart – Gucci and Quan. Those were my niggaz and no one or no mount of chips could come between me and them.

"Shit, my brotha," Tutsi replied with a humble nod. We didn't say much to one another. Actually, Tutsi didn't say much to anyone. He'd been antisocial and standoffish ever since Gucci had brought him into the fold. I'd tried to find what Gucci saw in him, but it didn't jump out at me. He had an animalistic will to survive, and I'd witnessed that shit.

***

It was about a year ago. He'd only been home for about two years and I had a caper planned, but no real goons to ride with me. Gucci was still on papers, so bringing him would have been too risky. Never know if the parole officer is following you, trying to track your moves, so they can track your paper. Anyway, I need a nigga who I could trust and Gucci had given me the rundown on

Tutsi's resume. After finding out that he'd been involved with the uprising in Sierra Leone, it was a lock.

We were set to hit an armored truck during an ATM machine deposit. I was sure that they'd have at least three or four hundred thousand plus in the mobile bank of American currency. I'd already trailed the truck for about three months, tracing every route that it would take. I wanted to know everything about the truck because this was going to be the come up of all come ups. I was getting two thirds and Tutsi was leaving with a third only because I'd put it all together. He was just the wing man, but it was mandatory that I had one.

Every third Thursday of the month, the truck would stop at a strip mall on Gratiot and 7Mile, to take a lift from the Credit Union, before swinging by the ATM on 8Mile and Hayes. I'd watched them, studied their route and was ready to go after walking Tutsi through what we'd be doing.

The third Thursday of the month rolled around and me and Tutsi were ready. I lay behind an alley dumpster camouflaged in cement grey fatigues. It seemed like the only color that wouldn't be detected by someone who was being nosy. Tutsi was at the telephone pole near the front of the 7Eleven, where the ATM was located, posing as a telephone maintenance man. I'd been a telephone service installer while I was on parole and kept the uniform when I quit because I was sure that it would come in handy later on.

Just like clockwork, the truck pulled up and the driver leaped out and walked around to the back, opening the hatch. The guard that was inside leaped out with his pistol drawn, taking watch as the driver got inside of the truck. While the driver was inside, Tutsi made his move. He gave the posted gunman a friendly nod but was not acknowledged although the guard was looking his way; he never noticed him. Tutsi followed through, not knowing that the guard hadn't acknowledged him.

"Sir, step back!" the guard said sternly and swung his automatic mini assault rifle toward Tutsi. His voice alarmed the other guard who then dropped his bag and swung his pistol from left to right. I was crawling near them praying 'God, please don't let this stupid ass nigga get smoked!' I was sure that Gucci wasn't going to let me hear the end of it if something would have happened to Tutsi. The two of them held some type of bond that was unlike the one that me, Gucci, and Quan had. It was deeper in some way and I didn't understand it at times. I kept inching toward them; until I saw the guard who had been loading the ATM pull his radio from its holster. 'Ah, shit!' I thought, knowing he was calling for a squad car.

BLOCCA...BLOCCA! I let off two shots hitting the guard with the mini assault rifle twice in his back. He didn't even see it coming. The other guard panicked, pressing the radio to his face while upping his magnum at the same time. BLOCCA! I popped him in his nose, sending him back to his essence with a single round from my .40. After I'd dropped the first guard, Tutsi jumped into the back of the truck searching for the bags. He came out holding two small sacks of money. Bitch! I heard sirens in the distance and knew that the law was on their way.

"Where are the rest of them?" I asked Tutsi, sure that there were more bags inside of the truck. He shrugged his shoulders.

"Not in the truck, brotha." He looked back and saw the bag that the guard had been tucking into the ATM. Tutsi rushed over, grabbing them and tossing them to me. The sirens were getting close and Tutsi looked backwards seeing them flickering.

"Get out of here, brotha!" Tutsi yelled, waving for me to run off. I didn't want to run off like a coward, but I could see the lights flickering louder as they hit the corner. 'Fuck!' I thought, running off into the alley. I was sure that I could make it back to the van, but Tutsi's ass was grass. I made it to the van and couldn't do it. Damn! I couldn't leave Tutsi behind because we had a rule against that type of shit.

"No hustler left behind," I whispered to myself, sliding a fresh clip into my .40 cal and cocking it. CLICK CLACK! I drove off hoping a miracle would happen and it did, but I didn't see it at first.

"What the fuck?" I asked myself in a whisper while driving by the scene, watching Tutsi holding his gloves in his hands, pointing and talking to the policemen. He looked calm as hell. I wondered what he was telling them and why they'd be listening to him – a nigga that had just taken part in a double murder robbery. Once I got home, I called Gucci and flipped out.

"Gucc! Man, what type of nigga is dude?" I asked; mad as hell because it was obvious that Tutsi wasn't waiting until he got to a holding cell. Instead, he was spilling the content on the pavement of the same streets that I'd just spilled a man's blood.

"What's up, Drake, man? What the fuck you talkin bout homey?" Gucci asked in a sleepy tone. He'd always complain about being in the suburbs, but at that moment, he sounded awfully comfortable to me.

"I'm sayin ya mans is a snitch!" I replied and told him the story while packing my shit. I was sure that they'd be kicking in my door at any moment, so I was bouncing. Gucci didn't believe me and assured me that Tutsi would die before he dishonored the game. 'Yeah, right, fool!' I thought, knowing what I'd just witnessed and it wasn't a man who was willing to die for his integrity.

I thought I had it all figured out, but Tutsi was a survivor. He'd survived the shit that he'd went through in his own country, and he'd escaped a life bid for the murders of those two armored truck guards.

After I took off, Tutsi went and lay on the ground by the telephone pole. He shielded his head and looked nervous. When the police drove up, he saw them and began running his con.

"It was that red car!" Tutsi said frantically, while running over to the policemen still ducking his head as if he'd been shot at. "There were three of them!" He nodded. "With guns!" His accent was as heavy as ever and it worked because they took his bogus name and number before letting him walk off, not knowing that he was the culprit that they'd been after.

***

Gucci walked back into the room and threw some papers at me. I looked down and immediately knew what they were. I'd done all of my time and didn't have any parole, but I'd known plenty of niggaz who had went through that problem. 'Oh, it's on now!' I thought, smiling as I read the release papers.

"So what's up? We gon eat or what?" I asked Gucci, hoping he was still down with candy sack snatching. He smiled over at me and I knew the answer before he could even say it.

"We gon eat, my nigga!" Gucci said and gave me a pound. Tutsi just casually nodded. His swag was as calm as it got, but he was a vicious monster when the street lights came on. That's what I liked about Tutsi: his gangster. I still didn't trust him enough to consider him my mans. My heart only has room for two – Gucci and Quan.

CHAPTER 7

GUCCI

I watched as my mans read the early parole release. Drake was always as happy for me as I was. Me, him and Quan were a team and I loved my niggaz, but they were going to have to accept Tutsi. Tutsi is my mans too. He'd been down when the rest of my team were tucked away in other prisons. Me and Tutsi had a bond that couldn't be broken because we'd been through some real trenches. When I met him, it was like any other prison friendship – I couldn't trust the nigga. Cats in prison all have the same swagger; either they're all major ballers or heartless killers. But when the veil comes off, they're usually neither. So I played it by sight rather than ear.

***

It was early fall, about a year before his release, when the real came out about Tutsi. Me and Tutsi had gotten cool shortly after I rode in. He was a strange looking muhfucka to me. He was thick and had a deep dark glare to his skin, almost like it was galvanizing. His lips were purple and his dark brown pupils were always wide, like the center of an egg yolk. At first sight, I thought he was a junkie, but something convinced me otherwise. Most fiends had an aggressive hustle hand so they'd do well in prison absent of their get high, and Tutsi didn't fit that mold. He was busted, but he had the respect of a made man. Niggaz wouldn't cross that line of respect unless they were ready to cross the threshold of the living.

I was in the weight room, pushing that steel up when a clique of Aryans rolled in. I'd been beefing with their leader, Sudz, over a debt that I refused to pay. There was something about handing over my money to a white boy that didn't sit right with me, so I refused to comply even though I'd lost fairly in a Texas Hold Em poker game.

Once they got inside, two of them blocked the door and then Sudz strolled in. 'Ain't this about a bitch!' I thought, knowing that drama was prevalent. I usually kept something heavy with me, either a pipe or a piece of sharp iron, but they'd caught me slipping. I rose upright and stared at him unshaken by his sub-par attempt to breed fear in me. I had clout in the system, so if I died, they'd be following me.

"What up?" I asked, raising into a defensive stance. I wasn't about to let them bust my head open without me sending someone to the infirmary too. There were four of them and two of them were suspect bitch. I looked over noticing a forty pound dumbbell lying near a weight bench. It was closer to them than me so I eased closer, trying to even the distance in case I needed a weapon. The Aryans weren't known for their hand work, but they'd stab a nigga with efficiency.

"I want my coins, boy," Sudz said with a deep southern drawl, causing a faint chuckle from one of his henchmen who stood beside the door. 'These niggaz playin!' I thought, knowing if they wanted to kill, it would have already been done. Sudz was a fraud just like his accent because I'd been around enough Klansmen and Aryans to know how they really got down.

"Coins?" I grunted and sucked my teeth. Although I was trapped in deep water without a raft, I wasn't about to bow down to those honkys. Hell nah! "I ain't got shit for you bro." I taunted them because they hated when black men called them bro or brother, especially when they called them a nigger. I eased closer to the dumbbell while tucking my hand behind my back. I was known for having a knife and not being afraid to use it so they stayed weary about rushing me. I kept an eye on each one of them and suddenly one fell to the pavement. He was bleeding heavily from his head and the others turned to see what had happened. Tutsi was behind them, standing on the outside of the entrance.

He'd slapped one of the goons across the back of the head with a padlock that was strapped to a belt. After seeing help, I rushed over to the dumbbell, snatching it up and cracking Sudz across the side of his head. WHACK!

"Bitch ass honky!" I spat, spinning and slapping another one across his mouth, sending a few of his teeth flying across the weight room. Tutsi had grabbed the other Aryan into a militant chokehold, squeezing the air from his body. 'Sheeit!' I thought, watching the Aryan's face turn as dark as Tutsi's. He was killing him. Nah, Tutsi! I wanted to protest, but he'd came to my rescue. If he wanted a kill, I wasn't going to be the one who stood in his way. He finally dropped the dead man's lifeless body to the rubber floor and we bounced.

"Come on, nigga!" I demanded, waving for Tutsi to follow me. I was air tight with the laundry porter so we slid into the laundry room, not alarming anyone of what had taken place and hoping that Sudz and his crew would G-code the situation.

Me and Tutsi kept quiet for the next month or so. We wanted to know the mood of the compound before we emerged from isolation. Prison had changed since the Penitentiary movies; muhfuckaz was snitching at an all-time high inside. I wasn't trying to get popped with a new sentence that had the letters LIFE! I peeked out into the corridor and saw Tutsi sweeping the range. 'What the fuck is wrong wit this crazy ass nigga?' I wondered, knowing that he didn't have a reason to be on the range because he wasn't a porter. "This nigga tryna get us popped," I whispered to myself while slipping into my state boots. I wanted to have some traction in case Tutsi wanted to get it on. H was massive, but I wasn't going to let him take me down the long green mile with his simple ass. Hell nah! Fuck that! I unjammed my cell door and crept down the range, thinking I was sneaking up on him. When I got to him, he chuckled. It was a cold snicker that sent a chill across my skin.

"My brotha," Tutsi said, never turning to face me. 'How the fuck?' I thought, knowing that I'd been in stealth mode.

"Tutsi? Why the fuck is you out here?" I asked, looking around making sure there were no guards on post to catch me. We were in a maximum security prison and I didn't have any business roaming the range without a pass. And neither did Tutsi's black African ass! He finally turned to face me. His hat was cocked ace deuce, like the nigga Adibese on that HBO show OZ. I chuckled knowing that he'd picked his new swagger up from that show.

"I'm staying, my brotha," he replied calmly, looking at me with an emotionless glare in his eye.

"What?" I asked boldly, hoping I'd heard him wrong because there was no way that anyone wanted to stay in prison. This nigga really is nuts! Everyone around the compound would sit around listening to his gruesome stories about shit that he'd been through back home, but I'd never bought into them. He was just a nigga on the prison yard trying to hold down a sadistic rep.

"I'm staying in prison, brotha," Tutsi said, smiling like he'd told me something hysterical, but there wasn't anything tickling about doing an extra day in prison, let alone a LIFE sting. Hell nah!

"My nigga," I shook my head defiantly. There was no way that I could let someone who had saved my life take the fall for a murder. I had street morals and knew that the souls of lost hood soldiers would haunt me if I didn't abide by them. "I can't let you do that, Tutsi, man."

"Let me? Brotha, I'm doing it," he chuckled and turned away continuing to sweep. 'Damn, this big as nigga gonna make me rumble with him,' I thought, reluctant to make that move, but if that's what it took to get his mind right, it was on. I pushed back down on him. This time I was more aggressive.

"Nah, Tutsi! We ain't doin no more time, brah," I said. I shook my head and stepped in front of him, blocking his path. He looked upwards with his eyes, never letting his head move, giving me a warning glance, but I wasn't scared. "Nigga! I'ont give a fuck 'bout your stares, muthafucka! I done cursed God so who the fuck is man to fear?" WHACK! Tutsi caught me across my jaw with a swift punch and swept my feet with the broom. 'Damn!' I thought, staring upwards at him from the ground as he brought the broomstick down across my throat. Nah, brah! I wasn't about to let him kill me. I had an outdate and was trying to keep it by leaving prison on feet, instead of being carried.

I kneed him in the balls and jumped back to my feet with an east side bounce. I was ready to do what I had to do to keep this nigga humble. WHACK! I connected with a leaping hook that caught him off guard. Just two months ago he'd killed a mind to save my life and now we were slap-boxing with one another across the 5 range of J-block. This nigga thought I was sweet! I tried shooting another jab, but Tutsi caught my arm, pulling me close to him and body slamming me. It felt like every bone in my body had broken when I hit the cemented prison range. I reached for my back before seeing Tutsi's huge foot coming towards my chest. I rolled over and tried making back to my feet. Whistles were blowing and I heard screams from CO's. "Down! Down.....Down!" they yelled, waving their batons in the air threateningly.

I was ready to lay it down, but Tutsi had just got started. He crushed the first guard's jaw with a single blow to the face, sending him to sleep. This nigga done did it now! I saw an officer crack him across the back of his neck with his club. WHACK! I couldn't let them beat him down like that. Not after what he'd done to help me so I went upside a guard's head and took an ass whipping along with him. After they nearly beat us to death, they drug us off to segregation. I had mixed feelings about being in the hole. I was glad that we were tucked out of population, but upset that my ribs were broken and uncared for. They wouldn't let us go to the infirmary because they'd went too far with our beating and didn't want it to get out.

I leaned onto the speak chute and called Tutsi. "Aye Tutsi!" I yelled down the range.

"What, my brotha?" Tutsi answered like nothing had happened between us. I was shocked and thought he was going to be a problem after our fight.

"Nigga, you still staying?" I asked with a chuckle, causing him to laugh as well.

"Definitely, my brotha," he replied with the same cold demeanor. "Especially after I put steel through one of those guards." He was calm, which let me know that he was serious. He wasn't trying to put on; he was just stating his actual intentions.

"Nah, man. I can't let you do that," I protested again, just as I'd done on the range when we fought, but he was adamant.

"Let me?" he chuckled, knowing that our conversation was déjà vu. "I'm doing it." We both laughed, knowing that he was mocking what had led us to the can. We talked through the chute for hours each day. He explained his reason of wanting to stay in prison.

Tutsi's life back home was worse than any poverty that we'd ever witness in America.

 Our prison systems were luxuries in comparison to Sierra Leone's living conditions for its citizens. He didn't have anyone in the states and preferred prison over a freedom into a racist American society that was built on generations of greed and torture of his lost people. He was kicking some deep shit and for the first time since we'd met, I believed his story. Being in segregation was cruel on a nigga's psyche. Tutsi's stories didn't help any because of their graphic detail, but his stories were like movies. After months, I finally convinced him to allow me to help. I was set to be released after him and wanted Tutsi on my team. He was one of the real ones who was cut from a rougher cloth than me and I was sure about his loyalty. He'd killed feeling obligated by association and that etched our bond in stone. It was written.

***

Drake passed me the papers back and gave me dap. He smiled while nodding his head. It was back on and we had a man to replace Quan until his release.

"That's what's up, nigga," Drake said coolly. I looked over to Tutsi noticing that he was somewhere else. It reminded me of another time when we were in prison, shortly after we met, when I gave him his street name – Tutsi. He was cleaning his feet before prayer when I walked down on hm. He was in a distant zone, away from where he was in reality, but I didn't let that stop me from disturbing him.

"What up?" I asked with a chuckle because his feet were jacked up, like he'd been running through jungles for real.

"Shit, my brotha," he replied and pointed to his dogs. "I'm cleaning my feet."

"You might really be one of those Tutsi muhfuckaz off Hotel Rwanda." We both laughed because he'd seen the movie. It starred Don Cheadle. From that day forward, everyone around the prison compound called him Tutsi. It fit him because he was a real soldier.

CHAPTER 8

TREY

I saw fury in Ship's eyes when he walked in. He looked from Ace to me, and then over to Rocsi. She was sitting with her legs crossed on an ottoman painting her toenails. 'Damn!' I thought, discreetly glancing over to her while she colored perfection. Rocsi done grew the fuck up! I wanted to fuck, but knew that Ship would be at my head. He was my guy, but putting dick in his cousin was where he drew the line. Me and him used to fuck all types of hoes back in the day, but a lot of things had changed about Ship since then. He was still a goon, but he'd become more cautious and calculating about everything, which was why I'd done as he asked and let Ace's wound bleed out.

"Who cleaned this fucking guy up?!!" Ship asked, furious about one of us deviating from what he asked. To Ship, saying 'fuck him' was saying 'fuck the team' and he would lay a nigga down for throwing those words at us. He walked closer to Ace and looked at the raggedy stitches that Rocsi had sewn into his head.

"I've been on this couch minding my muhfuckin business, pimp," I replied, making it clear that I had nothing to do with Rocsi's decision to go against the grain. She was a hardheaded hoe who needed a hand-checking if you ask me, but Ship wasn't willing to let anyone go upside her pumpkin. I glanced over to Rocsi, waiting on her to man up and confess that she'd been the one who showed Ace some mercy, but she kept quiet. 'This bitch is a brat!' I thought, turning my head back to the television. I saw Ship draw his heat and stand next to Ace.

"Who did it?!!" Ship asked again. I wanted to take a quick glance over to Rocsi to dry snitch on the hoe, but I simply kept my eyes on the TV. Ship was one of the shrewdest niggaz I knew, so putting the clues together, finding out who had done it wasn't too far away for him. There was only two of us here. He'd been on shift with Chico and I'd already let him know that I was innocent of that charge. So there was only one person left – Rocsi! Slap the young hoe, my nigga. I chuckled, hoping he'd feel my request and go upside her head with his roscoe. It wasn't beneath Ship because he was a womanizing muthafucka. I'd witnessed him slap plenty of bitches and niggaz. That kind of shit was just part of his blood thirsty nature.

Ace was nervous as hell. His whole body shook; even his lips. Goosebumps bubbled onto his arms and Ship nurtured his fear by placing his hand onto Ace's shoulder. Ace's eyes whipped toward Ship's hand, scared that Ship's next motion would be slapping him across the face. 'Slap that bitch first, my nigga!' I thought, looking over to Ship with a smirk that signaled my thoughts.

"Since you don't want to answer me, Roc," Ship said calmly before smacking Ace across his head with the thick metal of his .45, sending blood skirting into the air. Ace screamed a shrill groan that gave me a sudden pang of empathy for the nigga. He'd caught it bad, but he'd brought it on himself by trying to get rich in my parts. I wasn't Nebraska, but I was close because I had a certified lawman on my team who would use his license to kill at any given time. Ship knelt down and stuck the barrel of his thumper in Ace's mouth.

"Huh?" Ship taunted, knowing the whimpers that fell from Ace's tongue couldn't be mistaken for words. "Four pound has your tongue, huh nigga?" Ship swatted Ace's back, sending the barrel deeper into his throat, choking him. He was still cuffed and couldn't make any adjustments. He just gagged and tears fell down his face because he'd been broken. Ship took the pistol out of his mouth and chuckled while wiping the blood and saliva off his gun with the collar of Ace's shirt.

"All your hard work was in vain," Ship told Rocsi calmly. She looked over to him with pure evil in her eyes. It was a stare that I'd never witnessed her give to Ship. She hated me, so I was acquainted with that look, but Ship was her carnal god. Ship chuckled at her ugly stare, unfazed by her animosity. Her emotions no longer mattered to him because she'd used them to care for an enemy.

I shook my head, still hoping he'd slap the hell out of her. 'Ship soft for this bitch,' I thought, certain that he would have hit the roof if I'd been the one who cleaned up Ace's wounds.

SHIP

I took my pistol out of Ace's mouth and used his shirt collar to wipe the barrel clean. I wasn't ready to end his life and especially not with a slug from my police issued tool. Ace was a coward and I fed off of a sucker's fear, so I put the pistol into his mouth solely to feed my ego. I couldn't believe what I'd seen when I walked in. Ace was sitting in the corner of the room all cleaned up. His head had been stitched and bandaged and immediately I knew that it was Rocsi who violated. I wanted to be sure before I made an accusation, so I asked. Trey immediately sold her out by letting me know that it wasn't him. That was just as revealing as telling me that Rocsi had done it because they were the only ones allowed inside the apartment besides me and Chico and we were on duty.

Rocsi was getting out of hand and eventually she was going to have to find her another hustle. 'I'm not letting her take me under,' I thought, shaking my head while glancing over to her. Fuck that, cousin or not! She kept her heartless stare on me, but it wasn't frightening; at least, not to me. I'd lost fear four years ago around the time I found an old .38 in the alley near the garage of my grandfather's house. Since that day, I've known the value of an equalizer because steel would always even things up when a man was outmatched.

"Get your ass over there an d pull those stitches out of his head," I demanded calmly, not wanting to upset her any further because nothing good would come from her anger. 'Because I will slap the shit out of you,' I thought while tucking my heat back into my belt holster. When I looked down, I saw a stream beeline from the leg of Ace's pants. You nasty motherfucker! I stepped over the stream of liquid fear and leaned towards his face.

"Bitch!" I pointed to the stream while staring at him with a hateful grimace. "I know you didn't piss on my motherfucking floor, nigga." I wanted to slap him again, but it was useless. He would have shitted himself next so I kept my cool

Rocsi reluctantly walked over with her scissors and started taking the sutures out of Ace's head. I needed him to bleed until he bled to death, or bleed until he died from infection. Either way, I needed him to die from the wound that I'd given him during the raid. He was the one who I'd set up to take the fall for Reggie's murder. He had to die because he'd sing the national anthem to Internal Affairs. 'This nigga couldn't even hold water about the shipment of cocaine rolling in, so there was no way that he'd keep what I'd done to himself,' I thought while shaking my head and pulling Trey into the kitchen.

Trey followed me into the kitchen and straddled a stool near the breakfast bar. I wanted to talk to him about Khalid. I wasn't sure that Rocsi was still built for this kind of work. She'd been acting flaky lately and I was sure that it had something to do with Quan's release date approaching. I don't know why she even fucks with that punk ass nigga! I sat across from Trey and glanced out into the front room where Rocsi was taking the stitches back out of Ace's head. I wasn't sure why she felt the need to be so compassionate to a cat who we were hitting. It was suspicious as hell.

"Trey, man," I began before looking over to Rocsi again, making sure she was busy and out of ear hustling range before I resumed. She was a loose cannon and would flip out if she knew we were talking about her. Especially if she knew we were ready to ice her out. "I don't know about Rocsi anymore, bro," I continued in a voice discreet enough for her not to hear.

"What's up, my nigga?" Trey asked, pretending to be surprised, but he knew me. Rocsi had violated the team without reason. Despite the fact that she was kin, she was say out of line. I couldn't trust her anymore because my judgment didn't mean shit to her.

"I'm saying she shouldn't have cleaned Ace up. I bust his melon for a reason, Trey." I looked back into the front room, making sure she wasn't straining her ears to eavesdrop, but she was still removing the stitches that she'd put into Ace's head.

"A reason?" Trey asked with a subtle chuckle. Trey thought everything was funny, but this situation was a lot more serious than he must have imagined.

"Hell yeah, bro. I wanted to keep his wound open until he died and then drop him off into an alley near his safe house. He killed Reggie before running off and dying in an alley." I explained. I looked at Trey, hoping he'd catch on to what I was insinuating. I was barbaric at times just for the hell of it, but this was some strategic shit that I'd came up with. There was all types of CSI shit going on inside the department and I'd hate to be victimized by a police murder conviction from some high-tech forensic evidence. 'Fuck that shit!' I thought, waiting on Trey's response.

"Yeah. Damn, my nigga. That's some boss shit right there, baby," Trey replied, feeling every detail of what I'd suggested. I was sure that he'd doubted me, just like Rocsi. But, he stayed true to the game and trusted my judgment, unlike my own flesh and blood. 'They say family will get you first,' I grunted, hoping that it wasn't so with Rocsi, but knowing that the streets had a way of chilling a niggaz blood. People turned on their own daily in the hood; backbiting each other because everyone was trying to eat off of a small plate. The mint bred treachery with each dollar they printed because there were 300 million greedy motherfuckers trying to split it. Me and Trey kicked for a little while longer until Rocsi finished and walked in to join us. I couldn't look her in the face knowing that she'd shitted on my orders so I bounced out. 'That's the last one,' I thought, slamming the door as I walked out of the apartment. Rocsi wasn't getting another chance. The next time she violated the squad, she'd be dying. I'd build this shit from the ground. It was my child and trumped the love that I had for Rocsi.

CHAPTER 9

QUAN

'Son of a bitch!' I thought, walking into the recreation room. I was heated after hearing that the DEA hit Ace's safe house. I'd been working on that lick for about two years; only to hear that a snitch had beat me to the punch. After meeting Krispy, a major player off the west side of Detroit, I was sure that I'd have a smooth re-entry into the game.

Krispy was a fly muhfucka. He walked around the prison yard with the latest gear like he wasn't doing a life stretch for continuing a criminal enterprise. His Cartier frames had glaciers around the lenses and his Rolex watch didn't tic tock. Niggaz throughout the country who were getting money on the outside had heard his name at one time or another and they rode his bandwagon like he was a prince. I was one of them but my motives were different from the rest of his flock. I knew that he was fly – meaning that he had a fly swagger, including his mouth. Krispy would brag about how much cocaine he'd moved through the Midwest and how he'd done it. I was sure that it was only a matter of time before he'd give me the name of a come up, so I stuck around waiting.

***

Me and Krispy had gotten pretty close throughout his stay at Milan. We were the best representatives of the Motor City form his point of view. He'd always pop game at me about how he didn't fuck with niggaz, how he'd only used them to get what he wanted in life. I'd listen, knowing that I'd heard that same song from the rest of the camp. Although he'd say shit like that, he'd slap fives with almost anyone who was willing to touch his hand. The west coast niggaz stayed away from Krispy, though. I didn't know if it was fear, jealousy or they knew something that the rest of the camp didn't know. But prison had a way of exposing a nigga's character.

Me and Krispy were sitting at a picnic table near the entrance of one of the housing units when Suge, a huge muhfucka out of San Diego, rolled down on us. Me and Suge were always cool, so when he pulled up with a mean mug on his face, it surprised me. 'I wonder what's up with this nigga?' I thought, looking from him over to Krispy, who kept his head down, trying not to make eye contact with Suge.

Suge had gotten his name because he was from California and he resembled Suge Knight. He had that usual prison build – top heavy with no legs, so I immediately sized him up in case there was going to be trouble. A few more west coast cats rolled around the corner, assuring me that it was on. 'This coward ass nigga done got me into some hoe shit!' I thought, easing off the bench because I wasn't going to let them sneak me. I wasn't gonna let them put the pressure on Krispy either. He was a coward ass nigga for sure, but he was with me and I didn't fold on my team.

"What's up with you niggaz?" I asked, watching big Suge closely because he was the only one of their crew who might have posed a threat to me. I was young, but I wasn't a shorty. I'd put in my share of work during the four years that I'd had in at that time.

"Nah, lil brah," Suge spoke out, holding his hands in front of him, showing me no confrontation. "This ain't got shit to do with you." I looked back towards the bench and Krispy still held his head low. 'This bitch ass nigga,' I thought, looking back over to Suge and his squad. It was evident that Krispy was aware that they'd be coming, which meant that whatever they were there for, he was guilty of doing it. I didn't give a fuck, though, I was with him and had to take a stand for the Midwest because those DC niggaz was thirsty and would be at our heads if they heard we was bending.

"I'm here, so it's my business," I said and stepped closer to Suge showing him that I wasn't fearing his show of force. Ain't no bitch in me, pimp. I stared at him, letting the contempt in my eyes say what I was unwilling to let slide from my mouth. I'll body one of you niggaz! I felt blood rushing through my veins and my muscles tightened. I was ready to get it one, sure that Krispy wasn't going to be much help and it wasn't stopping here. The yard would be silent for weeks after the coast wars started. The Midwest had the largest gathering, but everyone wasn't gangster – especially Krispy.

"Hold up, Quan, man," Krispy finally interceded. 'About time, nigga!' I thought, looking back at him as he stood from the bench. He was still carrying a defeated and coward swagger, unlike his usual boisterous self. I guess ten niggaz ready to stomp your face into the gravel would make a coward expose his hand.

Krispy walked over beside me. He wouldn't take a step further, so we stood side by side. "Imma get at your guy, Suge," Krispy said, looking fearful as hell. "It's ugly right now, but we good, brah." He held his hand out, wanting to shake with Suge. Suge grabbed Krispy's hand, pulling his ear close to his mouth and whispered something to him. It was something that he didn't want anyone around to hear. It was something only for him and Krispy to know about, but I was sure that it wasn't pleasant. Suge let Krispy's coward ass go and looked over to me.

"We good, Quan baby?" Suge asked, wanting to know if we would be having any problems after this. Although I could have whipped Suge, it wouldn't have helped my situation so I nodded, letting him know we were good.

"Yeah, we good, but this my peoples, Suge," I replied, letting Suge know that a problem with Krispy was a problem with me. Suge nodded and smiled before walking away. He acknowledged something that most niggaz would have let slip by them. I was making a power move of my own by connecting with Krispy. 'Yeah, pimp!' I thought, still watching as Suge and his entourage walked off. I'm gon eat!

That nigga was the glue that brought me and Krispy together. He was sure about me, a nigga who seemed loyal. I was, but not to him. Saving him from a west coast head cracking had made him open up to me even more. Krispy was giving me information about his team on the outside that he should have kept to himself, because I was plotting.

"Yeah, young Quan," Krispy bragged one afternoon on our way out of the chow hall. "I had it all, baby. Porsches, Benzes, all of those joints and you're gonna have 'em too." He nodded as we walked the track.

"For sure, brah!" I agreed, although we were talking about getting it from two different angles. He wanted me to work with him, but I was more interested in working against him. My car was a three- seater for me, Gucci and Drake. Those were my guys and we had to eat by all means, even betraying a nigga who I'd hooked up with along the way.

"I'm telling you...my nigga, Ace. He's gonna hold you down when you touch," Krispy chuckled, knowing that I was all ears. He fed off of ass licking niggaz, so I played right into his hand.

"I'm sayin, though, how he tryna fuck with a nigga, Krisp?" I asked, wanting to get more into detail about who and where this Ace nigga laid his head.

"Remember those Cali niggaz who pulled on a gangster that one day?" he asked. I'm thinking, 'Nigga, the only gangster present that day was me!'

"Yeah," I answered, because there was no way that he considered himself a gangster, because the gangsters that I knew did gangster shit.

"I've been plugged with their connect for over five years, baby. Making it happen from behind bars. You feel me?" He nodded arrogantly, showboating as usual and I took it all in. "Ace be sitting on fifty, sixty bricks at all times."

"Straight up?" I acted surprised although I was certain that he was telling the truth. Fifty ki's had never sat in front of me, but for a nigga like Krispy, that was some every day shit. "That's have, my nigga! You west side niggaz be eatin!" I pumped his inflatable ego up like a hot air balloon.

"Damn right! I'm Krispy, nigga!" he laughed. "I got a weight house over off Outer Drive and Six Mile that's cranking!" Krispy bragged, telling me about the safe house that he'd set Ace up with. They were stashing a surplus inside the walls for the drought. Krispy loved that drought money because he could five to ten thousand tax on each bird, so he kept his vault stacked up with weight.

Throughout the next couple of years, me and Krispy became tight. He gave me the game full throttle and I soaked it all in. He was never a killer, but he was smart enough to keep real goons around him, like me.
***
I watched Carmen Harlan's broadcast about the raid. One of the officers who'd went into the house had been killed by Ace. 'Damn!' I thought, still watching the story. Ace done blazed one of those pig bitches and bounced! It was always good to hear about one of my own getting away. Especially after watching CSI and Law & Order for damn near seven years because no one got away on those cop shows. Krispy walked in looking heated and sat next to me.

"You heard, huh?" Krispy asked in a whisper, looking around making sure that no one else was looking. Any other time, he'd want all the attention on himself, but when shit hit the fan, he wanted it to blow into the opposite direction.

"Yeah, that's why I'm in here. I wanted to see the whole play," I replied, still watching the TV. Me and Krispy sat and watched the story before leaving the recreation room together. When we got some space from the other ears, Krispy went nuts.

"My nigga!" he started, looking hysterical. "There were over forty bricks left in there, brah! The law tryna play games talkin 'bout they seized twelve kilos. That's some bullshit!"

Krispy was mad as hell, but he wasn't half as furious as I was. He was already set for life, but I was hurting. I had about sixteen thousand on my account, which wasn't even bird money, so it was mandatory that I found another lick because being a broke ass nigga wasn't trendy!

CHAPTER 10

GUCCI

I walked into club Plan B, suited as usual, wearing a custom tailored camel tan wool gabardine suite with chocolate accented squares. My chocolate Mauri alligator shoes, belt and bow tie set the whole color scheme off. Niggaz in the D knew how to put on, but none of them could out stunt me. I was the only player in the city who could be gaudy enough to sport an alligator bow tie and get away with it. That's why the streets named me Gucci. I was a top flight nigga who maintained his hood swagger.

It was packed with women and I was trying to scout out my new wifey. I needed a bitch to hold down the house that this street money was about to build. I'd been locked down for damn near six years and was ready to get it cracking. Four years in the joint and damn near two years on parole had handcuffed a niggaz whole movement. I was restricted from everything I loved, because it was all in the game. Even the iron that I had tucked into back of my belt line was good to have back. Throughout the time that I'd been out of prison, I felt naked without my steel. It was a must have piece of hood apparel where I was from. I strolled over to the bar, getting a Grey Goose and lime. I didn't even like the shit, but I read a book called 'It Was Always us' by Earn, a nigga on the SoReal publication label. One of his characters said that drink accessories were always good conversation pieces. So I thought 'fuck it! Let's see.' There were a lot of fine bitches around to sharpen up my game with because I was kind of rusty. I'd been with April's pale ass for nearly two years and she kept my balls dry, so there was never any use to play. I mean, I'd seen several hoes that I wanted to pound out, but I would have to get around April's cum thirsty ass.

"Damn!" I whispered to myself after seeing Aries. She was one of Quan's girl, Rocsi's best friends and I'd been trying to get with her for years. She wasn't into hustlers back then, when we first met them, but the times in the city had changed. Women were losing their jobs by the bushels and were looking for an alternative source of income. 'Um! I don't know, though,' I thought pulling on my throbbing pipe because she was turning me on with that sexy ass walk.

Their whole crew had a mean stride, especially Queenie. Shit! Just the thought of her was arousing. Queenie wasn't the finest of the three of them, but she was definitely the sexiest. She had an ass like an Olympic track star and skin like copper. Queenie was cute, but there was something about those yellow bitches like Aries that held me down. I'd wife that hoe right now! I kept my stare glued to her erotic sway while making my way over to her. I ran my tongue across my teeth, checking for grit because I didn't want to step to a broad as cold as Aries without being proper.

I could tell that she'd kept herself together over the years that I hadn't seen her because she was still glowing and youthful. Most females, who had been ran through and thrashed, wouldn't have been as appealing as Aries was. 'Shit!' I thought, still admiring her soft features while easing up on her.

"What's up, Aries?" I asked, standing behind her smiling when she turned around. She stared at me briefly, trying to remember where she'd known me from.

"Do I know you?" Aries asked snobbishly. 'Yeah bitch!' I wanted to say and slap the hoe to the floor, but I kept my composure because I knew how much Quan loved Rocsi.

"Yeah, ma. We used to kick it at Skateland!" I replied, trying to refresh her memory, but she wasn't interested. She giggled and turned, glancing at her friend before looking back over to me.

"The kiddie disco, huh?" Aries laughed and walked away with her girls. I was humiliated as a muthafucka and wanted to snatch her up by her silky ponytail. I downed the vodka and pulled out my cell. After dialing Rocsi's number, I put the phone to my ear and waited until she picked up.

"Roc?" I said, ready to find out what had happened to Aries because she wasn't like that when I'd known her. She was a real sweet broad, unlike the cold-hearted bitch she'd been today.

"Yeah, what's up, Gucci?" Rocsi asked in reply. Although we didn't speak often, Rocsi was always happy to hear from a nigga.

"Roc, what's up with Aries these days?"

"Oh, I don't fuck with her anymore," Rocsi replied with a chuckle.

"Why?" I asked, wanting to know how they'd fallen out after being so close. Me and my guys argued all the time but there was nothing that would crumble our friendship. We'd been there for one another when no one else was, so in reality, we were all that we had.

"She's just difficult," Rocsi giggled again. "Too difficult for me and you, so stay away from the hoe, Gucci. You feel me, babe?" There was something in what she'd asked me about feeling her. 'Aries must have done something to hurt Rocsi,' I thought, wanting to know what it was because Rocsi was Quan's girl, which made her family by proxy. After being humiliated by Aries, I left. I wasn't about to stand around the club looking fly and knowing I'd just been shitted on by a high trotting east side bopper. I pulled up to the apartments and saw a flock of niggaz out front as usual. I walked up to Doug, one of the floor generals of the youngsters, who hung out front catching unfaithful customers before they could get inside. I'd been letting the disrespect slide, but without any restriction we could turn the building into a war zone, because I was that type of nigga.

"Doug?" I said, walking up to him peacefully. If the altercation was going to hit, it was going to be because he didn't comply with the terms that I set, not because I'd come at him with disrespect.

"What up homey?" Doug replied, giving me a pound. We were cordial and I liked Doug because he had an aggressive hustling stroke like me. I'd been a young nigga out in the projects trying to bring it all together in a nights grind so I was familiar with what he was trying to do.

"Doug, let's get this money together, my nigga. I wanna eat, but I can't do that if you and your soldiers keep stealing off my plate." I looked up after noticing the light in my trap apartment pop on. 'Tutsi must have seen me drive up,' I thought, knowing that he kept his eyes opened because he didn't like me creeping up on him.

"Stealing?" Doug laughed like I'd told a joke and I took that as disrespect. This lil nigga think it's a joke! I snatched him up by his collar, bringing him into a snug chokehold. He was a slim nigga, weighing about one-fifty, so scooping him off his feet was easy. I was benching well over three fifteen when I left prison so the strength was still there. I wanted to squeeze the life out of him until I saw his crew walking up.

"Look, bitch ass nigga. I tried to let you eat, but it's over. Take yo squad and find somewhere else to hustle," I said calmly, pushing him away, not wanting to scuff my alligators. Cheese and Tutsi ran out of the building upping their tools.

"What's the problem, niggaz?!!!" Cheese asked swinging his hammer into Doug and his goons direction. 'Cheese done manned the fuck up!' I thought, pulling my strap from the back of my waist too. If shots rang out, I didn't want to be the only one without my heat up. I saw Tutsi move in on Doug. 'NO!' I wanted to scream, but the flame from his heat sprayed too quickly.

BLAH! Doug's head opened from the other side and his lifeless body fell to the ground. His soldiers tried to flee, knowing that six feet deep beef was on the scene. Cheese spun and let off something thunderous from his .50 caliber. The barrel on his cannon was at least eight inches and hit the youngster in the back and off his feet, canceling his birthday wishes. I didn't even know Cheese was capable of dropping a body. He'd been around for a while, but I wasn't comfortable enough to make life sentence moves with him. Niggaz were trading two year bids in for life sentence information every day and I wasn't trying to be the one.

BLOCCA!! I put a single shot into the back of Cheese's head. "I can't take that chance, Tutsi," I said and wiped the .40 off, throwing it beside Doug's body. "We out, fam." Me and Tutsi scrambled through the corridor of dead bodies and hopped into my rental car, leaving the scene.

CHAPTER 11

ROCSI

Khalid had my arm snuggled tightly beneath his as we walked into the funeral home. His nephew, Doug, had gotten into a shootout at the Chalmers apartments. It was evident from the navy blue enamel casket that Doug had lost more than the gunfight; he'd lost his life as well. I looked around the room, seeing a small army of young soldiers and knew that there would be repercussions behind Doug's and his henchmen's murders. 'Damn!' I thought, while walking through the maze of goons toward the row of caskets. Those niggaz were serious! There were six coffins aligning the floor, all occupied by young cats. None of them had made it to twenty-five. That's the game, baby. I shook my head knowing that if I wouldn't have hooked up with Trey and Ship, I would have suffered the same fate years ago. Prison had taught me a lot, including how to surround myself with the right people because on the inside shit would get dark for a bitch who didn't know how to navigate.

There weren't too many older people at the funeral, letting me know that Doug and his crew were most likely products of their environments. Their mothers and fathers were probably junkies who had lost their children to the streets while the fathers were busy shooting that smack into their groins or the mothers were replacing their lipstick with crack pipe residue. Fiends were paralyzed by that shit. Too paralyzed to give a fuck about their own children – I know. I know from experience.
***
I was eight when I found out about my parent's truths. Before then, I thought the world of them, but seeing your family for what it really is, is a humbling experience.

I'd just come home from school. Early as usual because it was Friday and I had the cool parents who would let me skip my last class at least twice a week. We weren't like the other families in our hood – we were close. Me, my mother and my pops. Fridays were movie nights. We'd all cuddle up on the couch and eat popcorn all day while watching movies. This was a family ritual that had been going on since I could remember.

My mother was in the kitchen, dropping the kernels into the pot of cooking oil. I loved the smell of that shit. It signaled a night of family and fun. We'd play board games and all types of wholesome shit.

"Ruth?" my dad called frantically after walking into the house. He marched toward the kitchen without even acknowledging me. "Hoe, I know you haven't been getting credit from Tee without breaking me off!" He demanded nastily. My parents argued often, but I hadn't ever heard my father call my mother a hoe before. 'Is mom a hoe?' I wondered because she answered to it like it was her name.

"Nah," my mother replied, still shuffling the popping kernels inside the pot. She looked scared as hell.

"Bitch, you lying! I just came from around there!" he spat, reaching into her pocket and pulling something from inside. It was a sealed baggie of crack. I wasn't into the streets then, but growing up in a community drowned with drug dealers and fiends, it was common knowledge what crack cocaine was. 'My parents are smoking!' I thought, scrambling off into my bedroom and diving into my urine stained mattress. I couldn't believe that shit.

"Arrrgh! Ah!" I heard my father scream in a high pitched voice, unlike his usual deep sultry tone. I leaped up, tears still flowing from eyes after finding out that my parents were junkies, and rushed back into the kitchen. My father lay on the floor, curled into the fetal position, screaming, his skin sizzling. Kernels were still popping on his flesh as the oil cooked him. That night was more gruesome than any movie that we could have watched because it was reality – my reality. My mother was tucked into the corner of the kitchen loading her stem not being distracted by my father's screams as his flesh peeled away from his body. 'I'm a crack baby!' I thought, terrified by that stigma, but knowing that it was the truth because the smell coming from the tail of the sizzling crack pipe was as familiar to me as the Friday night popcorn. I cried myself asleep and my mother freebased herself into crack heaven.

***

After the funeral, as me and Khalid walked out, my arm still snug beneath his, a few of the youngsters approached us. Khalid released my arm for the first time since we'd arrived and gave one of them a pound. The youngster was tall with long dreadlocks that fell over his shoulders. His brown eyes and masculine sway gave him an arrogant swagger, but he wore it well. 'He's cute,' I thought, giving him a once over while standing beside Khalid. He wasn't my man and I definitely wasn't his woman, but I knew my position with him. I was his work in progress. I was cool with that because I was on a come up mission. He was cool with it because he thinks he's going to kiss the pot of gold at the end of this rainbow.

"Khalid, man.......this shit is wild as the old west in these streets, don," the youngster who shook his hand said while shaking his head with a distressed look on his face. 'Doug must have been one of Khalid's solders,' I thought, listening to the way the youngster had addressed Khalid. Don?

Khalid nodded before replying, "Yeah, but this is what we do. We live the streets and die the streets." He nodded like he'd said some real OG shit. 'That was a rap bar, nigga!' I wanted to say, putting this clown on blast. He was at his nephew's funeral, at a time of mourning and he was trying to spit a hot sixteen. I'd always known how corny Khalid, but that shit took the cake.

"Right," the youngster agreed with a nod before glancing over to me. I was sure that he liked what he saw because I was fly, but he didn't have enough in his piggybank to take a walk in this park. Too much for ya, young blood. I smiled, politely letting him know that I was out of his price range.

"Oh, my bad, Fatso," Khalid apologized and turned to me, introducing us. "This is a good friend of mines, Rocsi. And this is Fatso, one of my guys." He emphasized guys, wanting me to know that he had the youngster on his payroll. Khalid was like that, always trying to put on a show for someone.

"Good go meet you," I chuckled, not wanting to call the youngster Fatso because it was insulting. He'd picked up on my reluctance because he insisted.

"Fatso," he finished my sentence. "And its good meeting you too, baby girl." Fatso smiled, letting me know that he wasn't as humble as Khalid would have liked him to be. I guess real recognized real, because Khalid was a fraud whose soldiers didn't even respect him. I made a mental note of that because we might need someone further inside, and a little pussy could flip a nigga like fatso with the quickness. After shooting game with Fatso for a little while longer, me and Khalid left. He'd shown me what he wanted me to see – his community: a team of young goons who laid their lives down for his movement, not knowing that he was too coward to have done what they'd done himself.

***

After changing clothes, I slid over to the apartment to man my shift. I had been a month since the raid, but Ace was still held hostage in our apartment. We fed the nigga just enough to survive, but that was the extent of it. There were some days that I'd hear him wheezing for air. The sound of short air making me want to end it for him, putting a bullet through his forehead, but I couldn't.

I'd already violated the team once and a second violation would cause some ruckus – the type of ruckus that I couldn't handle on my own. I was sure that Quan would call Gucci and Drake to service if it jumped off, but I'd have to tell him about everything that I'd been doing since he'd been locked up. Quan and I had a don't ask, don't tell policy because it was better like that. How would a street nigga look in the streets, if the hood knew that his bitch was working with the drug task force. Even though me, Ship and Trey were hustling like any other clique in the city, the get down or lay down rule, a dope boy's bitch was held to a different standard.

I walked in and Trey was lounging on the couch watching SportCenter as usual. 'I swear you're a creature of habit,' I thought, rolling my eyes as I passed by him. We hadn't been speaking since he'd dry snitched on me about stitching Ace up. I did that shit for the team because Ace would have died if I hadn't cleaned up his wounds. I'm sure of that and we wouldn't have been able to make a move on their shipment this weekend. I couldn't understand why Ship didn't see it that way. Instead, he'd closed me out thinking I was against him. Fool! Ship was my cousin and I'd lay a nigga down for him, but his ego was too big to see past it. He thought everyone who didn't agree with his way was against him on a personal level. He'd saved me from myself when I was a young wild bitch. I wished I could return the favor, but Ship was too arrogant to take game from me.

I sat on the ottoman, away from Trey and the television while intently watching Ace's body movements. He was broken and numb, but his eyes let me know that he was still plotting. 'A nigga like him can't be willing to take this laying down,' I thought, still eyeing him. His hungered stare was pleading with me, but I wasn't the one. Niggaz always think the bitch is the weakest link. I chuckled, assuring him that I wasn't as empathetic as he thought.

I'd cleaned up his gash as an assurance that he'd live to give us the information we needed to get at his bag. And he did.

TREY

After watching the rest of SportCenter, I bounced. It was Rocsi's shift and we weren't cool enough for me to sit in the spot with her. Actually, I couldn't stand her. It was a love hate thing because I wanted to blow her back out. 'Shit!' I thought, grabbing my dick before hopping into my whip. Just the thought of sliding up in that young wet pussy was causing my manhood to rise. Rocsi knew how I felt about her, but she was caught up with a jailhouse nigga – Quan.

I didn't know who he was, but he had the pussy on lock. She'd fucked a few cats for the team, but recreation sex wasn't happening. I'd been shadowing her lately because Ship didn't trust her. He was on some other shit because Rocsi was a thoroughbred loyal bitch. I was blinded by those perky titties, but even I could see that. Ship was just self-centered and didn't like what she'd pulled at the apartment when she cleaned Ace up. I knew what she was doing, although, I wouldn't tell Ship. She was trying to keep the nigga living so we could keep our come up alive. Without Ace, we weren't getting to that shipment this weekend. Those California niggaz were sending the load on the pretense that Ace was still living and working; so without him, it was a no-go.

I pulled up to Pops' house. Pops was an old school cat who was still stacking paper. He didn't fuck with too many niggaz, which was why he was still in the game, but me and him been getting down for years. I liked the nigga and had never thought about sending Ship at him, but I had to make a dollar off of him somehow. He moved work into the streets of my city, so it was a must that I ate off his plate. 'I'm the prince of the city!' I thought with a slight chuckle while walking up to his porch.

I'd called earlier, but he was at Doug's funeral. I knew young Doug E. Fresh too and it was fucked up what had happened to him, especially knowing his hustling potential. A lot of hood niggaz felt Doug's swag and I was sure that whoever was responsible for his death would be seeing him again soon because Khalid's goons would be on the prowl for them. Pops' wife opened the door when I walked up to the porch. They'd been waiting on me. Pops was cautious like that and didn't trust anyone, so I know he was interested in who I'd have following me. Niggaz did that type of shit all the time – set a meet for a picture up (a picture was a look at the product), and have someone trail them to come in and lay everyone down after they were inside. I'd graduated to a grand hustle and put that petty stick-up shit behind me.

"What's up, Pat?" I asked after getting inside the house.

"Shit, I'm good," Pat smiled and pointed toward the den, where Pops was waiting and walked off. I caught a glimpse of all that ass that Pat was carrying around. She'd aged a little, but she still had it and I would always take a look when I came around. She knew it too; that's why she walked off twisting that mountain nastily. I walked into the den where Pops was doing what I'd just left from doing – watching SportCenter.

"What it do, Pops?" I asked and gave him a pound. Although we had a mutual respect for one another, it was written that weren't friends, so we kept it real cordial. Pops knew what I did because he had connects to people that me and Ship had hit before Ship joined the police force and an ex stickup kid one the narcotics force, as well as a best friend who was still knee deep into the game. These links were criminal intent in itself. He respected the principles of the streets – see no evil and speak no evil. 'Principles that I violated daily,' I thought, sitting on a couch that sat across from Pops.

"Trey, I'm sure you know about what happened to Doug," Pops said flatly, giving me the impression that he wanted to know if I'd had anything to do with it. Pops still on that fake Mafia shit! I chuckled and shook my head before answering. This was the part of the game that I didn't like – being trapped inside of someone's home making deals. I liked doing business on my terms, but thirty brick business was different. A nigga had to deal with who he could trust, and I trusted Pops.

"Yeah, I heard about that shit. That was some Harlem heroin wars type of gunplay there," I said, shaking my head, playing along with Pops' statement. I was sure that he wanted to right out ask me if I'd been involved and eventually manned up and did just that.

"How you know that?" Pops asked boldly, staring at me in an examining way. 'Nigga, I'm a boss!' I thought, smiling at his accusation posed as a question. You can't trip me up like that! And he should have known better.

"Nah, Pops," I replied calmly, shaking my head assuring him that I wasn't the culprit. I'm bigger than that old school. What would I gain from sticking a young nigga who was hustling outta the 'jects?" I met eyes with Pops, giving him the same cold stare that he'd given me.

"Nah, baby," Pops eased up and wisped a fake ass smile across his face. A rookie would have fell for it, but today Pops was fucking with a pro. "I wasn't putting that yon you, Trey." He leaned forward giving me another pound. I should have slapped his hand away, and would have if I was on my home court, but this was Pops' crib and I was sure that Pat was somewhere close. Probably posted with an assault rifle. She was cool with me, but fucking with a woman's meal ticket would get a nigga shredded.

"Yes you were," I relied with a nod, letting him know that I was game tight and knew that he'd implied. "That's neither here nor there, Pops." I dismissed the tension between us because I was more interested in getting the business straight. "Is you tryna get these slabs or what?"

"Slabs?" Pops asked curiously. 'Bitch ass nigga!' I thought, ready to go upside his head before remembering how old he was. I guess he saw the ill in my eyes because he leaned back.

"Pops, I thought you were playing games like I'm wired or something, nigga," I gave him an inquisitive stare, seeing if that was what he was doing. If so, Ship would be paying him and Pat a visit.

"Man, hell nah!" Pops replied, shaking his head convincingly. 'You just spared yourself, nigga!' I thought, still eyeing him because most hustlers could lie without pause, but Pops' eyes were vacant. He didn't know what a slab was.

"Well, what's up? I got thirty whole ones for fifteen a box."

"That's reasonable, but how many do I have to cash out?" Pops asked, trying to stall me out on paying the whole four hundred and fifty thousand. Pops, stop gaming, nigga! I chuckled, wanting to lean on his old ass. I'd came through, trying to show him some love and he was still trying to run game on me. Niggaz! I grunted while shaking my head.

"All of them or its twenty and you gotta cash out twenty." I was playing hardball with him now because I felt disrespected by his conniving demeanor. I'd been fucked by plenty of hustlers while I was coming up, but the tides of the ocean had changed and it was my turn to put pipe in niggaz.

"What?" Pops asked, shaking his head, insulted by how I'd came back at him. 'Yeah, muhfucka!' I thought, staring him down, knowing how he'd felt because I'd just had the same emotions.

"I said twenty a box and you gotta break bread for twenty of them," I repeated flatly, letting him know that I wasn't recanting on shit that I'd said. The friendly shit sunk when you tried to run game, old muhfucka. I sighed, waiting for him to answer. Cashing out twenty kilos at twenty thousand was still four hundred grand, so he was better off cashing out the whole thirty for the extra fifty. Pops sat across from me, still shaking his head. I was sure that he was trying to do the math on the two offers so I rushed him.

"Aight then, Pops," I said, standing up like I was ready to leave. Although I didn't want to, I would have bounced and found another taker who was trying to eat.

"Nah, nah," Pops said, stopping me from walking out. "I'll take them, but I need a few days." He looked up to me, hoping I'd give him that much leeway, but I couldn't. Sitting around with thirty bricks after making a proposition could be deadly if Pops was to get grimy.

"Hell, nah, Pops," I said adamantly, shaking my head and walking toward the door. "I ain't waiting around for you to send a few soldiers at me. Nigga, is you crazy?"

"I wouldn't do no shit like that, Trey!" Pops stood up and walked over to me. He was frail and didn't have a threatening demeanor, although, he was a monster back in the late seventies; when crack first hit the city. I'd heard about some of the gangster shit that Pops had put down, but this wasn't his era.

"Hold up, Pops," I chuckled, holding my hands as he approached me.

"Nigga. Please," Pops replied, chuckling at the way I held him off. "Cut that petty bullshit, Trey. I'm tryna get those hogs, baby. Let a nigga eat with you?" He pleaded, knowing that I'd given him an opportunity to reclaim his youthful swag. Thirty bricks had touched my hands a hundred times and I never had to buy one of them, but to an old school dopeman like Pops, that thirty would change the game for him. He'd become what he always desired to be, but never had the hustling potential to become a retired baller. Pops would be able to put the Pyrex down after this lick and I held the juice.

I stared at him; trying to see if there was any deceit within Pops' eyes. 'If you're on some hoe shit, Pops, Imma kill your whole bloodline!' I thought, still watching his demeanor closely.

"Fuck it!" I finally agreed. "We can do that. We shook and I pulled Pops closer to me, whispering into his ear, "If you play me though, Imma cut your eyelids off and make you watch me rape and kill Pat's fine ass." I smirked and turned to walk away. I was sure that Pops understood me and if he had any love for his wife, he should have listened because what I'd told him was the gospel.

CHAPTER 12

BLAST FROM THE PAST

Being behind the trigger of his 9mm Desert Eagle brought back memories for Tutsi. Growing up, mining the diamond fields of Sierra Leone was catastrophic on a dimension that an everyday guy couldn't imagine. The images of a country governed by a corrupt political system were devastating to a child; especially one who didn't see any future for himself. Tutsi was the son of a miner who panned the fields of Zimi, a small jungle region of Sierra Leone. Being the son of a miner led Tutsi to suffer his ultimate fate which seemed better than the 40 year life expectancy of the Mende people.

It was early June of 1991. The Liberian troops had already moved into the region but Zimi hadn't felt the full effects of their brutality. The Liberian guerillas called themselves the Revolutionary united Front or RUF, posing as a legitimate party seeking control of the Sierra Leone government. Their real aim was forming a stronghold of the rich diamond fields that aligned the country. Sierra Leone was a one rule party nation governed by the All People's Congress (APC) since the late seventies, but all that changed after the RUF invaded their country.

Tutsi was in the fields when he was captured by the RUF soldiers. They came into the fields chopping men, women and children down with their assault rifles. Women were ducking behind hills of clay that had been dug to pan stones trying to save their lives, but the militia wasn't having it. They came to slaughter and maim and that's exactly what they did. Tutsi, young and unwilling to die, chose his best fate after being held at gunpoint. The gunfire had ceased into a single shot minimum for the old and frail. Guerillas walked through towering their rifles to those who they saw fit to die heads and firing single shots into them, killing them instantly. They kept the youthful and agile because they would be used to man the fields panning diamonds for the RUF. A child soldier, only a few years older than Tutsi, held an AK47 to Tutsi's head. His arms trembled heavily. Tutsi noticed but didn't know if it was from the weight of the rifle or his fear to kill. They both stared at one another. Tutsi was unfazed by the imminence of death because he'd seen the most brutal part of life. 'Death can't be as bad as life had been,' Tutsi thought and stepped forward, pressing the barrel of the young warriors gun flush to his own forehead. He was ready to die, but the youngster wasn't ready to kill.

"Shoot him!" one of the RUF generals demanded of the child soldier, but the youngster's arms only quivered more. Tutsi's eyes widened. He'd just seen his father become a victim of the Bloodshed Squad, the unit who had just raided the diamond fields that he and his father panned. He wanted to get it over with because he had no one else to live for.

"Shoot him!" the general commanded again, this time walking over next to the youngster brandishing the cannon-like rifle. The child soldier was terrified and wouldn't pull the trigger. Suddenly, the general snatched the weapon and handed it to Tutsi.

"Kill him!" the general pointed to the teenage warrior who cowered after having Tutsi at gunpoint. Brutality was the initial premise of the RUF's movement and a coward had no place within their ranks.

BLAH! Tutsi fired a standard single shot to the side of the youngster's head, throwing his brains across the field.

That day, life changed for Tutsi. He went from field hand to squad leader. He was captain of the youth who commanded the Kill Man No Blood Unit (KMNBU). His team went into villages and provinces torturing and murdering civilians who resisted slavery and rape. On orders, Tutsi would carry out barbaric killings daily, being transferred from one team to another until he was finally placed with the KMNBU.

In late July of the same year that he'd been taken in by the RUF, Tutsi was sent as a tagalong with the KMNBU. Unknown to him, he was being groomed to lead the youthful team of killers. Ahmad, the general who had ordered Tutsi to shoot the cowardly soldier at the diamond field, walked Tutsi into a clay hut. It was filled with a family of crying women and children. An older man was being held down to a wooden table. Ahmad pointed at the man.

"Kill him! No blood," Ahmad commanded, letting Tutsi know that seeing red would be a failed mission of his. Tutsi nodded, knowing that a failed mission could cost him his life by savage means. He'd seen the RUF pillage his community and others with a pitiless ravage, and knew that his life meant nothing to them. He looked around the shabby hut and saw a claw hammer. It was probably used to pouch fig trees for honeycombs, but his use for it would be more uncivil. WHACK! Tutsi slammed the hammer into the man's chest, bursting his heart with a single blow. The sound of the man's ribs and chest plate crushing beneath his skin was so horrid that the other guards cringed. Tutsi threw the hammer to the floor. It was his first murder without shedding blood, but it wasn't his last. Over the next few years Tutsi soared through the ranks of the RUF, committing all types of felonious slayings and forgetting about his Mende heritage. He was a Revolutionary United Front Soldier.
***
Tutsi sat across from Gucci eyeing him, unable to trust his only comrade after what he'd seen him do to Cheese. Tutsi had spent a lot of time with Cheese at the trap house before Gucci was granted his parole and had grown to trust him. He wanted to question

Gucci about his putting a hole through Cheese's head, but Gucci was a general. Tutsi took orders and obeyed them so he kept quiet.

"What's up, Tutsi?" Gucci asked, noticing the way Tutsi kept cutting his eyes at him. He was sure that Tutsi wanted to know why he'd made the move he made, especially after seeing how close Cheese was becoming with them.

"Omar? I could have understood, but Cheese was my brotha," Tutsi said, not making eye contact with Gucci. In his camp back home in Sierra Leone, making eye contact while questioning a superior's actions was considered being hostile so Tutsi kept his eyes to the floor.

"My nigga," Gucci replied with a chuckle, letting Tutsi know that there wasn't any hostility. They were tight, but Gucci was sure that things could change between them at any moment because Tutsi was still unstable from being a child soldier. Gucci had grown up rough. He was the child of two generations of heroin addicts and being delinquent since the age of twelve. Gucci knew what poverty and hardship was like. But he couldn't fathom growing up with license to kill like Tutsi had, so he was easy with how he approached shit with Tutsi.

"Cheese wasn't your brotha," He mocked Tutsi's deep Mende accent. "I'm your brother and the only one." He nodded, hoping Tutsi understood where he was coming from. The rest of their team was cool with Tutsi, but they hadn't accepted him like Gucci had because they didn't know him like Gucci did.

"Whatevah," Tutsi dismissed the conversation and walked off into the kitchen. It had been a week and this was the first time that they'd been to the apartment since the shootout.

Gucci was familiar with Doug from seeing him hustling around the complex corridor, but he didn't know that Doug was plugged into some heavy hitters. The streets were screaming that Doug's and his team's murders were hits which made it safe for Gucci to move back in and set up shop in the Chalmers housing projects. Their flow started off slow because someone had moved in on their hustle while they were gone. Gucci was pissed about that and wanted to move on them, but the hood would be looking at him for Doug's murder if another nigga in the apartment complex was killed. It would surely look like a territorial thing. Although Gucci had Tutsi, one of the coldest hearts in the city, riding with him there was no way that they could hold court with Khalid's crew. He had a clique of young gunners off the north end that were born into the game and would die to continue their hood's legacy.

Khalid himself was an arched coward. Gucci, Drake and Quan used to cop work from him back in the day when they were young and on the come up. Quan wanted to hit Khalid, but Gucci and Drake kept it from going down because Khalid used to show them love.

"Gucc?" Tutsi called for him while peering out into the corridor. Gucci rushed over peeking through the thin curtains.

"Who the fuck is that?" Gucci asked, staring at the nigga who Tutsi was pointing to. He was a thin, light skinned nigga with a thugged out swagger. He had long locks that fell over his shoulders and a thick hooded sweater pulled over his head. They watched as he stood out front doing hand to hands with a couple of crack fiends. 'This nigga is looking for a slug!' Gucci thought, tapping Tutsi on the back and turning to walk out of the apartment.

Tutsi walked out into the corridor of the building followed by Gucci. He was already upset about Gucci's response to Cheese's death and was hoping that the soldier hustling their corridor would give him a reason to let off some steam. He rubbed his waistline making sure his heat was accessible. Gucci moved beside them as they approached the young gangster.

"What up, don?" The youngster asked as they approached. Neither of them was flashy so he had probably mistaken them for fiends. The youngster reached into his pocket while using his eyes to probe around the courtyard.

"Shit, nigga," Gucci replied, moving on the young goon. He wasn't sure if the nigga was digging for a strap or his sack of stones, so he wanted to be close enough to muscle him out of it, if it was heat. "I'm holding these 'jects down lil brah. Two of my mans already took it to bed out here, but we ain't burying no more of ours." At that time, Tutsi upped his cannon, ready to let it explode on anyone who opposed Gucci's rule.

"I'ont know who you with, pimp. But I ain't movin until these stones are gone," the youngster said, holding out his hand to show Tutsi and Gucci a palm full of boulders.

'Damn!' Gucci thought, staring at the size of the stones. He was sure that it was shipped because there was no way that a young cat like him would be selling straight drop in stones that size. Gucci gave him a once over. His initial reaction was to put pipe to the young street soldier's head, but he didn't know who he was working with, so he stayed cool. Tutsi still held his heat to his side, quiet and watching the dope boy for any sudden movement.

"Lil nigga, go head on before we light up this courtyard with these block rockers," Gucci demanded and pulled his .50 caliber from his belt. He was sure that the .50 would create the fear that the youngster should have had when Tutsi brandished his four nickel. He waved his thumper in a shooing manner, giving him a chance to run off, but the youngster didn't move.

"Lay me down, don, 'cause I can't go home without slumping these last twelve stones. Niggaz in my household in my household is hungry and I'm the onlyest muhfucka who tryna feed 'em. Feel me? So go head and lay me down because I can't leave here without this bread." The young goon turned around and walked back to his post. There were a few fiends waiting on some action and he wasn't about to let them slide through without serving them. He made his move and then pointed back to Tutsi and Gucci, who were staring at the young gangster in shock. Neither of them could believe how cold he'd been while staring down the barrel of two cannons. One of the fiends walked back towards them, startling Tutsi. He snugly wrapped his finger around the trigger of his .45 and watched the man closely.

"What's up, man?" the fiend asked with a compulsive shake. He was tweaking and Gucci immediately recognized it. The street soldier had sent two of the baseheads at them, breaking bread to show a truce. 'This young nigga is really hood!' Gucci thought, surprised by what the youngster had done. That showed game and million dollar balling potential and Gucci liked what he'd seen.

"Nah, brah," Gucci replied, nodding in the youngsters direction. "Y'all go ahead and spend with my guy over there." The youngster looked back and Gucci nodded, assuring him that he accepted his truce. The mood of the projects said let the young goon eat and Gucci didn't want to violate that.

"Let me holla at you, soldier," Gucci said, still searching the courtyard with his peripheral. He wasn't trying to miss anything. Not the law, not the ski mask boys, and definitely not a sell. He e was groomed into a seasoned hustler who was ready to eat by any means.

"I'm Gucci." Gucci reached out, giving the youngster a pound. "And this is my ace, Tutsi."

"I'm Hashes." He reached over to give Tutsi dap, but Tutsi just left his hand hanging out there. He stared at Hashes, wondering where he'd come from and not liking the way he'd stood up to them. Pictures of ways to slaughter the young hood were flashing through Tutsi's mind. He wanted to maim him before shedding his blood, but Gucci was thinking differently.

"Oh yeah," Gucci said, nodding at the uniqueness of the youngster's street name. "Hashes huh?" He glanced over to Tutsi, noticing that Tutsi was still clinched tight to his piece.

"Yeah, I used to push that chronic before I did my juvie bid. Feel me?" Hashes chuckled. "So niggaz started calling me the hash man and from there came Hashes." He nodded, knowing that his handle was as rare as his hustling capability.

"Yeah, I feel you," Gucci agreed with a nod while coolly rubbing the bridge of his nose. He was thinking, trying to figure out a way to make things run smooth for the both of them. He wasn't moving enough product to bless the youngster too well, but he could make room for him.

"Dig, Hashes. Let's get together this weekend so we can put something together, because you ain't the only nigga whose family is tryna eat. Feel me?" He mocked Hashes slang. Gucci had a habit of doing that – copying someone's swagger and making fun of it.

Hashes nodded, agreeing to meet up with Gucci on the weekend. He'd picked up on Gucci's arrogant mocking of his swagger, but it was useless to challenge him because he'd already won. He'd moved the rest of his stones and was rolling out before the hustler's curfew. At some point the ski mask boys would be coming out to scout their potential prey and he wasn't trying to be their victim.

CHAPTER 13

SHIP

I was out of my district doing an illegal and unlawful sting, but the move had to be made. I followed the semi as it connected on to 75 North expressway from Interstate 70. I was sure that it was the truck because the connect had described it to a science. It was a late model Volvo semi with a SKY company logo sticker across the back of the trailer. They had been moving for years on the same route, without paying their toll and it was about time for them to pony up on their dues. Chico patiently awaited the truck's arrival. He was posted up on the Michigan side of the Ohio/Michigan border and would pull the rig over on a routine traffic stop after we crossed over into the dirty glove. From there, I'd take the helm.

As I followed the semi, I peeked inside, sizing up the driver. He was an older looking Hispanic guy with a thick bicycle moustache and dark shades who probably didn't speak any English. And if he did, I was sure that he'd most likely pretend that he didn't. I'd done plenty of stings and most of them ended with us releasing the driver into the custody of customs officials. The cartels would recruit unsuspecting immigrants who were looking to make a quick buck into transporting their narcotics across the country for desperate wages. Sometimes they would get fucked in the game and catch a ten or fifteen year stint in the FED, but most of the time they'd just get released into their country's custody, which was worse for some of them.

I'd also canvassed the truck's appearance, trying to assess how long it had been on the road and where it had really come from. It was unusually clean for the distance that it was supposed to have traveled and that made me cautious. Looking around the immediate area, I couldn't be sure if the truck had a tail on it.

There weren't any cars that I'd seen more than once unless they were good enough to fool me also. There was supposedly a thousand kilos inside of the truck. A life changing amount of money could be made off of that amount of dope and there wasn't any telling who or where they were coming from, so I wanted to be apprehensive as ever with this stop because I wanted every one of the kilos on board.

Me, Chico, Trey and Rocsi had agreed to take only half, but taking half would be defeating the purpose. 'Fuck that!' I thought with an insidious laugh. I have to have all of those, baby! We'd usually leave a few bricks for the reports, making sure the district attorney and the chief was happy after a bust. But this lick was different because it wasn't supposed to be happening. No one from the department knew about the load, so we could do whatever we saw fit with the package, especially since Reggie's bitch ass was out of the way.

As soon as we passed the border, I saw Chico's squad car pull ahead of the truck. We wouldn't be stopping the truck there, in the middle of the interstate, because it would bring the attention from the highway patrol and foil our caper. Instead, we planned to wait until the truck entered the city limits, where we were in control of the movement and pull it over then. The semi slowed while passing a state trooper. 'Shit!' I thought, seeing the trooper's car darting through traffic and pulling behind the rig. It was evident that the truck was about to be pulled over.

"Go…go…go!" I yelled into my radio. The trooper was about to break an egg that I wanted to crack and I couldn't allow him to do that. I smiled after seeing Rocsi's van fly past me. She was hailing speeds of at least one hundred miles an hour. Trey showed up next, pulling onto the expressway from the Lincoln Park entrance.

BOOM! A thunderous roar of crunching metal rang out. ERRRRRRKKKK! Tires squealed as a Ford Taurus braked, sliding across the tarmac and nearly slamming into another car. Horns sounded after Rocsi slid into the rear of Trey's SUV and the trooper immediately dipped out from behind the semi, speeding over to the accident. I was sure that he'd seen everything because me and my team had staged it that way. We always kept a contingency plan because there was no telling when the unthinkable would happen – like it just did. I looked over as we passed the crash. It wasn't bad. Neither of them was hurt so me and Chico stayed glued to the truck as it cruised into the Detroit city limits. We were out of harm's way and able to put our play down without any interference from other law agencies.

Chico slowed and flashed his lights signaling that he was the law. The truck slowed and pulled over to the service lane. I pulled behind the truck, blocking it in. Chico jumped out of his squad car unbuckling his service issued pistol. I watched as Chico leaped onto the stairs of the truck's cab before getting out. By that time, I was sure that the driver had his eyes on the officer and nothing else, giving me the opportunity to creep around to the passenger door and crawl in. As I crept around, I heard Chico asking the Hispanic man all kinds of ignorant questions in Spanish. He asked about the headlights, the trailer and finally about the door locks. The driver popped them, giving me access to jump in with him. WHACK! I slapped him across the top of his head with my Berretta, instantly drawing blood from his cranium. He grabbed his head and said something in Spanish that made Chico chuckle. 'I'm going to find out what was so funny later,' I thought, slamming the passenger door and pushing the barrel of my heat into his side.

"Bitch!" I spat nastily and pushed the pistol deeper into the contours of his fat side pouch. "Don't even act like you don't speak English, because if you do, you'll be singing ten Hail Mary's after feeling this hot ass lead." I nodded, making sure he understood me. He nodded assuring me that he did.

"Okay....okay," the driver replied while continuing his frantic nod. E must have figured out that he was being robbed instead of arrested, because he was more compliant than the drug mules usually were.

"Where's the coca?" I asked flatly. I wasn't trying to waste any time playing games, especially knowing what was at stake. "Now, motherfuckers!" I demanded, raising the pipe from his side to his temple.

"Okay....okay...it's in the trailer. Far back inside." I could see the fear in his eyes and knew that he was telling the truth.

"Drive, then!" I commanded and he hit the emergency brake before dipping back into traffic. Chico trailed us to the warehouse that we'd rented for the drop. 'It's on, baby!' I thought, knowing that my life was about to change after getting hold of a thousand kilos.

We pulled into the warehouse lot and into the shed. It was a huge empty space that was used for dry food storage. I waited until Chico hopped out and made it over to the driver's door before getting out. Chico grabbed the driver, slamming him face down into the pavement and pressing his iron against his head of stringy hair. We didn't want him to make a run for it, especially if the package wasn't inside. Sometimes the loads came in twos, but the first would be the pick off load; the truck that would be stopped by the highway patrol, giving the other truck some leeway of sliding through unscathed.

I strolled around to the back of the trailer, opening it and seeing about seven to ten pallets with loads of bubble wrapped product on them. I jumped on and got pissed. 'This motherfucking Spic is playing games' I thought, ready to leap off the truck and go upside his head. The bubble wrapped skids were boxes of recycled paper towels. I walked over and snatched a Bounty box from one of the stacked pallets and opened it.

"Ain't this about a bitch!" I exclaimed, rushing off the truck and back around to the driver. Chico still held him face down on the cement at gunpoint. WHACK! I slapped him across the side of his head, sending a definitive message that I wasn't playing any games. A yelp flew from the man's mouth and he covered his head with his hands. WHACK! WHACK! I went across his hands, crushing his fingers before pushing the nose of my Berretta into his eyeball.

"Bitch! Where is my product?!!" I asked and swung the pistol back, threatening to bring it back across his head if he held out on me. I'd killed men for one brick, so there wasn't any telling what extent I was wiling and ready to go to about a thousand.

"Sir...." The driver held his hands up defensively. "Please! Por favor, senor! It's in the truck!" he yelled, still holding his hands out, trying to block himself from a gunshot or another slap of my thumper. I'd just checked the trailer, which was housing a shitload of recycled goods, so I knew he was lying or just crazy. Either way, I was going to find out something.

"Bitch!" I said, staring at him with menacing eyes that assured him of his imminent death upon a lie. Sweat had started to perspire from my forehead and saliva, from the thirst of getting dope boy paid, was dripping from my mouth. "You've got one chance to show me," I finally finished in a vehement snarl.

I pulled the driver to his feet and drug him to the trailer, pushing him inside. Chico and I kept a close watch on his every movement, because we weren't sure if he'd stashed a gun inside the trailer somewhere. Drug dealers used some of the deadliest tactics to protect their supply, so it wouldn't be beneath them to arm their mules. During a highway sting, when I first joined the drug task force, I met a mule whose family was being held hostage back in Guatemala. If he didn't get the bag delivered, his family would have been killed. I held my pistol on him while he rumbled through the trailer, pushing the first few pallets aside, while making his way deeper inside. Chico stood watch on the outside of the truck.

"Look!" the driver waved me over and pulled a Bounty box from the pallet. He opened the box, showing me about twenty individually wrapped kilos of cocaine. 'What a goddamn day!' I thought, shaking my head, knowing that my life had changed forever. I looked inside of a few boxes, checking to make sure that everything was there before pushing the driver out of the truck. I smiled and nodded to Chico.

"My guy, we're millionaires."

BLOCCA! Chico put a slug through the middle of the driver's forehead and we started unloading our newfound wealth.

CHAPTER 14

DRAKE

I watched as a young Latino guy and Rocsi tossed a body rolled into an Oriental carpet into an alley behind Ace's safe house; the one that had been raided about a month ago. 'What the fuck is Rocsi doing with these niggaz?' I wondered after seeing her dump the body out and burl back down the alley with the carpet, tossing it into a van and peeling out. I'd been keeping an eye on the area after talking to Quan, because his mans needed a lead on a nigga named Ace's whereabouts. Quan had warned me not to play too close to the hose because there was no telling who was still lurking, but he wanted me to kidnap Ace if I saw him. I was confused, though. I was wondering why he'd wanted me to case the spot out if Rocsi already had the drop on them. That was just like my mans, Quan, in the joint and still making moves; even having his bitch role-playing. He was a genuine street solder, who I trusted completely. When he called on me, I was there without any qualms – until now.

***

I was at Omar's house, smoking on a leaf of that Kush when I got the call. Quan was able to get straight through to my cell because he had a cell phone of his own, although he was in prison. He'd hooked up with some nigga named Krispy, who was supposedly the man, and had the drop on both sides of the prison walls. I saw his number and answered.

"What's up, brah?" I asked, happy to hear from my guy. Me and Quan were always a little closer to one another than Gucci was to either of us. I mean, Gucci was our family without a doubt or question, but me and Quan were just tighter.

"Drake," Quan replied with a slight chuckle. He always played it casual, like doing a bid was a walk in the park, but I knew better. Quan was a wild nigga, so being confined to a prison cell had to be fucked up for him.

"So what's good, my nigga?" I would always ask him that. I'd done a bid and wished I would have had someone to keep me eating and worried about my well-being, so I would do that as a constant reminder to Quan that he had his niggaz on the line holding him down.

"Brah, some wild ass shits been popping off out there," Quan chuckled again before going silent. He was usually twenty-four seven with the jokes and games, but that day there was something serious within his snicker. It was something, I was sure, he wanted me to catch onto so I let him know that I was paying close attention to what he was saying.

"Right, I'm listening, my nigga."

"Man, I got an address that I need you to check out," Quan said, before continuing, telling me about Ace's safe house had gotten raided and how thirty bricks came up missing. I'd been hustling, sun up until sundown since I was twelve and had never imagined copping that type of work, so just hearing about a bag that heavy was shocking. 'This nigga done met some power hitters!' I thought, still listening as he told me about the truck that was coming in from California. Krispy had set up a thousand kilo deal with some Colombians out of San Diego who were connected with Suge and was expecting the bag to drop soon.

At first, they thought Ace was dead. But after finding out that he'd been keeping in contact with their connect, Krispy thought he'd just laid low until the new shipment came in. When I heard the story, I wondered if this Ace nigga was working with The Alphabet Boys. I said as much to Quan, but he wasn't concerned about the FEDs. Quan's only concern was the hundred thousand dollar come up that bringing Ace and Krispy back in to

contact would bring us. Knowing that I had fifty coming was enough for me to be a willing participant.
***

After Rocsi and her guy jumped into the van and drove off, I leaped out of my truck, which was parked at the corner of the alley on the next block, and sprinted over to the body. 'Shit!' I thought, smelling the body before I could even take a look at it. His head was red with clotted blood splatter that had dried and caked up, causing it to turn into a growth of fungus. The stench stemming from the body burned the hairs in my nostrils, so I covered my nose with the sleeve of my sweater as I knelt over the thin remains. I grabbed the picture that Quan had sent me from inside my pocket and used my foot to flip the body over. I could see that the man's pants had been soiled, probably from his own piss and shit, and his skin was a dark purple. But it was definitely Ace. "Yeah, that's him," I whispered to myself and slipped back out of the alleyway before someone saw me and identified me as the killer. 'Sheeeit,' I thought, while pulling my hood over my head and dipping through a few backyards until I was back on the block that I'd parked my car on. That's the last muthafucka needs out here.

I'd done as Quan asked of me and now it was his turn to produce his part of the deal. His mans, Krispy, made a promise that I hoped he'd keep because I needed that fifty stacks in my pockets.

QUAN
I was lounging in my cell when Krispy rushed in, fuming. His eyes were bloodshot red with fury. He was out of breath from running up the tires to my cell.

'What the fuck's up, nigga?" I asked, leaping to my feet, thinking someone was going to rush in behind him. It was known by the entire prison compound that he was a coward, so running for safety wasn't beneath Krispy. He leaned over, putting his hands on his knees, while trying to catch his breath. I eased over to the cell door, peeking out. I wanted to be on point in case I had company coming behind him. The day room area was clear, but Krispy hadn't spoken up yet.

"Nigga, what's up? You runnin up in here like muhfuckaz was at those hot cakes," I chuckled and leaned against the wall, firing up a limb of good green. I kept some sticky ever since me and Krispy had hooked up. My whole bid had turned into a gravy train. All I had to do was keep the yard off his ass and he handled the rest because he had some major connections who moved whenever he needed them to.

"Quan, man...." Krispy finally replied, shaking his head and still gasping for air. I finally realized it wasn't the run that had him wheezing – it was whatever he had to tell me. 'This one must be bad!' I thought, staring at him as he tried to recover from his anxiety attack. I'd had one at my sentencing and knew how it felt to gasp for air, so I just stood back giving him his space.

"What's jumpin off, Krisp?" I asked, walking back to the cell door and looking out onto the range, ready to grab my steel and go to war because fucking with Krispy meant you were fucking with my food. 'And I gotta eat,' I thought seriously pulling hard on the limb hanging from my mouth and butting it out before tucking it back into the seam of my state shirt.

"Nah, brah!" Krispy relied, waving me back over to him, letting me know that this didn't have anything to do with the inside. He must have sensed my wariness and wanted me to chill before I caused us some unwanted attention from the guards and he was right. Hell yeah! I calmed down because there was all types of shit tucked into stashes around my cell that I wanted to keep.

"Quan, man...the load got jacked!" Krispy looked like he wanted to cry. I could have sworn I saw a tear forming in the corner of his right eye.

"What?   The load?   What muhfuckin load, nigga?" I asked, not knowing what he was referring to and not expecting him to say what he said next.

"The truck hauling those thousand birds, nigga!   That's what load!" He said, dropping his chin and shaking his head in disbelief. He couldn't believe what had happened and neither could I.

"Brah, you've gotta be bullshittin!" I couldn't believe what he'd just said.   'Hell muhfuckin nah!' I thought, certain there was no way that someone had lifted a truck carrying a thousand kilos of cocaine.   IMPOSSIBLE!   I was sure that someone had to be shadowing the load, protecting it from being licked.   Son of a bitch! I couldn't believe that I'd been naïve enough to miss out on that caper.   I was almost positive that Krispy had ran off at the mouth, giving another grimy ass nigga on the camp a chance to come up off of him.   Stupid muhfucka!

"Man, I bullshit you not!   It's over for me, Quan man…those Guatemalan El Salvadorian muthafuckaz are going to kill me, my nigga." He wiped his palms across his face and the tear that I'd seen forming, fell across his cheeks.   'This hoe bitch ass nigga!' I thought, wanting to slap the shit out of him for being such a pussy. Me, Drake or Gucci would have never bowed down.   Even if it was the US government on our asses, we'd fight until the end. That's how my team rolled when a motherfucker tried to take some food off of our plate.

"Man up, muhfucka!" I spat angrily, flashing a streak of fury in my eyes that had been brought on by his bitch ass ways.   His whining hadn't swelled any compassion within my heart because I didn't have any in me.   My emotions had vanished at the start of my seven year bid and there was no way that they'd be reappearing now that I was at the end.   "If you're with me……!" I aggressively pushed my thumb into my chest.   "I'm with you, and me or my niggaz don't die! Nigga, we kill shit!" I grabbed a towel from the iron bar post on my bunk and tossed it over to the chump. This nigga a real lame!

I watched as he wiped the puddle that had rose into his eyes away, knowing that he was a nigga who had been nested into the game. Myself, I'd been scratching the brick of the project walls, using the stone reside to make fleece rocks with and serving fiends fake crack on my come up. At one time, the whole project was looking to kill me for crack conning them, but I manned up and made it out of that motherfucker. 'But this clown ass nigga!' I thought, shaking my head while watching Krispy's defeatist behavior. I was certain that he'd been blessed into the game with multiple kilos of coke; a second generation kingpin or something. He'd been laying up sucking the life out of the hood while getting paid. Now that the ugly part of the game showed up knocking at his door, his soft ass was afraid to answer. Punk coward ass muhfucka!

CHAPTER 15

GUCCI

The sound of the premium stereo system in the club pounded like there was a live band in the house. I looked down as this fine redbone bitch dropped it in front of me. She'd been backing all of that ass she had up on me for about fifteen minutes, and I was starting to get hard. She leaned over, shaking her butt mountains from side to side, causing my dick to rock up. 'Damn!' I thought, feeling the vibration of her ass gyrating against the nerve ending of my bell head. I didn't even know this broad's name, but there was no doubt that she wanted to know mines. I tried to think about anything to bring my piece down, but the wave of the freak's ass was sounding the horns. This hoe has to be a stripper! I was certain of that. If she wasn't, then she'd definitely missed her money train because a stripper's pole was her calling. And from the looks of Hashes' and Tutsi's stares, I wasn't the only nigga in the club who noticed. They stood near the pool table, watching like they wanted to be in my position, and I didn't blame them.

"Damn, baby girl!" I said after she rose up and wrapped her arms around my neck backwards while still grinding her soft contours against me sensually. "We might as well fuck," I chuckled, but she made it evident that fucking her wasn't a laughing matter.

She spun around and breathed on my ear before whispering, "Where are we going?" She was bold and I liked it. Most women liked to play games, pretending that they weren't with one night stands when they were. This hoe was down for her crown. I glanced over to Tutsi and nodded, letting him know that I was about to step out with the broad, and he nodded back acknowledging my signal. I grabbed the broad's hand and led her through the club's dance floor and out into the parking lot.

"So what's up?" she asked, gently grabbing my whole sack, massaging it – dick and balls. 'Shit!' I thought, my knees buckling from her touch. Her palms were nearly as soft as her ass was.

"Where we going?" her lip gloss was double coated, making her mouth look wet and I wanted to slide my dick inside of it.

"Sheeit, we can get it in my Chevy!" I replied, anxious to feel that wet box between her legs.

She grabbed my hand and led me towards my Impala. 'How did this hoe know where my whip was?' I wondered while slowing up. This hoe is tryna set a nigga up! I snatched my hand away from the broad, pissed at myself for being so gullible. Not to mention, I'd left my heat in Tutsi's truck!

BLOCCA! BLOCCA!

I spun around after hearing two gunshots ring out. I was certain that they were thrown my way. "Shit!" I spat, ducking behind a Lexus truck that was parked beside my Chevy. These muhfuckaz wanna rock and roll! I crawled across the pavement, trying to make it over to Tutsi's Bronco. I wanted to grab my strap and even the battlefield up.

"Chop!" I heard the voice of the hoe who was dancing up on me scream and she darted towards the area that I'd heard the gunshots come from. 'Oh, this hoe is gonna just make it known! Like I'm a mark or some shit!' I thought as I eased closer to the truck. I was about two parking lanes away from the equalizer to this problem and tempted to dart over to the Bronco until I heard another two shots. BLOCCA! BLOCCA! Those two sounded more menacing than the first round of gunfire. Maybe because I heard feet hitting the ground, closing in on me as I rose to make a sprint to the truck.

"Gucc?" Tutsi called, giving me the courage to stand erect. I was sure that Tutsi had smuggled his strap into the club because he didn't go anywhere without it. 'It's on now, bitch!' I thought, seeing Tutsi and Hashes running toward me, both of them carrying their steel.

"I'm over here!" I yelled, waving them over to where I was. I was ready to grab one of their burners and chase that scandalous hoe down. "Bitch wanna peel me??!" I chuckled, noticing the rage in Tutsi's eyes when he got over to me.

"Give me yo heat!" I demanded, reaching for Tutsi's four nickel.

"Why? It's over. Let's go," Tutsi said and rushed off to his Bronco. 'Hell nah it ain't over!' I thought, running off towards my whip. I never forgot a face and was sure that I'd be seeing that freak's mug once again, but not as quick as I had. 'What the fuck??!!' I thought, staring at the broad's body sprawled across the concrete bleeding to death. She lay next to a slim nigga whose bloody body was contorted into a pretzel, pistol still clutched in his palm. I hit the gas, smashing out of the lot, not wanting anyone to ID my ride. I'd only been off of parole for a couple of months and bodies were dropping all around me. Shit had to change before I was trapped into a court in the streets situation because there was no way that I was spending another day in the penitentiary. 'Hell muthafuckin nah!' I thought, shaking my head and switching lanes, jumping onto the Ford expressway.

I pulled up to the apartments shortly after Tutsi. Hashes was already on post in the corridors, making sure none of our baseheads went up to the north building, as I walked up. He'd been on my trap squad ever since the day that he'd stood up to me and Tutsi. Hashes was a loyal nigga and I was starting to trust him because he wasn't greedy.

I was still edging my way up to the hustlers polls, only copping two kilos at a time, and the money was slow for us. But Hashes never complained, only asking for money to feed his siblings. 'Yeah, this lil nigga is the real deal,' I thought, walking up and giving my soldier a pound.

"What the fuck happened?" I asked, watching how Hashes' eyes canvassed the courtyard for whatever was to come. He reminded me of a young me. When I was posting up outside of crack spots and robbing the fiends before they could get inside to buy their fix. In a way, I felt like I was doing them a favor, keeping them from busting their hearts from freebasing.

"Man....." Hashes started, before seeing someone creep around the edge of the fire escape and up the back stairs of the north building. I could see the animosity bubble into his eyes. It was the same anger that I'd hand once I realized the hoe at the club was trying to pull a jack move. He finally took his eyes off of the loose fiend and finished what he'd started saying. "You was slipping. You s'pose to be giving me the game, but I had to lay down the law on that sheisty ass hoe." Hashes shook his head, looking disappointed in me. 'Shit!' I thought, wondering how I'd missed the play in the first place. That wasn't like me because I was usually aware of shit like that.

"So you peeped it going down, huh?" I asked, feeling fucked up about that tramp catching me sleep. It's the suburbs! I shook my head, knowing that living in the suburbs for the last couple of years had made me less attentive to the gangster shit that was lurking around me.

"Nah, that shit was Tutsi's call for real. He's the nigga who saw it going down," Hashes explained. He told me about Tutsi seeing the young slim nigga's eyes chaperoning the broad's every movement. While I thought they were watching in envy as the hoe ground her ass all up on me, they were actually catching my back. When me and the freaky little skeezer walked out of the club, the rail thin cat followed right behind us. Tutsi tapped Hashes, letting him know what was about to go down and they followed behind the jack boy.

When they walked out, they saw the youngster reaching for his metal, confirming what Tutsi had initially thought was going down. The hoe was leading me right into a robbery. Her man was going to catch me with my pants down and take me for a little pocket change. 'Dumb dead muthafuckaz!' I thought, still listening to Hashes break the whole play down.

Tutsi immediately upped his heat and blasted the scrawny looking young nigga, sending to the pavement in a backflip. He landed with his foot close to his head, breaking the bones in his leg. Right after the blast, Hashes looked up and saw the slut who'd been draping me into a caper running toward the dead man's body, so he whipped his strap and put two into her voluptuous body, laying her down beside her man. 'This nigga a young G!' I thought, giving Hashes dap as a thank you for putting in work.

"You dropping bodies like that, nigga?!" I asked, excited that I was in the company of another goon. Me, Tutsi, and Hashes had formed a team of our own. Drake and Quan were still my mans, but my new team was everyday rock solid like cooked coke.

"Yeah, it ain't shit, Gucci. I've been out in these streets since I was ten and ain't too many niggaz showed me the love that you have. Feel me, don?" Hashes kept his eyes glued on the fire escape that the fiend had taken up to the trap spot in the north building. I was sure that he was waiting on him to come down.

"No doubt!" I nodded, letting him know how much I felt him. It wasn't every day that a nigga put in work to bail his mans out of a death sentence, but Hashes had done just that. Him and Tutsi.

"Go on up, don. Tutsi's waiting on you," Hashes said and walked off after seeing the crackhead nigga sliding down the banister of the fire escape. He looked happy as hell, so there was no question that he'd gotten some love from the north building niggaz. 'Imma catch up with those niggaz and kill something!' I thought, tailing behind Hashes. He was my soldier, but I wasn't ready to let him go handle up alone, especially with some cloak niggaz who we hadn't even seen yet. They hustled like moles, pushing their product through door chutes, not even letting the fiends see who they were. Tutsi wanted to ransack their unit, shooting our way in until everything inside was dead, but I wasn't ready to own that war. Especially after what we'd done to Doug E Fresh and his crew. 'Fuck that shit!' I thought, knowing that we wouldn't be able t make a dime if four more bodies dropped in the Chalmers projects.

"I'm with you, Hash," I whispered as we rounded the corner to the fire escape. Hashes nodded, letting me know that he'd heard me. He whipped his heat and hid it against the blind side of his leg, so I followed suit. I wasn't about to be caught with my pants down again.

"Bitch!" Hashed said, in a muffled tone, through clenched teeth. H didn't want to bring any attention from the hustlers in the north building. He snatched the addict into a snug choke hold and drug him beneath the fire escape. 'Hashes bout to kill this nigga,' I thought, looking at the way he was handling the fiend. He was being rough as hell, throwing him onto the urine stained concrete and slapping him with his heat.

"Please, Hashes!" the fiend begged in a high pitched voice, whining like a bitch. His head was leaking from the iron going across it, but his palm was wrapped tight, protecting those stones that were inside of his grasp.

I told you I was gonna do something nasty to you if I caught you over here buying from these nigga again….didn't I bitch?" Hashes' eyes were demonic. This was a side of him that I hadn't seen.

"Please, Hashes!" This time, the fiend's beg was in a quiet whimper. 'This nigga sounds like a hoe,' I thought, giving him a once over and noticing the chipped pink nail polish on his fingers. He's a punk! I'd seen some freakish shit in my lifetime, especially while I was in the joint, but this nigga took the crown. I couldn't see his hair because he was wearing a dingy knitted skull cap.

"Hoe, get naked!" Hashes demanded angrily. I looked over to him, wondering what the fuck he was doing. Not only was he telling a dope fiend to get naked, he was telling a male fiend to get naked.

"What the fuck kind of shit is you into, nigga?" I asked, hoping he wasn't a homo because that was a deal-breaker for niggas who I hustled with. 'Don't say it, nigga,' I thought, shaking my head and hoping he wasn't gay. Please don't say it. Hashes had been a certified goon until this point, but I'd kill him as quick as I'd killed Cheese.

"Imma gut this bitch," Hashes replied with a demonic snicker. 'Nah! My nigga!' I thought, pulling the hammer back on my roscoe.

"Is that a pussy?" I asked, looking down at the fiend, who had stripped asshole naked beneath the fire escape. 'Damn!' I thought, staring at the hairiest manhole that I'd ever seen. She was a broad – an ugly one, but a hoe nonetheless. "Shhh!" I sighed, relieved that I didn't have to let the hammer of my tool fly. Hashes was a good nigga to have on the team, but raping a man would have sealed his fate.

"I told this hoe, Gucci!" Hashes spat, taunting the fiend as he unbuckled his pants. 'This niggaz gonna actually do this shit!' I thought, watching in horror; wanting to stop him before he made a life changing mistake. She could have AIDS!

"Nah, Hashes, baby," I finally tried to intervene. "You probably don't wanna do that, my nigga." I shook my head, cringing my face from the horrid smell that crawled from between her legs. I was certain that she hadn't washed in months, possibly even years.

"Yeah, don," Hashes chuckled. His eyes had a deranged glare in them as his pants fell to the ground around his ankles. His dick was flagpole high in the air and he hiked his shirt up, holding it with his chin. "You probably saying some shit like this hoe could have AIDS or she's a fiend, but I'm thinking: fuck it!" He slid his log into her ass causing her to yelp in pain.

"Hah....shes!" she whined, as he pounded her ass hard and stiff. My mans is a fucking nut! I watched, listening as he lectured me about his lifestyle.

"I'm figuring," Hashes shrugged his shoulder, still roughly pushing his dick in and out of her, her bony ass slapping against his thighs and his pistol still hanging from his hand. "Imma die out here in these streets before I die from whatever this crack hoe can give me. Sheeeit..." He laughed, "I might be giving her something." I continued to listen as Hashes candidly talked to me while brutally sodomizing the fiend. He thrust hard into her, busting a nut and snatching her hat off her head, wiping the blood and shit off of his piece. 'You nasty muthafucka!' I thought, staring at Hashes who was now beating the dopehead bloody. She curled into the corner of the fire escape naked, shielding her body from his blows, all the while still clutching those stones in her palm. After all of what she'd just gone through – getting raped and beaten, even slapped across her head with a pistol – she refused to let a crumb of her get high fall loose.

CHAPTER 16

TREY

Me and Chico stacked the bricks atop of each other. Rocsi sat in the barn covering her nose. 'Stuck up bitch!' I thought, glancing over to her fine ass. She acted like she'd never smelled horse and cow shit before; or like her own shit didn't stink. Ship had handfed that hoe too long and she'd forgotten what it was like to be out there with the wolves. If she wasn't Ship's cousin, I'd show her. I slammed the last of the five hundred kilos on the pile.

"Ship, we're done, my man," Chico said, waving Ship over to the neat pile of millions. I'd already made a few calls to some trappers that I knew, including Pops. He'd cashed me out on the thirty slabs that I'd fronted him last week, and was ready for another load. Luckily, we'd just hit the motherlode of cocaine heists so I'd be able to supply him for the rest of the fall. Ship strolled over to us, still flashing his conniving ass smile.

"I have to go see about something, but I'll be back real soon," he laughed and looked from me to Rocsi and over to Chico. "Can't have you thirsty niggas around all of these ki's for too long. Y'all might try to oust a brother."

"Whatever, nigga," Rocsi said, waving Ship's remark off, still using her sleeve to cover her nose.

"Yeah right, hombre," Chico chimed in. I stayed silent because I knew that the remark was really directed toward me. Although me and Ship were tight, there was always a question of loyalty between us after he joined to police force. I couldn't trust him and wondered if he'd turn me in to save his own ass. After all, he was the police and had taken plenty of street niggaz out of the hood in cuffs. 'Sheeit, nigga,' I thought, watching as he walked through the barn and out of the door. Ain't no telling what a nigga might do for five hundred slabs.

I turned to Chico and asked, "So what was so urgent that Ship had to bounce so sudden?" Being sixty miles away from the hood made me feel trapped, especially with a thousand pounds of dope around. If the police came nosing around the joint, we'd al be doing life sentences in the FED.

"I don't know," Chico replied flatly. I stared at him, seeing the deceit within his eyes. 'This nigga is lying!' I thought, wanting to know why they were being so secretive about their movement, especially with so much at stake. We all should be reachable in case something went wrong.

"Yeah," Rocsi reiterated, "he did just roll out all of a sudden." She finally took her sleeve away from her nostrils and walked over to us. 'This hoe must have been thinking like me,' I thought as she crossed her arms, looking like she was doubting Chico's ignorance. Chico looked from her to me and shrugged his shoulders.

"Shit..." he nodded, "he might have went to the station. You know he's till on shift until five." Damn! He's right. I knew that Ship's schedule required him to be on post until around eight because he'd always remind me and Rocsi that he was the only one of us who had a nine to five.

Rocsi glanced over to me, twisting her lips, letting me know that she still didn't believe what Chico had said. 'Ain't this some shit!' I thought with a nod, not letting Chico see that me and Rocsi were communicating. This was the first time since I dry snitched on her that she'd saddled up with me. Rocsi was usually against everything I said, especially when I concerned Ship.

"Well, I've gotta split too, but I'll be back," Chico said, breaking the silence that had overtaken the room. The farm that we'd been stashing our criminal rewards on belonged to Chico's aunt and I didn't like sitting around while he wasn't there. Something ain't right. I stared at Chico as he stumbled over his own feet while walking out.

"Rocsi, I'm telling you. I know Ship and those two muthafuckaz are up to some underhanded shit," I nodded, assuring Rocsi that I was right wand we were about to get fucked.

"You think so?" she replied, questioning me sarcastically. "Because I'm sure of it." She turned facing the door that Chico had just disappeared through.

"Hell yeah," I said, looking over to her fine ass. Even though I couldn't stand her, 20/20 vision wasn't a requirement to notice how sexy her body was. 'Bitch I hate this,' I thought, knowing what I was bout to ask of Rocsi would cost me in the long run.

"Why are you eye-fucking me, Trey?" Rocsi asked, noticing the lustful stare that I was giving her.

"Shut the fuck up with that hoe shit," I replied, waving what she'd said off, although she was dead on because I'd fucked her in every position in my imagination. "You gon have to follow them muthafuckaz, though." She looked at me, seeing if I was serious. I nodded towards the door, signaling her to rush off behind Chico. I was sure that he'd take Rocsi right to Ship and whatever they were hiding.

ROCSI

I jumped into my truck and sped off, trying to get behind Chico. Trey was thinking the same thing that I was thinking. I knew something was up when Ship took that fake phone all. I'd heard his alarm ring thousands of times, so hearing it sound off and him answer it like it was a phone call made me suspicious. 'There he is!' I thought after seeing Chico's car weaving through busy freeway traffic. Bzzzzz Bzzzzz! My cell rang from inside of my purse. I grabbed it and looked at the caller ID. "Shit!" I spat, not wanting to answer because it was Quan.

"Hello?"

"What's up, ma?" Quan asked after I answered.

"I'm in the middle of something," I replied, keeping my eyes glued to the rear end of Chico's car. I wasn't about to let him slip away because I'd never know what they were up to then. Ship was a slithery motherfucker and I was sure that this would be and Trey's first and last opportunity to expose his bullshit.

"In the middle of something?!" Quan asked nastily. "Fuck you mean, you in the middle of something??!" His attitude got shittier, make me wonder why he'd called. 'He must have gotten shitted on by a CO and now he wants to fuck with me,' I thought, grunting loud enough for him to hear me. I knew how it was because I'd been there; having a fat CO motherfucker telling you to ride your bunk like you ain't shit, so I knew what he was faced with.

"Quan, I'm on your side, babe," I said politely, not wanting to agitate whatever he was feeling. I love Quan and wanted him to be happy even when I wasn't

"Who is that Mexican nigga, Roc?" Quan asked me boldly, surprising the hell out of me. 'I know he's not talking about Chico,' I thought, wondering how he knew that I was following him. He'd been telling me about a nigga named Krispy who he'd hooked up with who was supposed to have juice on the bricks, but I hoped he wasn't using it to stalk me.

"What?" I asked, curious to know what the hell he was referring to and why.

"My peeps saw you in the alley, Roc. Feel me?" he asked and I swerved, nearly slamming into the median. He knows about us dropping Aces' body off! I caught the steering wheel and looked up, noticing that Chico's distance had widened. I had to make it up quick because I didn't know where he'd be exiting. We were about fourteen more miles from the city so his stop had to be close.

"Quan, let's not. Not right now, okay?" I stayed casual, not trying to alarm him and not wanting to hurt his feelings by telling him to stay the fuck out of my business. I was aware of how fragile prison niggaz egos were. If I would have told him how I felt, it would have melted him, so I spared my baby's feelings.

"Bitch! I'm Quan! I decide when and if something can wait! Do you know who the fuck I am, hoe?" Quan asked, barking at me the same way that my father did my mother before she scorched his face with cooking oil.

"Yes, Quan," I replied, holding my temper to a calm sigh after replying. 'Slow down, babe,' I thought, hoping he didn't make me hang up on his ass or worse – tell him about himself. I don't know who the fuck he is anymore, having a nigga following me.

"You better act like it then and have your ass down here Tuesday!" he demanded and hung up before I could reply. Tuesday was less than a week away, so I wasn't sure if I could manage. Quan was my baby without a doubt, but my split of these kilos had to bet taken in before I made any sudden moves.

Chico came up on the Harper exit, in the middle of the hood and I cautiously followed behind him, dipping between cars like I was an agent. I had picked up a lot of game being around them throughout the years, including when someone was full of shit. And his scandalous ass was definitely full of shit! I slowed as Chico pulled into an abandoned carwash. "These shady motherfuckers!" I said, looking at him and Ship slap fives before disappearing into the car wash. 'These no good niggaz must have gotten something extra out of that truck!' I thought, peeling off. I'd seen where they were hiding their stash and would be checking in on it when they were out of sight. Ship and Chico had violated a law of the teams – thou shalt not steal from each other. Now that the rules were tarnished, a bitch like me would be violating them all. I picked up my cell and called Trey.

"Hello, Trey?" I said after he answered. "Unless Ship is helping Chico fuck his wife, we're good because Chico went straight home." I lied and hung up. Ship and Chico had started a streak of betrayal in our clique and I saw fit to continue that trend. 'Because a bitch gon eat!' I thought while pulling into HarborTown condominiums and called upstairs to Khalid. There were some things that me and him needed to discuss.

SHIP

Chico walked up smiling like a motherfucker. We'd pulled it off – a lick that would change both our lives, starting with me quitting the force. I'd done too much dirt and knew that it was only a matter of time before I got caught up. And I wasn't trying to be victimized by own treachery.

"We did it, my nigga," I gave him dap and we walked into the car wash. The car wash was an old building that I'd bought about three years ago. I planned on fixing it up and turning a profit out of it, but the real estate bubble burst, destroying my plans. 'Fuck it, though!' I thought, knowing that what it was being used for was more lucrative than the few grand that I would have made off of a short sale flip. Chico was my guy and could keep his mouth shut. We'd been robbing drug dealers and prostitutes for about four years together and I knew that partners like him were hard to find.

"Ship, bro, your cousin was asking all kinds of funny questions," Chico said, nodding like there was more to it. Something that I should be hearing between the lines.

"And??" I asked, prompting him to give me more because I didn't know where he was coming from. Rocsi was always inquisitive, like the average bitch. Just because she was in the game – hustling, robbing, and setting niggaz up to be robbed – didn't mean she wasn't a hoe.

"Hombre, I'm telling you that....she was just asking and asking, man," Chico reiterated, still trying to convince me that Rocsi wasn't being herself.

"That's the kind of shit that bitches do, my brother," I laughed and patted Chico on the back, letting him know that it was okay. "You've been married for too long. I'm going to have to take you to the bounce. Everything's on me."

Chico chuckled at that because although he didn't go for pleasure, he knew that neither of us had to pay when we dropped by there. We'd been shaking them down for years, taking money and sometimes I'd fuck a few women depending on who was working.

"Fuck off, cabron," Chico's accent went deep when he was serious about something. 'What's up with this motherfucker?' I wondered, hoping he wasn't going to make me end our friendship with a single slug to the back of his cranium. "I'm serious, bro. Something wasn't right about her....and that fucking Trey." He nodded, assuring me that they were somehow in cahoots against us.

"Hell nah!" I shook my head defiantly, knowing that he was mistaken because there was no way that Rocsi would do anything with Trey. She hated him and if Chico couldn't see that, I was going to have to start questioning his real motives. Now what the fuck are you trying to pull? I stared at him, examining his demeanor. There were five hundred kilos of powder cocaine stashed in the chemical closet of the car was, the other half of the dope that we'd taken from the truck load, and two armed men in the font of the building who knew where the drugs were. Chico had been solid throughout our dealings, never once trying to shiest me, but the shit that he was implying? Trying to convince me that

Rocsi and Trey were backdooring us made me question who he really was. 'Is he trying to divide and conquer?' I wondered, walking away, moving closer to something that I could duck behind if pistols were drawn.

"So what's the deal, brother? Where do you want to move yours to?" I asked, after getting into diving distance. Chico was a decorated marksman. We'd been to the range and we'd taken target practice on countless thugs, so there was no doubt in my mind that he could make a fifty foot shot. 'Tell me, Chico,' I thought, with a chuckle after reading Chico's body language. He was nervous and must have realized that I was onto him.

"Bro, mines can stay with yours. You're the only person in this that I can trust because Trey is..." Chico whistled while twirling his finger around his ear, gesturing that Trey was crazy. "He's loco, man."

"Nigga, I've seen you kill at least ten motherfuckers and Trey's the one who's..." I repeated what he'd just done, mocking him. This motherfucker is trying too hard. Me and Chico had just snaked Rocsi and Trey out of millions and he expected me to trust him. 'Shit!' I thought, watching his every move. I don't even trust me.

"Fuck it then, bro," Chico said, shrugging his shoulders. "If they come, I'll be on point because I don't trust them....but you might get caught asleep." Chico turned and walked off, giving me a change in heart. Maybe this motherfucker did see something?

I stuck around for a little while longer after Chico left. I wasn't sure if he'd be trying to double back and run off with all five hundred of those cakes. "This shit is wild," I said in a soft whisper while shaking my head. I'd heard that money made everyone around it paranoid. And I didn't believe it until now because all of the people who I'd trusted at this point. I had contaminated our circle with deceit and retribution was seeing that same deceit in everyone on my team. Damn!

CHAPTER 17

GUCCI

I pumped every inch of this stiff dick into Pat's tight little pussy. She was an older freak, who liked it from the back, so I made an extra effort to please her. I'd been copping work from her for about three months and she'd been playing her hand right so far. So, I figured I'd let the hoe live instead of sending my team at her. Good thing Quan still had a couple of months left in the pen because he would have definitely pulled rank and sent in the troops. Drake would have backed him too. They didn't think that I had recognized, but I knew about their closeness. 'It's cool, though,' I thought while staring down at Pat's ass riffling with every stroke of my hammer. I had Tutsi and Hashes now. Hashes was an animal muthafucka, but he was part of my crew so I had to accept the good, the bad, and the nasty shit that he'd done to that fiend the other night.

"Oh shit! Gucci, baby, I'm about to cum…." Pat panted, my thighs slapping hard against her ass as I pounded deeper and harder into those wet walls. 'That old nigga can't be hitting this pussy right!' I thought, keeping an even stroke as she groaned erotically.

"Yeah, bitch!" I spat, knowing that she liked to be talked to nastily. Pat was a young nigga's dream because she was a freak who had a tight wet pussy and couldn't get pregnant. I can hit this pussy raw all the time, baby! "Hold it in and wait for me, hoe!"

"I….I….I can't! Please, daddy! Ooooh..I wanna cum all over that fat ass dick!" Pa was the nastiest talking whore that I'd ever fucked. The young generation of tramps needed to take some lessons from her and step their game up because Pat was an animal. I scooped her legs up, grabbing her ankles into a wheelbarrow position, still hammering her. She moaned sensually, which was something that I liked about her because she'd go from naughty to sensual in a heartbeat. Her walls got wetter and I knew that she'd beat me to the climax.

"Yes, oh yessss!" she rolled her hips in a slow tantric motion. That shit drove a nigga nuts.

"Sheeeit!" I switched from a long stiff stroke to automatic, pounding her wet box like a machine gun making the hose pour. I should be getting those three birds that lay in the corner in a duffle bag for free after the way I'd just laid pipe on her ass. She was fine as hell to be a vet, but I'd just fucked the old hoe like she was prime real estate, instead of rehab property. We both lay across the bed breathing heavily. Me, thinking about grabbing the bag, putting a hot rock through her dome and leaving her inside the trunk of her car in the parking lot of a local supermarket.

"So what's up Pat?" I said, looking over to her. She lay on her stomach showcasing that mountain of ass she had. "We been popping nuts off at each other for a couple of months and we still ain't broke bread." I was making a plea for her to at least drop her prices to below twenty thousand a slab.

"Yeah, we have," Pat chuckled and looked backwards, watching me caress her bubble. "and you've been enjoying yourself too."

"No doubt, but it's time to mix business with pleasure."

"Oh, so you don't think twenty a ki is fair since we're fucking?" Pat snickered, bringing the veteran out. She was a shrewd businesswoman. I'd met her through a stripper who danced at The Grind while I was scratching the ground trying to come up. Back then, I couldn't do business with her because she didn't fuck with short money niggaz. That was a good thing too because I would have definitely licked her ass. She hung out with a lot of bitches, but I hadn't met her man yet. He was a mystery who I wasn't sure even existed.

"Hell yeah," I stated boldly, letting her know that I was ready for her to break bread. "About seventeen...no more than eighteen five, sheeit." I slid my hands between Pat's ass cheeks after feeling her pussy moistening again. I wasn't sure which had made her juices flow – me rubbing her ass or us talking money. Whichever it was, the evidence was glistening across my fingers. Pat smiled and leaned upright, my hand slipping from between her cheeks and her titties jiggling freely. She'd definitely been blessed because the old bitch had the total package. 'A hard body and thunder beneath the hood of that muthafucka! Shit!' I thought, shaking my head as I waited to hear what she'd have to say next.

"Cool, we can do that," Pat said casually before grabbing my dick and pushing it into her mouth. 'Goddamn!' I thought looking down at how she'd taken it into her mouth in one gulp. Pulling and pushing it back out without me feeling any teeth. I'd just burst a monster nut, but my mans was ready to get it on like Marvin Gaye!

"Damn, baby. Just like that, huh?" I asked making sure she was serious. Although I liked to get my dick slurped on, I liked swelling my pockets more. She slid my pole out of her mouth, her tongue still attached to the head and nodded.

"Mmhmm!" she hummed and pushed her throat back down on my meat. We'd sealed a business deal over an hour of kinky sex. 'What gets better than that shit?' I wondered while laying back waiting on my eruption.

After Pat left, I scooped the bag up and bounced over to the apartments. It was time to whip it and chop it. Everything was booming for us. The doors of our trap apartments were swinging like they revolved and the customers were tweaking. A drought had hit in a major way, loosening shit up for my team. Me, Tutsi and young Hashes were about to blow, especially since I'd just fucked the prices down per bird. Pat was lucky; little did she know, because denying me what I wanted would have caused me to take it. 'But she's a down ass bitch,' I thought, snatching the slabs out of the back seat and rushing up to the cooking apartment

We'd rented an extra unit and had been using it just to drop our coke, turning it into rock. The fiends loved that shit because we brought the eighties freebase style of crack back, letting it fall and freeze. Even that fiend who Hashes had raped, sodomized, and beaten was a faithful customer. I gave a grimy looking ass addict a hood head nod on my way up the stairs. I usually took the fire escape because it was less traffic, but the stairs were a shorter hike. BOOM BOOM I kicked the door twice, letting them know that I was there. Tutsi's voice came through the door.

"Who data is?" he asked, the bass in Tutsi's tone was deep and hardened. I was a street nigga and could hear death in his words.

"It's Gucci, my brotha," I replied, mocking the way he'd say 'my brother' after every sentence. I guess that was a Sierra Leone swag or something, and Tutsi owned that shit. Tutsi opened the door, giving me a grim look about teasing him. He'd become real sensitive lately, ever since I knocked Cheese down.

"Fuck is you lookin at, black as nigga?" I laughed and walked inside, tossing the duffle bag onto the floor near the sofa. I looked around for Hashes. "Where's the youngster at?"

"Don't know, brotha," Tutsi replied, shrugging his shoulders. He walked over to the window, peering out into the courtyard. There was something about that window and Tutsi. He'd be sitting there all day watching, but I didn't know what he was watching for or why.

"Why are you always looking outta the window, Tutsi?" I looked over to him while grabbing the Pyrex from beneath the kitchen sink. I liked to use Pyrex because it was see-through and I could keep an eye on the coke as it fell to the bottom. Most hustlers dry cooked their coke or microwaved it, but that shit was gooey in the middle. It didn't sizzle and refire like that shit I was bringing out of the kitchen.

"Come look," Tutsi said, waving me over to the window. The last time that happened, we'd almost had to put Hashes six feet up under the city and I wasn't ready for another incident like what had went down with Doug E Fresh.

"What's up?" I walked over, looking out into the direction Tutsi was pointing into. 'Shit!' I thought, staring at a pair of fat ass titties with nipples the size of half dollar coins. "Daaayum!" She was stepping out of her shower, water still dripping from her chocolate body. Her hair was silky and fell across the back of her neck. I couldn't see what that ass looked like, but if her top was any indication – she was proper. I know this hoe has some shorties. She lived in the projects and most of the females there had at least two, but her body was still tight.

"That's what I've been looking at, my brotha," Tutsi said, holding out his fist and giving me dap. He had good taste in women because this broad was a dime!

"Who is she?" I asked, still watching as she carefully rolled on her deodorant. Everything about how she moved was woman-like, unlike most of the boppers who lived in the hood. I wonder what her attitude is like.

"I don't know, but she's beautiful, my brotha," Tutsi nodded, staring at her like she was a shrine or something. She was fine, I'd give her that, but she wasn't cute enough to have me posted in a window stalking her all day. 'Fuck that shit!' I thought, shaking my head while walking off, back into the kitchen. It was time to make it quick like Jiffy mix, baby. BzzzzBzzzzz My cell phone vibrated so I pulled it out of my pocket, looking at the caller ID before answering. I wasn't about to let just anyone fuck up my flow, but it was my mans Drake. We were down and I couldn't screen him out like that, because he'd never do me that way.

"What up, Drake baby?!" I asked, excited for two reasons. This seventeen five deal was going to help me bubble into a street giant on the creak scene, especially knowing that Pat could keep them coming my way throughout the drought. She'd sworn that her connect had plenty and would supply as long as I could move them fast. And I was always amped to hear from my guys. We'd been crew for decades and nothing would come between that.

"Everything, nigga," Drake replied with a chuckle.

"Everything like what, my baby?" I wanted to get to it because I had business on the floor. Three kilo business that I wanted to cook and tuck before something catastrophic happened. It was always like that for a hustler. Whenever a nigga is making his climb to the top, some bullshit from the bottom snatches his ass back down. 'And I ain't tryna be that nigga no more!' I thought, shaking my head and looking at my watch while listening to Drake rambling. I was loosely listening until he said something that hit me like a ton of bricks.

"What!!!?" I asked, after Drake said something about Rocsi dumping a body into the alley. Hell nah! I was sure that he was mistaken, but he assured me that what he'd said was the hood gospel.

"That's on the team, nigga! Hood gospel, brah brah." Rocsi was running with Mexicans, dropping bodies in alleyways and shit. 'Impossible!' I thought, before having a change of heart because there was a time when Rocsi was making moves in and out of town with us. We were young and more courageous. Back then, we were trying to be crack kings. A certified goon is a certified goon until the grave, and Rocsi was alive and hustling just like me and the rest of our clique. Quan was even making moves from the inside. 'Just like that nigga, too,' I thought, shaking my head with a quiet chuckle. I missed Quan and hadn't spoken to him in months. I'd sent a few dollars, keeping him on point because I'd hate for his bid to be like mines had started, but we hadn't spoken. I've gotta get in touch with my nigga.

"So what's the straight talk about this shit, family?" I wanted to know what Quan wanted to do about her. I knew he loved her, but her snuggling up with a gang of Mexicans would probably bother him. He wasn't as forgiving as he seemed, especially to someone who had betrayed his trust. 'We might have to body this hoe,' I thought, still waiting to hear what was said.

"Nah, she good for now. Quan said they're s'pose to visit this week and he'll let me know what's what from there. Feel me?" Drake asked, his voice implying that I read through the lines and I already had. Rocsi's days were numbered if she'd crossed my mans in any way that he saw unfit. Of course, he'd gone for almost seven years and had to know that she'd sat it out. But to what extent? If she was cooning niggaz, it had to be more intimate than just a friendly fuck because that kind of trust was dangerous.

"Hell yeah," I replied, pulling a limb of Kush from my shirt pocket and blazing it up. "I definitely feel you, my baby," I coughed, letting the smoke from my lungs cloud the kitchen and putting some heat on the sauce pot filled with water. "I gotta go, though, Drake. Just let me know, aight?"

"No question, my nigga.....Oh yeah, Omar wanted me to ask if he could cop a whole one form our peoples too?"

"Hell nah!" I replied, wondering where in the hell Omar had gotten bird money from. Just four months ago, he was sitting on the couch of my trap spot looking for a handout. 'Where in the fuck is this nigga hustling at?' I wondered, thinking maybe he was getting money out of town because I hadn't seen him around in a while. I hadn't missed him, but on second thoughts, if he'd come up with slab fare in a couple months, I wanted to be in on that come up. "Well, I guess he cold cop from me for about twenty four a log," I'd be making seven grand off of every kilo I sold the clown, and there was a drought so it wasn't like he had too many options. All of the major hustlers around the city had disappeared, fearing they'd get jacked while it was so tight for the little man, but I still had drug flow.

"Damn, Gucci! What the fuck is that about?" Drake asked, evidently wanting to know why the prices were so high. He wasn't into the dope game anymore, only robbing and extorting, so he must not have known what the streets were looking like.

"Nigga, its Sahara desert dry out here in these muhfuckin streets! A nigga can't get em whole at all. I'm tryna do the lil nigga a good one, family." I tried my best to sound convincing. Evidently it worked because Drake fell right on top of my bullshit.

"Word, well I guess it's on, my nigga. I'll tell him and we'll go from there because he don't wanna fuck with you after what happened to Cheese."

"It's on." I hung up, not wanting to explode at Drake for what he'd said. This bitch ass nigga mad about Cheese too? I was fuming and all types of thoughts breezed through my head. He was supposed to be my number one nigga and he was letting his bitch ass cousin bad mouth me. I'd never let Tutsi or Hashes cross him or Quan out. I sighed, dropping an eighth of a kilo into the Pyrex jar, disappointed that Drake was letting Omar's bitch ass talk shit behind my back. He was Drake's cousin, which was his hood license because if not, I would have laid him down. 'Should have charged his ass twenty-six!' I thought furiously, while watching the powder cake and drop to the bottom of the Pyrex, turning into gel.

"Tutsi?" I called, disturbing his view of the apartment window where we'd just seen that thick broad naked.

"What's up, my brotha?" he chuckled, already knowing what I was about to say.

"You know what time it is?" I grabbed the box of Arm & Hammer, shaking it into the air jovially.

"What time is it, my brotha?" Tutsi played along, still smiling, showing all thirty-two of his yellow ass teeth. This was the only time that I could get a laugh out of him. Any other time he was straight faced and cold.

"It's time tooooooo..."I began, my voice sounding synthesized and robotic. "Rock rock planet rock, don't stop!" I danced around while shaking baking soda into the gel and running cold water over it, making that shit rock up. We'd always do that while we were cooking our product. Hashes was a silly ass nigga. He'd get up and dance around the front room like there was a party going on. I guess I liked him so much because he was a product of the same game that I'd grown up in. Watching my mother prostitute herself for heroin only to have my father beat the shit out of her and take her keep. Seeing that made me callus, not giving a fuck about another human being, but having a team around me like Drake and Quan kept me from going too far over the edge. And I planned on being that nigga for Hashes – the one who kept him from going too far over the edge because what I'd witnessed him do to that fiend was gruesome and reminded me of where I'd come from: THE MUHFUCKIN GUTTER!

CHAPTER 18

Pat walked into her home carrying a paper bag filled with big face bills. She smiled and kissed Pops on his cheek, setting the money beside his recliner and walking off into the bathroom. She'd brought bread back in a bag, but the fish was on her body. She was sure that she smelled of nasty sex with Gucci. They'd been sexing for the last two months and she loved the way he paddled her from the back and talked to her like she was a piece of shit. 'Oooooh!' she thought, rubbing her thighs together, feeling her walls get moist from the thought of Gucci and the way he'd just blew her house down. She dropped her pants and examined her thighs, knowing that they'd be bruised from the way he man-handled her.

Gucci reminded Pat of how Pops used to be back in the day, when they were at the top of their game. Pops would even bully her out of the pussy when she was on her period and she loved it. But, his age had caught up with him while she was still in the prime of her sexual life. 'Fuck that!' Pat thought with a smirk while admiring the way her titties perked at her age. She was sure that there weren't too many women at forty-two years old who could rock a young nigga like Gucci into a sleepy coma. She massaged her breast while running a bath, her pussy still moist from the way he'd tickled her clitoris before falling asleep. She wanted more, but he was out of it. She reached into the medicine cabinet and pulled out her bullet. It was silver and had two velvet prongs on the tip that vibrated.

"Oh shit!" she cooed while sitting on the edge of the bathtub, letting the velvet prongs to vibrate on her clitoris. . Per pussy expanded and she played with its walls while letting the bullet do its magic. "Aaaaah.......ooooooooooh..oh!" she continued her long and erotic moan, wanting Pops to come in and finish what Gucci had started, but knowing that he wouldn't. Her legs quivered and she moaned loudly knowing that she was climaxing;

a feeling that she'd been getting from every minute with Gucci. "Ooooooh!" Her body convulsed with a lascivious spasm and it was over. She threw the bullet onto her vanity and got into the tub.

Pops was out front, his dick had swelled into an erection fit for a teenager, but he wasn't about to waste it on Pat. He loved his wife and wouldn't let her get away from him for the world. But, it wasn't about a sexual chemistry because he'd lost that for her years ago. He could trust her.

Pops knew that Pat would get down and dirty with him, doing whatever was called for when it came to making that dough. She was the one who had shown him how to recompress cocaine, turning three bricks into four and two into three if the product was good enough. The problem was the product that they'd been getting throughout the years was already watered down and couldn't take the synthetic mixture until now.

Pops continued counting thought the money that Pat had just brought in: a hundred and seventy thousand after selling Gucci ten birds. Gucci had really come up over the months since he'd hooked up with Pat. Pops knew that he could have charged him more because his coke was still good even though he'd been whipping the powder, but he wasn't like Trey.

Trey had been fleecing the hell out of Pops since the drought had hit, selling him kilos for seventeen a slab – two thousand more than what they had originally agreed on. Trey was gutter like that; always trying to make an extra dollar from everyone. Pops was sure that it would be catching up with him soon.

There was something fishy about Trey being the only nigga in the city with cocaine, especially while a drought was going on. The word on the streets was that a truckload of cocaine had been hit by the FEDs, but there wasn't any record of the bust. Everyone in the hood was on pins and needles. All of the major hustlers had disappeared, leaving the city just in case there was a major sweep by the FEDs. Meanwhile, Trey was around the city balling out of control. He wasn't spending any money or showboating, but he was dropping bricks off to Pops in bundles.

"Scandalous motherfuckers," Pops whispered to himself in a quiet grunt. He was almost certain that Trey and his mans, Ship, were pulling jack moves on dope boys in the city. Ship and Trey had grown up together robbing and extorting niggaz in the hood before Ship joined the police force, which mad Pops' antennas go up. He was sure that a badge couldn't turn a bad boy good, especially a grimy hoodlum like Ship. 'They're probably the ones who jacked that truck!' Pops thought, tucking the money back into the bag after counting it.

"Pat, come out here," Pops called. He was ready to put the next load of coke into the cloning machine. Pat walked out, her body glistening from the body butter that she rubbed across her cocoa complexioned skin, and her titties swinging freely. She had a pair of French lace boyshorts on and nothing else. Pops stared as she walked up, knowing she was giving him every signal known to man that she wanted to get fucked. But his young bitch was at home waiting for him. 'Damn Pat's still looking good!' Pops thought, watching as she posed in front of him, legs popped backwards and hands on her thin waist.

"What's up, baby?" Pat asked, smiling after noticing the way Pops stared at her. He hadn't given her that kind of look in years and she was sure that it had everything to do with her young stallion. 'Yep, I've been fucked real good today, baby,' she thought, still smiling at her husband, wishing he'd at least suck on her pussy.

"I need you to shoot out to the baker and put those other twenty together. I got twenty-eight out of the last pile so do whatever it is that you do so well," Pops chuckled after flirting with her with his eyes.

"Okay, I can do that, baby," Pat smiled and walked away, twisting her ass making it riffle nastily. 'That's a start,' she thought, noticing how he'd just flirted with her. She was sure that Pops had a young project bitch who kept his balls emptied out, but she wasn't about to lose her man. She was sure of it because who else could do what she did? And he'd just assured her that she did it well. She looked back, seeing Pops take a stack of cash out of the bag before disappearing down the hallway. Pat was certain that it was for whoever he was tricking with; but it was change in comparison to the stash that she'd put away in case of a rainy day.

After getting dressed, Pat shot over to one of their rental properties in St. Clair Shores, a suburb right outside of Detroit. There wasn't a lot of crime out that way and Pops knew that his product would be safe there. That's where the magic happened. They would each spend a few days a week out there, making it seem like they were an average working family, but inside was a coke factory where they mixed and recompressed each one of the bricks that Pops got from Trey. Pat watched the way Trey looked at her and wanted to know what his dick game was like, but she didn't want to cross that line with Pops unless the game called for it. Pat knew that Pops hated Trey and would have killed him years ago, but Trey was consistent and kept the business good between them. He'd never tried to backstab Pops other than upping the price, but Pops could handle that because it was a stretch from what had happened to most of Trey's people. They were either swimming at the bottom of the Detroit River or found slumped atop of a pissy mattress in an alley.

She parked in the attached garage and walked through the breezeway into the house that they referred to as the bakery before throwing her purse onto the couch. She'd brought back thirty-one off of the last batch. It was the purest of what they'd gotten and a lot purer than the first thirty birds that they'd bought from Trey. He'd been bringing them in, but Pat knew that they weren't from the same connect. She didn't know how or what he was doing to move in spite of a drought, but he was definitely doing it.

'What the fuck was that?' she wondered, looking out into the backyard after seeing someone running through her backyard. "Must be some kids playing or something," she said to herself after peering out into the yard from the window and not seeing anything. Knock Knock Knock Pat walked over to the door after hearing someone knocking. She saw a middle-aged white man standing on the outside of the door. His skin was pale and he wore a cheap pair of wire rimmed glasses that were pushed up close to his face. 'Who in the fuck is this nigga?' she wondered, opening the door and smiling politely. Her .38 was tucked into her purse which was on the couch, but she didn't think she'd be needing it.

"Hi," Pat said, unlocking the screen. "May I help you?"

"Sure," the man replied with a deep Hispanic accent and swiftly puling heat from inside of his jacket, pushing his way into the house and closing the door behind him. "Bitch, where is my cocaine?" he asked, shocking Pat. 'His coke?' Pat thought, staring down the barrel of the white man's revolver. He had the .357 pointed at her forehead and looked like he wasn't afraid of using it. "Wha....wha....what are you talking about?" she finally mustered up the courage to ask. Pat wasn't a coward, but she wasn't a fool either, so she played it cool. Letting the nose of the Hispanic gunman's tool guide her backwards through the house. She was sure that he was checking to see if there was anyone else in the house. Unfortunately for her, there wasn't.

"Puta!" he said nastily, slapping her across the side of her head with his pistol. Blood gushed out of her head and she got dizzy. "Where is my coca, whore!!?" He pressed the barrel flush into her face, sending her a clear message. 'He's about to kill me!' Pat thought, standing beneath the nozzle of a killer's burner. He drew the pistol back and asked again.

"Where is it? We put a GPS in the shipment and it lead us here! So where is my product, mami?" He used his free hand to grab his cell, pressing send and putting it to his ear. "Come!" he said flatly and ending the call, putting it back into his pants pocket. Pat knew the call could only mean something bad for her. When she was younger, she'd always thought that she'd be dying in the streets, but after being in the game for a hustler's lifetime, she thought that she'd slipped that trend. Fuck! She eased backwards toward the couch, hoping to get to her purse. She had something inside of it that would send him to his quintessence.

"GPS and product?" Pat asked, looking frightened, but all the while taunting him, hoping for a violent response. "What the hell is that?" Her face cringed bracing herself for the slap that she saw coming. WHACK! Her hands flailed into the air as she fell backwards onto the couch. Her purse lay beside her open, with her heat laying on top. It was her freedom from being left dead in the living room of the bakery.

"Please!" she cried, curling up and scooting closer to her purse knowing that she had to make her move because someone else was on the way. She discreetly slid her hand into the purse and looked back, catching him glance at the door. BLOCCA BLOCCA! She threw two hot rocks into the intruder's chest and immediately hit the closet, snatching up the duffle bag of cocaine and rushing back into the garage where she'd parked the car, stashing the drugs in her whip. She called the police, telling them what happened.

"I've just been assaulted by a black man! Come quick!" she screamed frantically before giving the police the address to the house and running next door. She was sure that they'd already heard the shots and had called the law before she did. 'Fuck it!' she thought, banging on the next door neighbors screen door. I can't be there when those other motherfuckers get there! She'd heard the Hispanic man who she'd just killed call for back up and was sure that his goons were on the way. "Come on motherfucker!" Pat said in a whisper after seeing someone peeking through the window blinds.

She could hear the police sirens in a short distance, and knew that they were coming with the force of their entire county. She'd purposely said that she'd been assaulted by a black man, knowing that an all white county would assume that she was white and come with menacing rage. A middle-aged woman opened the door, first taking a quick glance around the surroundings before opening the door and letting Pat inside. Pat breathed heavily. The adrenaline of being close to death had her pussy walls drip juices that had puddled into the crotch of her panties. She loved the thrill and excitement of the game that came along with it – including young hustlers like Gucci.

"Are you okay?" the woman asked with a deep concern in her eyes. Pat's original fright had dissipated after seeing her assailant's chest burst open, squirting red as bright as the flames which had just flown from her pistol. She gave the woman her best impression of a woman who had been terrified.

"He tried to rape me!!" Pat's face cringed into a hysterical frown and tears suddenly fell from her eyes. The woman, whom she'd only seen in passing, pulled her into her embrace protecting her from her fraudulent feelings. "Just like in the movies!' Pat thought, wanting to laugh at the woman who had welcomed her into her home. The ambulance and police showed up together. The paramedics wouldn't allow Pat to answer questions, telling the police that she was in shock. A Dodge Durango drove by as Pat was being hoisted into the EMS truck. She glanced over to the truck seeing a younger Hispanic man with tattoos covering his face and neck. He sucked his teeth and nodded to her, assuring Pat that what had started with his peoples being killed would end with a funeral line following her casket. 'What the fuck has Trey's grimy ass gotten us into?' she wondered, laying back onto the stretcher, her face frozen soled while playing disoriented.

Pops pulled his Viagra induced dick out of Aries, his young bust it baby, making a sloshing sound as it slid out. 'Who in the fuck is this?' he wondered, picking his cell up off of the floor and looking at the caller ID. Someone had left him an anonymous text message. While he stared at it, deciding whether to open it or not, Aries knelt between his legs and sucked her juices off of his balls. Slurp! The sound of her wet mouth massaging his sack was hot. She pulled on his shaft and nibbled on his crown while he opened the text message.

    "What the fuck!" Pops spat, surprised and upset by what he read. A hospital attendant had texted him letting know that Pat was in the hospital in a state of shock. They didn't explain what had taken place, only leaving him a message about her medical status. He pushed Aries off of his pole. She looked up at him with a nasty stare.

    "I don't know what your problem is, but I'm not one of those hoes you fuck with on the streets, Pops!" Aries said, still staring at him as he grabbed his pants, sliding them on without attempting to look for his underwear first. She wondered what happened because Pops had never run off on her during sex. They'd been together for a few years and he took real good care of her. She was aware that she was second to Pat and she was building momentum to take the number one spot.

    "Bitch!" Pops spat, standing at the door, holding the handle and looking backwards to Aries as she knelt naked on the plush carpet of their bedroom. "I run you, you don't run me, hoe!" He spit some real old fashioned game on her and she gasped for air. Over the years, since she'd been getting caked by Pops, Aries had become rotten in every way. She was already conniving and disloyal, which was why she'd lost all of her friends. But the money that Pops had dried her bitterness up into something more horrid. She stared at him with a hateful glare in her eyes.

"It's that bitch Pat, huh Pops?" Aries asked tearing up. She'd been pulling that one and Pops wanted to let her know that he'd been hip to her game. He walked over to her, snatching her up by her hair and pulling her naked body close to him. Rage had filled his eyes. Knowing that something happened to his wife and seeing this bitch disrespect him to his face had sent Pops into a brazen fury. WHACK! He slapped her across the face, still holding a hand full of her thick silky hair, making sure she didn't hit the floor so he could pull her into a vicious chokehold.

"Bitch! Straighten your muthafuckin face when you're talking to me!" he looked around, pulling her by her hair, making her see what he saw. "I bought this shit, hoe! That means it's mines, ya dig?" His swagger was seventies pimpish when he checked Aries. Pops would never attempt to manhandle Pat. He knew that the consequences were deeper than being hated because she was the same streets as him – streets that didn't believe in unearned mercy. "Now pack it up, hoe. It's over!" He finally pushed her back onto the floor, spitting on her before walking out of the house. 'Who in the fuck is this hoe playing with?' Pops wondered, getting into his Navigator and driving off. He was sure that the house he'd been sharing with Aries would be one of two ways when he got back: destroyed and burning or clean with a naked bitch waiting to make up. He preferred the latter, but expected the worst. Either way, what he'd done had to be done or he would have been lay-a-waying some unnecessary bullshit from the hoe in the future.

CHAPTER 19

DRAKE

I sat in a stolen van that I'd lifted from a grocery store on the southwest side of the city, waiting on this clown to come out of his apartment. His wife and son had already left and I knew he wouldn't be too far behind them. They had the same daily routine that ran like clockwork. I'd timed and scheduled their weekly routine and knew that this was my best shot at getting him without being seen.

When Quan asked me to hit this nigga, I was shocked. We'd done all kinds of shit together, but kidnapping wasn't one of them. I'd never had to do it, but for the type of paper that nabbing homeboy would bring in, it was one. Quan had sworn that snatching the Hispanic cat would help us to get to the truck that had been jacked. 'A thousand muthafuckin birds!!?' I thought, knowing that moving them would put my name in the baller's hall of fame. "Shit!" I said, seeing the guy stroll out of his crib. I opened the van door, ready to leap out and smack him with my heat, but stopped short. An unmarked police car pulled up. It was a double black Charger with the flashers planted into the grill. 'Imma hustler, mutha fucka!' I laughed. Can't get me like that, fam. I watched as the Hispanic cat jumped into the passenger side. "This punk ass nigga's a muthafuckin snitch!" I spat angrily. I didn't know the guy personally, but a snitch was someone who shouldn't have been able to recycle the same air as a real nigga like me. Him and everything that he stood for disgusted me. At that moment, I'd made up my mind. 'Imma coon that nigga!' I thought, all of my reservations about kidnapping someone had vanished. It was on.

After watching the cop drive off with the Hispanic cat, I swung by the Chalmers projects. My mans, Gucci, had upped his crack game because fiends were running around everywhere. It was like a scene from New Jack City and Gucci's trap apartment was The Carter. I hopped out of my whip and rushed through the courtyard, pulling down the fire escape stairs. On my way up, I ran into some unexpected shit. 'Dayum!' I thought, staring at young Hashes pounding a fiend from the back. She breathed and panted heavily as he pushed deeper and faster, not being bothered by my presence. Hashes' eyes rolled into the back of his head, hypnotized by addict's wetness.

I stared at her, noticing how thick she was. 'Maybe she ain't smoking...?' I thought because a basehead's body wasn't anything like I was looking at. She had a short bob cut hairstyle that came to her neck and her ass was wide and muscular like she worked out. Her lips were chapped like she'd just taken them off of a pipe, but other than that, there were no telling signs that she fucked with that rock. Her perky titties swung beneath her as he ground into her, trying to gorge the bottom of her canal. I shook my head and walked past them, never saying a word. Gucci had already told me how Hashes got down and I swore that he'd been exaggerating, but the truth had just been exposed about the youngster. Thump Thump! I knocked on the kitchen window with two quick thumps, letting them know that it was someone from the clique. Gucci was sensitive about us being coded around his trap because niggaz had taken the game back to the old school money, mack or murder style. It wasn't about hustling because niggaz had abandoned the game, only worrying about how they were going to eat and saying fuck principles. Tutsi looked out and nodded before opening the window and letting me climb inside. "What' up, Tutsi?" I asked, giving him dap. He nodded and locked the window, pulling the armor-guard back over it.

"Everything is good around here," Tutsi replied. "How about you, my brotha?" I smirked, wanting to laugh after hearing his hitch.

"I'm good. Where's my mans at?" I asked about Gucci because I didn't see him in the front room. Tutsi shrugged his shoulders.

"Don't know," he replied flatly and walked over to the front window that looked out into the courtyard. Tutsi stayed on point, ready for whatever the game would bring. But there was off something about him – something that I didn't understand, something other than him never being interested in popping a nut off in a hoe. Something peculiarly deranged and inhuman.

"Tutsi, man, I got a lick up for us that's about some serious ends," I said, pouncing onto the couch and looking over to where he'd posted up in the window.

"Like?" Tutsi asked, glancing over to me, letting me know that he was interested. We'd already made a few moves together and shit always went well. Tutsi was professional and I like that quality in him. He wasn't my mans, but I liked the way he got down because he was gangster about his shit.

"Quan hooked it up," I started, before filling him in on what was going on. I let him know that our mark was a snitch and that sold him on it. Tutsi had been sold out by an informant on his bank robbery case, getting him seven years in the pen where he'd met Gucci so he had an intense hatred for rats. "Man, we get fifty stacks even if we don't find the work," I finished with a nod, assuring Tutsi that we'd been offered a good deal.

"When?" Tutsi asked flatly, still looking out into the courtyard, although he'd been intently listening to me, his eyes hadn't left the corridor. There was something keeping him from making eye contact with me. 'What the hell is he looking for?' I wondered while staring at him for a sign.

"We can move on him any time this week. I already know the nigga's routine. Feel me?"

"Yes, my brotha."

"Yes what?" I asked, not knowing exactly what he'd agreed to – feeling me or doing kidnapping with me.

"Both. I feel you and I'm in." He agreed without any protest.

"You think Gucci's gonna roll?" I asked, not knowing if Gucci was willing to jeopardize what he was already doing. He was my mans and had never bailed on me when I needed him, but things had changed over the years. We'd grown apart, partly because he'd groomed another team of his own and partly because of the beef between him and Omar.

"No telling these days. Me, my brotha," he pointed to himself. "I'm in and I'm doing it because I trust you, not for the money. I already have plenty of money. Plenty." He glanced over to me and smiled, assuring me that plenty was abundant. Tutsi didn't spend money because he didn't have any habits, so I believed him. 'This booty-scratching muthafucka probably has small faced bills,' I thought, shaking my head at the sight of his teeth.

"You need to get some dental work with it, my nigga," I laughed, causing Tutsi to chuckle too.

"Fuck you, my brotha," he kept chuckling while still gazing out into the courtyard

GUCCI

After pulling Pat's car into his garage, Gucci pulled the duffle bag out of the trunk. She'd tuck it into the tire compartment before running next door. Gucci peeked through the garage door window, making sure he wasn't being set up because what Pat had offered him was too good to be true. 'Maybe this hoe is tryna jack a nigga...' I thought, clutching the bag tightly while gazing out into the street. There weren't any signs of trouble so I walked out, rushing the bag into the house. I wanted to get the bricks into a safe spot. Somewhere that only me and God knew about because thirty kilos was enough work to cause a bi-coastal war. I set the bag on the floor beside the couch and rushed to the front window, looking out into the streets again. I didn't want any surprises from Pat. It wasn't like she was incapable of them because it was known that she'd fleeced her plug for the coke that was supposedly in the duffle bag. I rushed back over to the bag and opened it.

"Thank you God!" I said with a sigh of relief, and looking up to the heavens because I was sure that all of my suffering had been alleviated. 'It's on!' I thought, closing the bag and debating whether I should break bread with my team and cut Pat out, or keep my promise and cash her out ten thousand a brick. I could turn around and move each one for twenty-five, especially since it was drought season, so I'd still be pulling a major caper. Or I could break each slab down into stones and push them rock for rock and get rich.

I tucked the bag beneath the couch and left. I had to get back to the trap. Tutsi was there and Hashes had finally popped back up after being missing for a couple of days. He was like that, always vanishing and returning a few days later. I didn't like it, but Hashes was a little off and had a strange way of doing shit. I kept an eye on him, though, because a nigga could never tell about someone out in these streets. Especially after seeing a glint of the foul shit Hashes was capable of.

Hashes had been molesting all types of fiends. Sodomizing them, raping them, and even making them perform bestial shit. I'd even stopped taking the fire escape because it had become his deviant playground – the place where he did his sadistic strong-arms.

One afternoon, I'd just finished hooking up with Pat and was climbing up the fire escape with three kilos of cocaine when I ran into Hashes making a hype suck a dog's dick. I walked up and the nigga gave me a hood head nod like he wasn't doing anything immoral.

"You see this hoe!?" Hashes said excitedly, pointing at her as she slurped on the dog's piece. I looked from him over to the fiend and back to him. 'This muhfucka gotta stop this shit!' I thought, outdone by what he'd been having someone do for half of a stone. He was too stingy to give them a whole twenty. Instead, he'd break it in half and sell the other half for twenty still.

"Man, you a sick muhfucka, homey." I shook my head, disgusted by what he was involved in and walked past them. The sad part was that the fiend didn't seem to mind. Actually, the bitch looked more interested than violated. After that, I'd started taking the front, walking through the courtyard of the projects.

I hopped out of my car and rushed over to our building. As I walked through the corridor, I sensed that something was off. There aren't any addicts running around. 'That's strange,' I thought, looking around and wondering what had happened. My first thought was that Hashes had raped or beaten one of our regulars and ran everyone off for a few days. There was no telling when he'd explode, because he hustled with an iron hand. I looked towards the north building and my blood rolled into any immediate boil. My customers were posted around their building.

"They must have gotten back on," I said to myself and rushed into our complex. 'It's a muhfuckin drought! How did these clowns get on?' I wondered furiously while rushing up the stairs to the apartment. THUMP THUMP I kicked the bottom of the door, letting them know it was family. No one had keys to the apartment. That was a rule at the trap because if the law came in, whoever was holding the keys to the unit would be the nigga with the cast. Tutsi opened the door and gave me dap.

"Tutsi, man some crazy shit is going on!" I said, never seeing Drake sitting on the couch as I walked in.

"What's that, nigga?" Drake asked, chuckling because he knew that he'd caught me slipping.

"What's up, my nigga?" I walked over and gave my guy some love. It was always good to see Drake, but I didn't expect to see him in the chill apartment.

"So what is it, my brotha?" Tutsi asked.

"Them muhfuckas in the north building are slumpin again!' I replied, remembering why I'd been upset in the first place. I'd just came up with thirty whole ones and needed to move them quick and that wouldn't be happening if those north building niggaz were around. 'These are my 'jects!' I thought, wanting to take Tutsi's route and head over there blazing heat to all of those fools.

"Yeah, Hashes noticed earlier today," Tutsi said and Drake chuckled. I guessed they had an inside joke that I wasn't aware of and I wanted to know that it was.

"So what's up? How'd he find out?" I waited and Drake butted in...

"Hashes caught one of the fiends strolling over to their trap and you know the rest," Drake said, grabbing his crotch, letting me know that Hashes had put his usual down on one of our scattered flock. I didn't condone what Hashes was doing, but it worked because the baseheads were in line whenever he was around.

"It's on, Tutsi. We going in that muhfucka tonight!" I nodded and walked over to where he stood by the window. I was sure that he'd been watching for that fine ass broad to give us a show again and I wanted to take a peek. I wondered if she'd seen us and was leaving her curtain open on purpose, just to get us hard. Some women were like that.

"Tonight?!" Drake asked with enthusiasm. I looked over to him seeing a sanguinary twinkle in his eyes. 'I'm hanging out with some sick muhfuckaz!' I thought, shaking my head.

"Nah, brah. This shit is for the trap," I replied, letting Drake know that he wasn't welcome to ride. Besides, I had Tutsi and Hashes, two of the sickest niggaz I knew, rolling with me so I was certain that hitting them would be a walk in the park.

"What? Why not, nigga? We hood!" Drake stated boldly, being persistent about moving on the north building hustlers with us. I looked over to Tutsi, who shrugged his shoulders, and back to Drake who looked at me like he was upset about me not wanting him to troop up with us.

"Nah, I can't live with it, brah. If you was stacking this cake with us….I'd be alright with it, but it's our trap and our problem." Talking about me, Tutsi and Hashes, who I looked around for, but obviously wasn't there. "Where in the fuck is Hashes?" I finally asked, trying to change the tone of the room because both drake and Tutsi didn't understand why I'd been so adamant about Drake not suiting up. I knew my guy and was sure that he was down to ride or die, but this wasn't his problem – it was ours.

"Last I saw, he was on the fire escape busting some fiend's back out," Drake said and chuckled. I was sure that it was some gruesome shit if it involved Hashes. 'That must have been what Drake was laughing about earlier,' I thought, curious to know what Drake had seen. Although I wasn't into those types of fetishes, the shock of seeing some of the gross shit that Hashes did was intriguing.

We sat around for a while and Drake filled me in on the caper that Quan had set up. Quan's man, Krispy – a nigga on the inside with Quan – wanted us to find out what happened to his shipment of coke, starting with the Mexican who had dropped the body into the alley with Rocsi. Tutsi had already agreed to roll and I was definitely in because they were my niggaz. Plus, the payout was heavy. "Hell muhfuckin yea, my nigga!" I said, nodding my head, agreeing to get at that paper. Me and Tutsi had done kidnappings in prison and wouldn't hesitate to take a rat off the streets for the sake of all thoroughbred hustlers out there in the game. Knowing that made everything else a bonus because downing one of them would take the real street niggaz up a point.

"Come!" Tutsi said, waving me and Drake over to the window. 'It must be that hoe!' I thought, getting up and rushing over to the window.

"Drake, man, this bitch is fine!" I said after getting to the window and seeing the chocolate honey getting naked. Shit! I finally caught a glimpse of her ass and it was proper – round as an onion with hips to match.

"Gucci, I'm good," Drake laughed at us and waved us off while getting up. "Y'all niggaz trippin." He walked toward the door and I followed behind him locking it after he left. We'd been waiting on him to leave before setting up our hit, because it was definitely going down. I rushed back to the window to finish watching the show. I'd been looking for that freak all week. 'Imma get at this bitch!' I thought, seeing the way her titties fell from her bra, exposing those thick nipples. Tutsi was quiet, staring at her like a sick voyeur who was stalking his prey. I was sure that wanted her probably more than I did, but I was one move ahead of him. A move that would make the best man a winner – me

CHAPTER 20

SHIP

After picking Chico up, we shot over to the apartments. I'd gotten some bad news from Trey. The shipment that we'd heisted was bugged with GPS monitors and one of Trey's customers had taken a bad loss as a consequence. 'I don't know why I didn't think of that?' I wondered, knowing that I'd been slippin because I was usually more cautious. I'd been sidetracked by all of the money that we stood to make off of those kilos and it almost came back to haunt us.

"Chico, we have to burn Trey's people, bro," I said as we got out of the car and walked up to our building. I didn't want the gunplay from whoever's truck we'd lifted to boomerang back to us, especially with me quitting the force. If that happened, I was sure that people would start talking and put two and two together. I was only thirty years old, far from retirement age, leaving a job with good benefits – and being chased down and shot at by cartel members. Everyone in the force would be taking heed to that and I'd be having a lot of meetings with internal affairs. Hell no! I shook my head, not wanting to suffer that fate and knowing what needed to be done in order to escape it.

"Yeah, hombre," Chico agreed with a solid nod. "I was thinking the same thing, huh bro." I used my key to get into the apartment. I saw Rocsi sitting on the couch, looking nervous, when I walked in. Chico came in behind me and closed the door. Trey came strolling from the back of the apartment stretching like he'd just woken up.

"What the fuck happened?" I asked, wanting to know how we'd let something like GPS trackers slip by us. We were supposed to be professionals and we were being as sloppy as amateurs. 'This shit better be good!' I thought, staring at Trey who looked like it was worse than I'd originally thought. He'd been moving the bricks fluidly, bringing in over a million cash already, and I'd had no complaints until now.

"We missed the muthafuckin trackers!" Trey replied, still yawning from his sleepiness. He walked further into the room, rolling his eyes at Rocsi and nodding to Chico. 'And Chico thought something was up between them!' I thought with a short swift grunt.

"I knew we were moving too fast," Rocsi added, looking over to Chico and I. She shook her head and landed her attention on me. "Remember when I said let's go through each of them?" She stared at me before glancing over to Trey. "Remember Trey?" she said.

'Ain't this a bitch!' I thought, staring at her in shock. Right then, I'd had a sudden change in heart. Maybe these motherfuckers are plotting on me... Rocsi had never used Trey as a co-signer, which made their sudden duo suspicious to me.

"Yeah, Ship," Trey nodded, agreeing with Rocsi. They'd been at one another's throats before the heist, only to become bosom buddies a few weeks later. That wasn't like Rocsi. She'd usually hold a grudge; at least, until she could get even with the person who had betrayed her.

"So what's the deal? Where do we go from here?" I asked just to see where everyone was at. We'd grown apart and it was all over money. We were thieves who knew that there was really no honor amongst us. Larceny was embedded in our hearts and we'd kill one another to come up. I looked around from Rocsi to Chico to Trey, wondering which of us would be the one to go bad. 'Which one of these motherfuckers are going to try to sink the Ship?' I wondered, glancing at each of them.

"Sheeit, I already made my next move," Trey said, ending the silent stares between us. I guess he could feel the tension rising and wanted to ease the animosity that had overtaken the room. "I shot out to the farm and went through every one of the last four hundred."

"Was everything good out there?" I asked, hoping he'd have something good to add to this fucked up situation.

"Yeah, hell yeah. We're on point out that way, but who knows if they'd already tracked the farm before I pushed those last thirty off on old school Pops."

"Right, I feel you too, Trey," Rocsi nodded, their sudden camaraderie bothering me after hearing her agree with Trey. 'Maybe they're fucking?' I thought, hoping that's what it was because any sign of betrayal would cost them their lives.

"Damn! So we have to find another place to hold them."

"What about that car wash that you copped, Ship?" Rocsi asked, causing my head to whip into her direction. 'She knows!' I thought, staring at her for any sign, but she didn't give. Her eyes were vacant.

"That's a good spot for them too. Thanks Rocsi," I added, trying to throw her off in case she'd been on to what me and Chico had going. There wasn't anything in the wash so I had plenty of room for storage. I saw Chico glance over to me and knew that he was wondering what I was doing. I'd made the right call, I was sure of it, and after I explained it to him, he'd be gain to go with it. We couldn't send a guilty message to Trey and Rocsi. They were hood and looking for any type of deceit in us.

"Nah, brah brah," Trey said, shaking his head defiantly. "I'ont think that'll be a good idea. That hood is grimy as fuck and niggaz is looking for a come up." 'Thank you, Trey!' I thought, wanting to leap from my seat, but remained poised. I simply nodded.

"What? That's some bullshit, Trey!" Rocsi blurted, looking upset that Trey had finally went against her call. "He's had that wash for years and no one has gone in there to steal before." Her lips curled into a doubtful smirk and she started picking in her nails.

"Yeah, but ain't nobody been pulling up in Lexus trucks and shit either!" He was referring to Rocsi's truck, noting that the jack boys would be paying attention to an old dilapidated car wash with nice cars coming and going. I guess that spelled kilo safe haven in the hood.

"You're right, Trey," I finally chimed in, shutting the conversation about moving the dope into my car wash down. I didn't want Rocsi to come up with a better proposal after Trey had shot her down. She was my cousin and I'd groomed her in the game and was certain that she could out-think everyone in the room, including myself. "I've got somewhere, though. We can leave them here and lock the apartment down. Only letting Trey come and go." I looked around to everyone. Trey nodded agreeing and so did Chico, but Rocsi only shrugged her shoulders. She must have felt like her input didn't matter. I was relieved because she'd almost sprung light on what Chico and I had pulled off. I was leaning towards them knowing about the other load of dope being stashed at my car wash, but her and Trey's disagreement assured me that they didn't. 'I'm letting my own paranoia fool me,' I thought, shaking my head, giving Trey a pound and hugging Rocsi before walking out of the apartment followed by Chico

ROCSI
I was mad as all hell when I left the apartment. Me and Trey were supposed to be airtight against Ship and Chico. I was sure that something was up and whatever it was, it was going on inside of Ship's car wash building. 'What other reason would they have to be over there?' I thought angrily while jumping into my Lexus SUV and driving off.

I was on my way to see Khalid. Although he'd started off as a mark, me and him had gotten kind of close. I didn't feel him enough to give him any of this sweet thing, but we had bonded in an odd way. He wasn't like Trey, always trying to get a glimpse of my ass; Khalid was different. What had started as a regular paper chase eventually turned into something personal. Me and Trey would never be like that, especially after he'd just sold me out again.

I couldn't trust Trey. That's why I'd been holding out about Ship and Chico leaving the barn and going to the car wash. 'He'll probably start some hoe shit between me and Ship,' I thought, knowing that it wasn't beneath Trey to tell Ship about me tailing him and Chico. Shit, maybe they were doing some real police shit! I battled with a lot of different options, not knowing the truth, but sure that it would be coming out soon because there was something shady brewing. Something that Ship didn't want me and Trey to know, but Trey was blinded by his oversized ego and couldn't see what the fuck was really happening. There were a thousand kilos in that truck! I knew because Quan told me when I went to visit him.
***
A strange feeling overcame me as I walked into the visitation room. I'd been a frequent visitor and knew what to expect when I walked through the prison gates onto the compound, but this feeling was something different. I knew that me and Quan's relationship would be changed by what I had to tell him, but I wasn't looking forward to hearing what he'd had to tell me either.

I sat, legs crossed exposing the soft shimmer that using Ama La detoxifying body polish gives my skin. Quan loves to see me in skirts and dresses. Sometimes I'd come commando as a bonus for him. As usual, niggaz had their eyes glued to me, never paying any attention to the bitches who they were visiting with. 'I'd walk out on these niggas!' I thought with a grunt because there was no way that I'd ride backseat to a bitch who was here to see someone else. "Hell nah," I whispered, smiling and shaking my head because a nigga would have to have all eyes on me.

Quan walked out. His swag was on high, like always, but he wasn't smiling. There was a seriousness in his stare. One that assured me that we'd be at each other's throats. There wasn't a doubt that we'd still be together after I left the visiting room. He's my baby, but I couldn't let him bully me. I stood up, ready to give him usual hug and wet kiss – Quan loved the way I applied my Smashbox lip gloss because that shit made my lips look dick sucking ready. He got to our table and sat down, never attempting to touch me. 'Ain't this about a bitch!' I thought, staring at him, hands on hips, ready to explode. I wanted to slap the shit out him right there in the visiting room, sending him back to his bed area with a story to tell.

"Quan? I know you're not gonna play me like that?" I asked, still standing over him. I'd been waiting to see him all month and wasn't about to let him just shit on me like that. He chuckled while coolly rubbing the bridge of his nose.

"Bitch!" he snarled at me, still staring at me with vehemence. "Sit your lying ass down!" he pointed to my chair, scolding me like he was my damn father or something.

"What's the problem, Quan?" I asked, sitting as he'd asked me. I'd promised myself that I'd act reasonable, but there was only so much a bitch could take. 'Don't make me do this, Quan,' I thought, giving him a warning stare. I could have cut a fool on his ass and walked out, still holding my head high, but he'd have to back into the prison population with the stigma of being shitted on by a bitch.

"Who is you runnin with?" he asked nastily. "Don't come with no muthafuckin games either!"

"Why? I'm making sure you're good, ain't I?"

"Hoe, I ain't ask you about me!" Quan looked over to the guard, realizing he'd gotten loud. "I asked you about that Mexican muthafucka."

"He's a friend of Ship's, Quan. Why are you doing this?" I wanted know because he wasn't the jealous type, at least not until now.

"Because you a hoe," he pointed his thumb into his chest. "My hoe and I ask whatever I wanna."

"I know who I am and who I'm with, Quan. And I'm not going to be too many more hoes and bitches."

"You gon be whatever I want you to be, bitch! I thought Ship was the police now?"

"Yeah, he is, but he still does his thing too," I nodded, hoping he'd change the subject because I wanted to talk about something different - something that didn't concern Ace's body or Chico.

"So Ace was Ship, huh?" Quan asked and my head whipped into his direction. I couldn't disguise my shock. 'How does this nigga know Ace?' I wondered, staring at Quan with my mouth hung wide open.

"Ace?" I asked, still shocked that he'd known him. "How did you know him?"

"I did and don't worry about how. I'm asking you the questions."

"Yeah that was him. But why?" I wanted to know what interested Quan in what Ship had going on, especially about what he had going on with Ace. We'd let Ace die of starvation before dumping him into the alley behind his dope spot. He'd suffered throughout his death because the wounds in his head that Ship had given him at the raid and refused to let anyone clean up had gotten infected, blinding him and causing him to get gangrene.

"So who got those thousand slabs off of the truck?"

"Thousand slabs?" I asked, knowing he'd gotten he number wrong because there was only five hundred kilos in the truck that we had jacked.

"Yeah! Bitch, don't act dumb now. Who got that work?!!" he stared at me, searching for deception. Quan was the only person on earth who truly knew me. Maybe because we'd spent so much time in the prison visiting room talking and getting to know intimate shit about one another or maybe we were just soul mates. Whichever, it didn't matter because the fact was that I couldn't lie to him.

"We hit the lick, but there were only five hundred cakes in the truck."

"Nah, Rocsi. Somebody is holding out on you, baby." At the sound of my name, I knew that the tone of our conversation had changed. He'd started believing me. He knew that I wouldn't lie to him because I trusted Quan with my truths.

"Are you sure, Quan?" I asked, wanting to know if he was picking me and blowing smoke up my ass.

"I'm positive. This is us, Rocsi!" he nodded, assuring me that he wasn't playing games. *This is us* was his way of saying he promised and I believed him. 'That dirty motherfucker!' I thought, shaking my head as my blood boiled. I wanted to kill ship. He was my cousin, but what part of the game was he in? Fleecing his own peoples after we'd all taken penitentiary chances to hit that lick I could have died in that accident with Trey. Or worse, I could have killed him and gotten stuck with a life bid behind that shit.

Quan finally opened up, telling me about Krispy and how Ace was on his team. I couldn't believe how loose-lipped niggaz were in prison. Krispy had been feeding a shark all of his business, not knowing he was being preyed upon because once

163

Quan was hungry – he was gon eat! And get fat at Krispy at Krispy's expense.

***

I pulled up to Khalid's hair salon. All of the females stared out the storefront window, wanting to be in my position because I was papered up and flaunting it. I stepped out, looking good as usual. My hair was already shredded into a short spiky do with honey blond highlights. It was disrespect to step into a salon with your hair already done, so I made it my business to make a weekly appearance with the flair of a certified street diva. My hips swayed from side to side, gyrating my onion, making it look like heavy artillery. I didn't have a mountain like Buffy the Body, but I wasn't working with a molehill either. 'Ya heard!' I thought, with a flashing smirk and chuckle while walking past the reception desk. Toya, a bitch from the east side, was manning the desk. She ice grilled me and rolled her eyes as I walked past. 'I know, bitch,' I laughed, taking my Giorgio Armani Dragonfly frames off. I'd left the sun outside, but the light from my shine was blinding the other bitches in the shop.

Khalid's face lit up when he saw me. He walked over, hugging and kissing me like I was his property. The fact that we weren't fucking was a secret between us that I'd be keeping if he played his hand right. Everyone was plotting to slide me the soap, so I had to do some underhanded work of my own. The D raised killers, cons, and bitches who used niggaz as ponds. And I'm that bitch.

"What's up baby boo?" Khalid said, stepping back and giving me a once over. He loved my style, and spent more time admiring the way I looked in my jeans instead of trying to get me out of them.

"Nothing," I replied with an innocent façade. My girlish smirk hid the deceit in me and I sat into a styling recliner. I discreetly watched as all of the haters turned their faces up at me.

Oh, these hoes are hating! I chuckled. "So where are we going?" I asked, sure that Khalid had something good planned. There wasn't a party in the city that he wasn't invited to. He was the man. Making moves with real Mafia connects and everyone who was someone in the game knew it.

"My mans is throwing something nice at the State Theater," he said and nodded to the alligator boots that I was wearing. He'd bought them when he was in Monaco earlier this year.

"So you decided to wear them for me, huh baby boo?" Khalid laughed after asking me that. It was an inside joke because I'd questioned their quality before looking at the label. I was like, "If these ain't Mauri, I'm cool." Not knowing that he'd slid me a Manolo Blahnik boot box. A pair of stompers running about fourteen grand and I was ready to protest about some five thousand dollar Mauri's. That's when he became a jack move because niggaz with money that long could stand a shakedown from the squad.

"Right," I replied with a quaint chuckle. "I still didn't get a chance to properly thank you." I made sure the rest of the shop heard me and I wrapped my leg around him and pulling him toward me. He smelled hypnotic too. It wasn't an intrusive smell either; it was subtle like how Quan smelled. I kissed his neck sensually and heard gasps from all over the salon. The kiss was more to ruffle the bitches in the shop than to arouse Khalid.

"Chill out, baby boo. This is my place of business," he laughed, backing away from me because he knew that I'd put on a real show. I liked attention, whether it was good or bad, and Khalid knew that. We sat around for a few minutes longer before leaving out. We both had to get dressed because a night out with Khalid required more than some alligator boots and Roberto Cavalli jeans.

GUCCI

It was time to move. Tutsi stood beside me and Hashes took the rear. I wanted to lead by example because this would be my last time soldiering up. I'd made a nice piece of change fucking with the game and I wanted to start enjoying it, which let me know that it was time for me to take a back seat to Hashes. He was guerilla enough to handle the helm and the nigga could think too, which made my decision easier. 'Fuck it!' I thought, knowing that my mans Tutsi had stacked up a good piece of hood currency too.

Tutsi was a gutter ass nigga. His African roots had traveled across the ocean with him. He lived the bare necessities in life. Never buying shit. He'd trick with the young bitches around the projects occasionally, but other than that, Tutsi was fish pussy tight with his cash.

"Tutsi, put a spark to this wick," I whispered as we strolled up the stairs to the apartment where the north building crew was serving their product. A basehead was coming down the stairs. "Hold up!" I pulled the cocktail back. Although we were masked and blacked out, I didn't want the fiend to see what we were about to do. We had too much to lose, including our freedom.

"Come here, bitch!" Hashes said, grabbing the junkie into a swift chokehold. He was squeezing the life from the piper's body. 'This nigga's a monster!' I thought, grabbing his arm, making him loosen up on the fiend's neck. It was the same bitch that he'd raped on the fire escape. After all he'd done to her, she still managed to sneak back over to the north building. 'What are these niggaz shaking their work up with?' I wondered because their fiends were obviously more loyal than ours.

"Chill nigga! Let that bitch go," I demanded, but Hashes wasn't having it. He shook his head and we stopped at the top of the stairwell.

"Hell nah, don! This hoe knows who we are. Fuck that shit!" He upped his mini 14, pressing it against her throat.

"Hold up, lil brah. We can make the hoe get the chute opened," I nodded, trying to convince Hashes that my idea was air tight. "Feel me?"

Tutsi nodded and smiled, showing his rotted out and yellow teeth. "I feel you, my brotha." Hashes nodded too and grabbed the fiend by her throat, pushing her in front of us. Now he was leading the way. I walked slowly, not wanting any of the jet fuel to leak from the forty ounce bottle. Fuck that shit! I chuckled to myself because I knew a nigga who had killed himself like that while trying to firebomb his baby's mother's pad. The gas leaked onto his clothes and when he lit the bottle, he lit himself up too.

"Knock on the chute, bitch! Three knocks and a stomp! Just like they told you," Hashes said. I looked over at Tutsi. Tutsi shrugged his shoulders. He knew what I was thinking. 'How does this nigga know the knock?' I wondered, watching as the dope fiend bitch tapped the side of the chute. Tutsi lit the cocktail and I stood beside the door, out of view because I didn't want anyone to see me. The flame swooshed and suddenly the chute opened. I threw the cocktail inside and leaned back on to the wall. Hashes and Tutsi were on the other side of the door. Hashes still held the basehead hoe in a snug headlock. The chute never shut and screams came from the apartment.

"Put this shit out, Tex!" someone yelled from inside before the door flew open. Hashes pushed the fiend ahead of him and swung around the corner, quickly letting his .50 caliber follow her. BLAH BLAH! I heard his handgun sing and I quickly followed behind him.

My intentions were to go in ahead of Hashes and Tutsi, but Hashes had really shown up, letting me know that he was down for his crown. The war on the streets was starting in the north building and Hashes was leading the way. There was a body sprawled across the floor. Shit! It was the fiend's body. I recognized her from her hat. It was missing a side of it, where Hashes had blown a chunk of her head off, but it was definitely the same dingy skull cap that he'd wiped his dick off with. He must have smoked her after pushing her through the door.

I saw Hashes moving quickly through the house. His mini 14 slung across his back and his .50 held in front of him. 'Where the fuck is Tutsi?' I wondered. BLOCCA BLOCCA! Two shots rang out behind me. I swung, pointing my thumper into the vicinity, but there wasn't anyone there. The flickering of the loose flames were scattered throughout the unit and I saw a shadow. It was Tutsi and he was standing over a body and shaking his head. His pistol was lowered and looked like he'd made a mistake. 'Oh shit!' I thought, rushing over to him. I was sure that he'd made a mistake and smoked Hashes, but he couldn't have. I'd just seen the youngster rushing towards the back of the house. Maybe it was the fiend's body and he thought he was the one who had killed her.

"Tutsi?" I called, moving closer to him and the body that lay on the floor beneath him. I walked up and nearly lost my breath. "What happened?" I asked, looking form Omar's burned and bullet riddled body to Tutsi who stood over him with a smoking Roger. He'd smoked Drakes' cousin.

"He was inside," Tutsi said with a solemn glare.

"Fuck em then. Let's roll out," I said and patted him on the back. Hashes came back into the front room with an insidious smirk on his face.

"We cleaned house, don," he said. I gave him a head gesture to follow behind me as I bailed out. I was sure that the other tenants had called the police. Although niggaz in the ghetto played by a certain set of rules, there were those few who were good Samaritans who would call the police anonymously and pretend to damn the traitor who had violated the hood law.

After getting out of the building, we all split up and went our separate ways. That was just a precaution that we took in case the police ever got behind us. That way they would only have a fraction of what it took to snatch our plate.

ROCSI

My and Khalid walked into the party looking like black royalty. Me in a tan Michael Kors pants suit, those chocolate brown alligator boots with a four inch heel that Khalid had bought me in Monaco and a chocolate Prada scarf wrapped around my waist that matched my boots. It was still early fall so I left my eggshell beige mink at home or I would have really killed the game. There were a few females in the atmosphere who had put on in a major way, but none of them could outshine me. 'I'm Rocsi!' I thought with an arrogant snicker while canvassing the open room. Khalid had my waist pulled snug against him, letting the crowd know that I was with him. His gabardine suit, tailored in Italy to fit him, was a woman magnet. Females swarmed around us like sharks. I was sure that all of them believed they could rock the sheets better than me, wanting to do all kinds of strange sexual shit for a chance to be with Khalid, thinking that would give them the leverage to take my place. But the thing was – me and Khalid weren't even rocking like that. He'd stopped trying to get a taste of my girly girl a while ago. We still kicked it strong, but I'd actually grown to like the nigga, but wasn't about to get at my goodies; especially with Quan so short to coming home.

We walked over to the bar, Khalid still hugging my waist. There was something that he wanted to portray, an image of having a bad bitch underneath his wing. He wanted to look like a don, even at the expense of being a fraud because I definitely wasn't his diva. This nigga's a trick. I watched as he ordered to bottles of Louie and walked off towards our table. I tensed up when Chris Webber, a nigga who balled for the NBA, walked up to us. He was tall and handsome. A momma's boy looking motherfucker, but he still had that hood swagger like he'd put hands on a nigga for principles alone. Chris smiled at me, giving me a once over before slapping five with Khalid and embracing him. I figured they must have known one another because their embrace was genuine like they'd been friends for years.

"Hey Khalid," Chris said, still smiling a slightly buzzed smirk and chuckling. "I see you came right this year." He looked over to me and smiled, letting me know that I'd already known – that I was superior to any bitch that he'd been fucking with.

"Yeah, no doubt," Khalid replied and wrapped his arm back around me waist and pulling me snug against his body. I smiled while thinking, 'damn this nigga is fake!' I looked at Chris who seemed to know what I was thinking, because his smirk was telling. Everyone and anyone who knew Khalid knew how fraudulent his personality was. He'd paint a Picasso look-alike knowing it was a Walmart mass production knockoff.

"Yeah, Chris. This here is my baby boo," Khalid bragged like I was really his woman or some shit and I just smiled.

"Hi, I'm Rocsi," I reached out my hand and we shook. 'Damn this nigga's hands are soft!' I thought, shaking firmly. I liked to shake hands with men because it let them know that I'm a serious bitch. Other females like to play that kiss the cheek girly shit, but Ship had warned me against that kind of submissive shit early in the game. Letting a nigga kiss your cheek is like telling him you're willing to cook and watch his motherfucking kids. And Rocsi ain't the fucking one for that shit!

"Nice to meet you," Chris replied and leaned over, whispering something into Khalid's ear before walking off. Whatever was said had to have been a joke because Khalid burst into laughter. We walked over to our table and uncorked a bottle of the champagne that he'd ordered. I didn't like the shit. He could have gotten me a couple shots of Grey Goose and a top shelf Long Island to chase it down and I would have been fine. He probably would have had a better chance at sliding between my legs too, but he was too lame to foresee that.

171

Sometimes I believed Khalid was intimidated by me because I didn't need him. I had my own hustle and my own money. Whatever he brought to the table was just a bonus and I'd usually send it to Quan as sort of a rental fee to Khalid. 'Look at this nigga,' I thought, smiling as Fatso walked over to our table. He'd cleaned himself up pretty good. He was vined out in a dark navy blue suit that hung too loosely from his broad shoulders. The color and the suit was fly, but it wasn't a good enough fit to party with narcissistic niggaz like Khalid. His dreads were draped right, though. They fell across his neckline looking like he'd just come from getting them twisted. And his skin looked butter soft. He was more attractive than he'd seemed when I met him at Doug's funeral. 'Plus, I'm a sucker for a thug in a suit!' I chuckled and took a sip from my flute, flirting with my eyes, although he wasn't in my league by a mile.

"Khalid, what's up, don?" he gave Khalid dap and stepped back primping his suit. He fumbled with the lapel and smiled. "What you think, don?"

Khalid nodded. "Yeah, you're proper, but you're asking the wrong person." He looked over to me. "What do you think, Rocsi?" Khalid asked. Fatso turned facing me, still holding that same pose. I chuckled because these two niggaz looked up to me like I was the damn fashion police. I came to have a good time and get away from the game for a night, but Khalid wasn't going to let me. I respected him trying to add me into their thing, but Fatso was his little friend, not mines.

"I would have laughed at you and walked away," I said boldly and took another sip of the bitter champagne in my glass. Fatso was cute and Lord knows the nigga had some of the most adorable brown eyes, but his suit wasn't tailored right. I could tell that he hadn't put much time or money into his look and it would have been a turnoff for me.

"What?" Fatso's face turned demonic. I'd offended him with the truth. I looked over to Khalid thinking, 'Khalid, you'd better get your little friend.' I knew I looked cute, but I'm ghetto and had brought seventeen niggaz from the hood with me. They were in my purse, lining the clip of my .40 caliber. A bitch stayed strapped and ready for these clowns, including Fatso.

"Khalid, this hoe's trippin. This's Armani, don!" He flipped his lapel showing us the tag. I guess he hoped I'd get offended by his insult or be impressed by him showing me the designer tag on his lapel, but I was neither. This chump's a lame.

"Chill, Fatso baby. This is my peoples, nigga," Khalid looked from him to me and back to him. I never took my stare away from Fatso as I slid my Chanel bag closer to me and unbuckled the flap. 'Do it, nigga!' I thought, reaching my hand into the bag and clutching my strap as we stared one another down.

"Let me holla, don?" Fatso asked, and walked away with Khalid following behind him like a chump. If a nigga would have played me like that in front of Quan, Quan would have laid him down flat like a motherfucking doormat. But this sucker was a short distance from the table networking with Fatso, a nigga who had just called me a bitch. At that moment, all of the feelings that I'd developed for Khalid vanished. He was just a mark to me again and I'd use my heat to slug him just as quick as I'd bury Fatso's ass.

I watched them talking, wondering what they were discussing. 'What the fuck are they talking about?' I wondered, assuming that Khalid was probably trying to talk him out of slapping me, but I didn't give a fuck. If Khalid knew Fatso's ego was too frail to hear the truth, he shouldn't have asked me for my opinion. He knew that I wasn't a lay down type of hoe and wouldn't flatter a nigga to stroke his shallow ass admiration of himself. Hell nah, fuck him!

I rolled my eyes and continued watching as they talked, thinking the whole conversation was about me. 'Look at this punk,' I thought, certain by the glance that Fatso had given me before walking away, that he wanted to slap the shit out of me but I would have slung something scorching through his chest plate. After a while, I couldn't take it, so I walked over to them hoping I'd catch something, but they froze up, stopping their conversation mid-sentence. 'Ugh!' I thought, coughing after smelling a nasty fume coming off of one of them. I'd been with Khalid all day and knew that it wasn't him, so that left Fatso. Either this clown has paper or he's an idiot! I shook my head with disgust, knowing that he'd pumped gas in Armani.

I walked off toward the bar. I wasn't about to spoil my night arguing with a chump like Fatso. I was too fine and too fly and by the looks that I was getting from the ballers swarming the bar, it was obvious that I wasn't the only person who thought so.

CHAPTER 21

DRAKE

Me and Tutsi were posted outside of Chico's apartment building when I saw his Jeep driving up. His wife and son were already inside. We'd watched them go in earlier. Tutsi wanted to snatch them up and make the hit a family event but I wasn't with it. I just wanted the drop on the coke that had been lifted. It was dark and I hoped the darkness wouldn't alarm Chico, but we needed it like that. Tutsi had climbed the light poles that aligned the small parking lot, busting the lights. We needed the lot to be dark so we wouldn't be detected by any eyewitnesses when we snatched Chico's bitch ass up. Quan had gotten the word from Rocsi that Chico wasn't an informant, he was the police. He worked with Ship, Rocsi's cousin. When I heard that, I wanted to renege on the caper because I wasn't about kidnapping detectives and shit. Getting caught would cost me my life or a lifetime of suffering because the dirty ass police in Detroit would send me to prison maimed. 'Fuck that shit!' I thought when I first found out that our mark was a lawman. Later on, though, after I found out about the whole story I fell in.

Ship, the nigga who had started their whole movement was a grimy ass cat from the west side of town. He'd been sticking hood niggaz for over a decade, even after he joined the police force. His badge had given him a freedom to fuck over any nigga with felonious tendencies and that type of foul shit wasn't good for the game. I'd grown up watching the police shake niggaz down, but the law did it with a promise to protect a hustler's hustle, unlike what Ship and Chico were putting down. They were strictly out to fleece niggaz. And they had an inside connect who was instrumental in all of their jacks. His name was Trey.

Trey was a nigga from the same streets as Ship. He was a major baller and the hood loved him because he kept the right complexion on his product – tight white. The type of coke that flaked up with crack crystals when it was cooked. Trey was known in the streets as a crack general, instead of a rat no one knew about his credibility as a DEA informant because they embraced the lame like he was a hood legend although Trey was closer to being an officer than a dope boy. He would set street niggaz up to be robbed by Ship and his drug task force team, breaking the code of the game while stripping niggaz for major work that he'd put back on the streets at wholesale. Everyone in the game thought Trey was a legitimate hustler who had an out of town connect, never imagining that he was pushing the same shit that their mans had gotten popped for a week earlier. He was a real double dealing muthafucka and me and my squad had a special box of hot rocks for his ass.

Chico jumped out of his Jeep, never seeing Tutsi as he slid from beneath our van. He swiftly moved between cars and was at Chico's throat before he could move.

"Hands on chest!" Tutsi commanded, snugly pressing his four nickel against Chico's throat. Chico must have felt Tutsi's seriousness because he quickly obeyed what he'd demanded, putting his hands flat against his chest. Tutsi knew that Chico was a policeman and didn't want him to reach for his service pistol, so he made him put his hands where they were visible until he could pat him down.

I opened the rear doors from the inside of the van and smiled as Tutsi pushed Chico's rotten ass up to the back door. I jumped out and patted him down, pulling his piece from the back of his waist. It was a blue steel Ruger. 'This clown really think he's hood!' I thought with a faint chuckle before slapping across the back of his neck with his own heat. WHACK!

"Get in, bitch ass nigga!" I spat and pushed him into the back of the van making him split his head on the doors. Tutsi kept his heat at Chico's dome and climbed into the back with him while I ran around to the driver's seat.

"Hey, bro!!? What the fuck is going on?!!" Chico asked with a deep Hispanic accent. I was sure that he was wondering who would be gutter enough to nab his knowing that he was a cop. 'Me, muthafucka!' I thought boldly while driving off. Tutsi kept quiet, never answering him, while roughly hog tying him. The silence sent Chico a message that said we weren't playing any games. After Tutsi finished, he slid himself into the corner of the van and lifted his pistol to Chico's chest.

Chico followed Tutsi's lead and fell silent. He'd come to terms that his kidnapping was not negotiable and that we didn't give a fuck that he was a cop. We were taking him to an old dilapidated building in Highland Park, a small intra-section of Detroit that set inside the middle of the city. Me, Gucci and Quan used to strip stolen cars inside of the run down warehouse building back in the day. It was like a safe haven for the squad and would most likely become a final resting place for Chico because after we bled him for the information we needed, we'd leave him there dead because he was too connected to let him breathe.

GUCCI

Pat rolled over and stared up at me. I could tell what she was thinking and she was wrong. She probably thought it was her, but it wasn't. My piece going limp had nothing to do with her. 'Hell nah!' I thought, staring at her well defined naked body. Pat was a fine ass bitch, regardless of her age. I just couldn't stop thinking about Omar's bullet riddled and burned body.

I couldn't believe I'd been sleep to his game all along. He'd been smashing work on my block for months, right up under

177

my nose, without me knowing it. 'Shady ass nigga,' I thought, shaking my head. He'd even sent Drake to cop work from me during the drought. Had me and my team wondering where they were getting on from and it was our coke all along. Shit! It hit me like a ton of steel. 'Maybe Drake was in on it,' I wondered, unknowingly questioning myself out loud.

"What?" Pat asked, wondering what the hell I was talking about. Her voice brought me out of my trance. I'd been blindsided by Omar's deception and nothing else mattered to me right then. I only wanted answers. Answers from a dead muthafucka and I wasn't ready to visit him to get them, so Drake would have to translate. He was my mans, but money had brought treachery out of the loyalist of cliques. From the looks of what had taken place, mines wasn't an exception to its scheme.

I shook my head while flashing Pat a fake smile. "Nah, mami. I was just thinking about some shit," I said and she nodded. She was a real veteran hood bitch and I was sure that she'd been had a few times and had gotten over on a few fools herself. That's the way the game went. Everyone was trying to get fed, even at the expense of someone they hustled with.

"I understand, but damn, baby," Pat cooed and slid closer to me, rubbing her soft well-manicured hands across my bare chest. I hadn't been to the gym since I'd gotten out of prison, but my rips were still impressive. She kissed my oblique and purposely brushed her stiff nipple across my dick. Pat's tits were still firm and still full of youth.

"Ooops," she whispered in a knowing manner before kissing the crown of my pole. The salute became alive, rising to attention and Pat gave it the respect of a five star general.

"Shit!" I grunted with excitement as she swallowed the length of my pipe, slowly sliding up and down while massaging its thickness with her tongue. I grabbed the back of her head and guided her as she handled her business. She wasn't as efficient as

April, but what she was doing was good enough to make me sound the fuck off. I exploded, filling Pat's mouth with all of my frustrations. Semen slipped from her lips and she smiled while leaning toward me.

"Hold up!" I held her back with my hands. 'This bitch done lost her muthafuckin head!' I thought, ready to slap the cum out of the hoe's mouth. She was about to kiss me with a mouth full of DNA. "I'ont get down with that snowball shit! Bitch is you outta your mind?" I'd heard a few white boys bragging about that kind of foul shit while I was in the joint - red wings was where they'd eat their girl's pussy while she was on her period or snowballing like Pat had just tried to do to me. Just the thought of her trying to play me made my hand wrap into a tight fist. I should punch this hoe!

"Ugh, nigga yous a nasty motherfucker for even thinking some shit like that," Pat said and reached behind me, grabbing her panties and spitting the semen into them. 'Oh,' I thought, and shrugged my shoulders. Fuck it! I didn't know what the hoe was trying to pull. She'd been good to a nigga and a bitch would try anything when they'd given so much of themselves. So I wanted to make it clear that I wasn't about the bend for a bitch. Besides, real niggaz ain't that flexible. I chuckled and slapped Pat's wide ass.

"Nah, brah," Pat chuckled and glanced over her shoulder. I fucked a lot of hoes but there was something different about Pat. The bitch had her own and I liked that because it eased the pressure of wondering if she was out for mines. We had a good time and we did good business, which was why I didn't fleece her for the bread I owed her.

"Pat, you alright with me," I chuckled because Pat wasn't trying to hear me. She twisted her lips and waved me off, but I was being real with her. She'd smoked a nigga for trying to come up off of her and I respected a nigga who would ride for theirs, especially a bitch who would lay a muthafucka down for snatching food off of her plate.

"Whatever, Gucci," Pat laughed. "Nigga you've already gotten your dick sucked so cut out the games, brah." She was candid as hell. Bold enough to make me be real about the situation. 'The head was alright, but that was the extent of it,' I thought, wanting to tell the hoe just that.

"Nah, Pat. Real talk. Ain't too many hoes out here slinging iron to these niggaz for jacking muthafuckas, so a female whose repping for the streets is what's up."

"You don't even know, Gucci. I swear to you, you don't know," Pat replied, shaking her head like she wanted to tell me something and believe me, I wanted to listen. I'd been curious about her whole ordeal and wanted to know what happened, but I wasn't about to ask until now.

"What's up? Is this something I gotta take care of?" I baited her, wanting to get something out of her. Although I'd grown to care about Pat, I wasn't about to kill shit for the hoe and hoped she wouldn't call me on it.

"Nah, brah," Pat laughed. "I handle my own, but it wasn't what you think. Those bricks that I fronted you." She sighed while shaking her head. A snide smirk wisped across her face, letting me know that she'd pulled a shrewd caper for them – something I'd already concluded.

"You robbed a nigga?!!!" I pretended to be shocked. Pat probably thought I was as naïve as I pretended to be, but it was a façade. Something that kept the streets sleep to what I was really capable of. I'd been around underhanded muthafuckaz my entire life. Although Pat wore a skirt, the bitch was no different from any of the other goons running the streets of Detroit. 'I knew it!' I thought, still looking shocked as Pat nodded, agreeing that she's hustled someone out their bag.

"Yep," she chuckled after admitting what she'd done. "My husband."

My eyes bulged and this time I really was shocked. 'This hoe is married!' I thought, staring at her trifling ass. I guess there isn't any honor amongst thieves because Pat had hoodwinked her own husband. "Your husband?" I asked in disbelief, wanting to hear her say it again. 'Bitch! Your husband?' I thought, waiting on her reply and she nodded.

"Mmmhmm," it was drawn out hum and nod that said he'd deserved it. 'Maybe he'd been putting his foot in her ass?' I wondered, trying to justify what she'd done but I couldn't because there was nothing that would condone her taking a mouth full of my semen back to her husband. I'd kill a bitch! I shook my head and cringed at the thought of a bitch back dooring me like that.

"Damn, Pat. You're colder than I thought," I laughed while thinking 'I gotta watch this hoe.' If she'd schemed on her own husband for thirty kilos, there was no limit to what she'd do to me

"He let a motherfucker say he'd rape me." Pat's eyes filled with contempt. "This fraud name Trey, told him that he'd rape me and make his hoe ass watch and he didn't protest that shit!"

"Straight up, ma?" I asked. Now I was really interested in what had taken place. 'Trey?' I thought, knowing that he was one of the niggaz that we were supposed to be hitting for Quan. Maybe those thirty birds were part of the thousand that had been jacked? "So what's up? You want a nigga to go upside that clown's head?" I asked, knowing that Trey would be getting dealt with anyway. Drake and Tutsi probably already had Chico, the Hispanic cop who ran with Ship, hog-tied with a pole up his ass.

"I'm okay," Pat replied, smiling and I was sue that she was thinking I'd really meant what I'd proposed. She was a gangstress, but just as much hoe as the next bitch, so knowing that I was

181

willing to protect her was admirable to her. We talked for a little while longer. Pat told me about the Colombian who had tried to put a hollow point through her skull.

Pat's husband, Pops, had evidently copped some of the dope that had been jacked. Unfortunately for him, they'd gotten the coke with the GPS monitors and the henchmen had come to collect. 'Damn, this hoe is a G!' I thought as she detailed the way she threw the hot lead through the goon's body. It was like reading a SoReal publication novel. They dropped the finest urban fiction in the game and Pat's story could have easily been one of their plots. My cell went off. Bzzzzz Bzzzzzz I looked at the caller ID and it was Drake.

"What up doe, my baby:" I asked after answering. I was sure that Drake had gotten the drop on the hijacked truck of drugs, but I'd picked up an earful myself.

"We gotta get together, brah," Drake's voice came through my cell phone. We'd already planned to meet up at the warehouse, so I knew the destination.

"Aight. I'm on my way," By the time I hung up, Pat was already slipping back into her pants. She tossed her cum soiled panties into her Hermes Birkin bag and flashed me the middle finger.

"I should have snowballed your ass," Pat laughed, but I didn't think what she'd said was funny.

"And I would have slapped your muthafuckin head off of your shoulders." I responded with a stiff nod, assuring the hoe that I would have done it. Pat was my goonette and I loved having a veteran bitch like her around to make moves with, but spitting semen in my mouth would have gotten the hoe knocked the fuck out. I slipped some jeans on and we both slid out together. I had a meeting with my team and thanks to Pat, I wasn't coming empty handed.

CHAPTER 22

Pops pulled up to Khalid's hair salon. They had been trying to get in touch since Doug's funeral but the game had kept them at ends. Khalid was laying low, respecting the call of the streets because shit had gotten too thick for him and he had too much to lose. Exposing his connect and losing his freedom was at stake while The Alphabet Boys were in town and Khalid was trying to dodge both of those fates.

Pops peeked through the storefront window of the salon and saw Khalid standing in front of a fine light butter pecan complexioned female. He hopped out of his whip and strolled into the shop. Pops was an old school player to the heart and his swagger reflected that. His Kangol leaned hard to the left falling right above his forehead. He slid a fresh toothpick into his mouth after nodding to the receptionist. It was a peppermint scented toothpick in case his breath had a stench to it. Pops didn't want to offend the honey who held Khalid's attention. 'Shit!' Pops thought with a swift headshake that represented his admiration of her good looks.

"Khalid?" Pops called out while approaching him and the female. Khalid spun and gave Pops a hood head nod after seeing him.

"Sup, my guy?" Khalid greeted Pops with a pound.

"Shit, you know what it is, baby," Pops chuckled and glanced over to Khalid's female friend. She was bowlegged with a thin waist and a nice little onion. The shape of her ass was perfect and she shoved her hands into her back pockets, giving herself a nasty look that sprung Pops. She wasn't as thick as Aries, but she was definitely finer.

"Pops, this is Rocsi," Khalid introduced Rocsi and pulled her snug against his body. He'd always make her appear to be his property, but in actuality, Rocsi was her own woman. She called her own shots and some of Khalid's; but his starched ego would never let that get out.

"Yeah, this is my baby boo, Pops," Khalid nodded, letting Pops know that Rocsi was off-limits. They'd both grown up in the cop and blow era, but Pops trying to cop Rocsi would cost him his life because she was something that Khalid was unwilling to part with.

"Yeah, I feel you," Pops replied with a nod of his own, letting Khalid know that he acknowledged the subliminal message that he'd sent. They'd been down for a while and knew when to back off – and this was one of those times. Khalid slapped Rocsi across her tender bottom and sent her off walking towards his office. Her hips swayed seductively tempting Pops to take a peek, but he managed to stay focused. What he had on the floor was more important than taking a look at Rocsi's sensuality.

"So what's on your mind, my guy?" Khalid asked, as if he didn't know what was really going through Pops' head. Pops had called him earlier wanting to know the drop on the truck that had been trapped by the FEDs. Everyone wanted to know what was up with that. The driver or the drugs hadn't been found and the streets were still dry as the Sahara. Street soldiers were starving and the generals weren't trying to break bread, including Khalid.

"So what's the deal on that truck, my nigga?" Pops kept it simple, not wanting to beat around the bush because the information that he was willing to sell Khalid could become lucrative. He'd lost thirty kilos during the attempted recovery of the coke that he'd stashed at the bakery (his and Pat's safe house) and he wanted to recover the maximum amount of payout for them, even if it was from Khalid's pockets. 'Sheeit!' Pops thought quietly. It ain't like the nigga can't afford it.

Khalid was one of the biggest dealers in the city and had a bankroll and a flamboyant reputation to prove it. He was almost untouchable because he had inside connects with the local politicians. He kept a few made men in his pockets and wasn't afraid to call in a few favors whenever it was warranted.

"The truck?" Khalid answered with a question followed by an obnoxious chuckle. Khalid was an arrogant motherfucker and Pops immediately picked up on his sarcasm.

"Yeah, nigga. The one with all of those birds on it. And I ain't talkin 'bout the ones that fly either," he nodded after sliding in a glib remark of his own. Pops wanted to slap the hell out of Khalid. Pops wasn't a gangster by any measure of the word, but he was sure that he could put Khalid down. The streets had been testing Khalid's gangster for decades, exposing the bitch that he really was. Pops knew that and wanted to put a press on the nigga, but the money that he stood to make prevented him from busting his head.

"Oh, that truck," Khalid played surprised and naïve. He knew what the streets had been saying, but the truck wasn't his. The buzz around the city was that his supply had been intercepted by the FEDs and that he was facing a secret indictment, but that was some fraudulent shit that a hater had put out there on him. There was plenty of swagger jackers out there trying to take his place, but Khalid was a real general in the game. He made moves and ordered the kill whenever it was necessary and would put dollar signs on whoever let that hate mail about him go viral in the streets. He had the hood behind him, so he couldn't be stopped.

Khalid was known as a coward in the streets, so his hood credibility was something new. He'd caught wind of his newfound respect when Doug, his son, was killed. The youngsters and the veteran players turned out in numbers to show support. Niggaz from everywhere had soldiers on the prowl trying to find the killers so they could avenge Doug's murder. It was the way of the streets and Khalid had his top henchmen on it. Fatso was digging a ditch for the niggaz who had fucked over his son and would be burying them in it when the gun smoke cleared. Rocsi rubbed Fatso the wrong way, almost making him shift gears on the whole idea because Fatso wanted to off her after their run-in. He was a heartless motherfucker with one of the coldest pistol hands in the game. He'd filled a lot of thugs with hot rocks and wanted to send something special delivery to the niggaz who had laid Doug down.

Khalid looked from Pops over to the receptionist and back over to Pops. He was checking to see who was paying attention to their conversation. He had a strict code to trust the people in his company, but there were some things that he wanted to keep private. "Come on, my guy." He swung his head signaling Pops to follow him into his office.

Pops trialed Khalid into his office followed by the stare of the receptionist. She was Khalid's pitbull. A down ass bitch who locked the shop down and grabbed the straps when they disappeared into the office. It was the look that Khalid had given her.

"Imma step out, babe," Rocsi interrupted them, pretending to want to leave, but she really wanted to stay and soak it all in. Whatever they were about to discuss concerned her and her team unbeknownst to them. 'They were in on those slabs?' she wondered while raising from the couch. Khalid held his hand up.

"Nah, you're alright, baby boo." He wanted Rocsi to stay. She knew that he'd want to boss game it in her presence because he was a showboat like that. Pops looked from Khalid to Rocsi and back to Khalid.

"Khalid, are you sure about that?" Pops was skeptical about talking in front of Rocsi. He didn't know whether his mans had known her long enough or good enough to make moves in front of her and was sure that he wasn't willing to shot-call in the company of a hood bitch. He'd seen women like Rocsi destroy the coldest of thug dynasties throughout his years in the game and effused to let her fine ass pull a gangster bitch move on him while back dooring Khalid. 'Hell nah! Fuck that shit!' Pops thought, watching as Rocsi's face turned up at his response to Khalid's openness. He and Pat had hears invested in their trust and he wasn't even sure that she was keeping the game one hundred lately.

There was something about the cocaine at the bakery getting snatched from her that didn't sit right with Pops. 'Why would the other goon run off leaving his mans to die?' Pops wondered, giving what had happened a brief thought. He'd already known about her fucking around with Gucci, a young baller from the east side of the city. Gucci was a small time hustler who had just come home from a short prison stint, but the hood was talking. He'd been on a supreme rise to the top of the food chain and that puzzled Pops because Gucci was still hustling although there wasn't any dope in town. These hoes gonna get burned playing with fire! Pops shook his head, still defiant about talking in front of Rocsi because suspecting his bitch of bending made him lose all hope for a gangster's bitch to stay gangster. Rocsi was just like any other chick out of the ghetto – she'd stay down until the hustle laid down. Pops walked toward the door.

"No!" Khalid held up his hand in protest and Pops turned around facing him. 'I knew this clown would change his mind,' Pops thought with an arrogant chuckle, unaware of what Khalid was about to say.

"I wouldn't walk out of that door if I were you, Pops," Khalid rose his eyebrows, giving Pops a cold stare as a warning not to leave the room because the receptionist was on the other side of the office, ready to spray whomever left before Khalid's approval to her. Pops looked from Khalid to Rocsi and then to the door before glancing back at Khalid and sitting. He wasn't sure how Khalid had turned the tables on him, but he had.

"Fucks up, Khalid, man?" Pops asked, wondering what the threats were about. He'd come to extort Khalid out of some cash for the information that he had, but Khalid had picked up on his game.

"Muthafucka, you know what it is," Khalid chuckled. It wasn't a lighthearted laugh. Instead, it was a conniving snicker that assured Pops that he'd been caught up by his own greed.

"Nah, Khalid. I'ont know what the fuck is going on, but...." Pops was cut short by Khalid's palm. He had a way of making people feel inferior to him although he was the biggest coward in the streets. Of course, he was a major player, so he had a team of soldiers who would squeeze the trigger at his request; but he himself was a bitch.

"Who got that bag, Pops?" Khalid asked while calmly walking toward Pops. He could tell by the nervous look in Pops' eyes that he knew something. Something that could help him recover the shipment that had been stolen from Khalid's main man, Krispy. A team of thieves had lifted the truck before it reached the city, and Khalid was sure that Pops had an idea who the cocaine pirates were.

"Man.....Khalid, brah," Pops shook his head, wondering how Khalid had pegged him. How in the fuck?!! Pops wondered how he'd let himself be trapped in Khalid's office in the first place. Khalid finally made his way around to Pops. Standing in front of him, Khalid smirked.

""Look here, you bitch-made muthafucka!" Khalid pulled a butterfly knife from his front pocket made its blade do a few fancy acrobatics before tucking it back into his pocket. Rocsi grabbed her mouth, trying to keep herself from laughing at him, because his attempt at being gangster wasn't convincing.

'I know this nigga wasn't trying to scare him...' Rocsi wondered, still watching as Khalid tried to probe information out of Pops. She'd seen Ship bring the bitch out of the most heartless niggaz and what Khalid was doing wasn't the way to do it. Pops was more afraid of what was on the other side of the door than what Khalid was capable of doing to him. Rocsi dug into her purse, pulling her heat from inside. She knew how to get shit done and wasn't ashamed to take the lead when she had to, which was most of the time with Khalid. The thing about power was that it only existed when someone felt inferior to the person enforcing it and Rocsi knew what it took to show her power. WHACK!! The sound of Rocsi's blue steel .40 cal crushing the side of Pops' head was felonious. Khalid's head whipped toward her. He was shocked. He didn't even know she carried a cannon and was definitely unaware that she'd be hood enough to go upside Pops' head with it.

"Nigga!" Rocsi's voice was high pitched and demanding when she spoke, swinging the barrel of her thumper back again. "Who got the bag?!!" she slapped him across the side of his face, sending blood gushing from his cheek. Rocsi had another agenda that didn't include Khalid. Instead, she wanted to know what Pops knew about her team snatching that truck. Rocsi had seen the strength of Khalid's street team and knew her squad would be outnumbered in a war, but wouldn't be outmatched if they had a heads up on their opposition.

"Khalid! Man....get your peoples, brah!" Pops squealed. Blood poured through the creases of his fingers while he tried to cover the head wound that Rocsi had caused. A stream of red crept across his face, dripping onto his shirt. He was bleeding bad and Rocsi was ready to make it worse.

"Nah, nigga! Who holding that bag and this gon be the last time I ask," Khalid snickered and nodded over to Rocsi. "Next thing Imma do is let my baby boo get at you." At that, Rocsi slid closer to him and pushed the .40 cal flush against Pops' head. The felonious tint within her eyes assured Pops that he'd be a memory if he tried to hold out any longer.

"It's a nigga name Trey!" Pops blurted, hoping she wouldn't squeeze the trigger of the pipe pressed against his head. 'If this bitch don't bust, Imma coon her ass!' he thought between prayers that she didn't kill him. Pops' plan had fizzled into a plea for his life. He told Khalid everything that he knew; putting Trey's crown on a chopping block right in front of Rocsi, not knowing that she was a major component in the truck heist.

"Let this coward breathe, babe," Rocsi said, and tucked her heat into her belt line. Khalid was relieved that she'd decided to let Pops live. He didn't want the blood to stain the white leather sofa that Pops was stretched across. Not to mention he was certain that Toya, his receptionist, would have pumped lead through the door of his office, risking everyone being smoked.

"Yeah, I was thinking the same thing, baby boo," Khalid pulled his cell from inside of his blazer and called Toya. "Tee Tee, he can leave, mami." WHACK! Khalid slapped Pops across his face and pointed toward the door, while tucking his phone back into his jacket. "Bounce, nigga." Pops leaped to his feet and rushed out of Khalid's office, still holding his head. Toya was tucked behind her desk with a tech 9mm sitting on her lap. She filed her nails while eyeballing Pops' cowardly ass scurrying out of the salon. Khalid was sure that this wouldn't be the last thing he heard from Pops, especially after being humiliated by a bitch, but he wasn't worried because he had Fatso on speed dial.

Khalid grabbed the cell from his pocked and punched in Fatso's digits. "Fatso…..man, it's urgent," he said and hung up, placing the phone back into his pocket. He was sure that Fatso got the gist of what he meant. They'd been playing the streets together for a while and knew the call of drama when it was present. Rocsi grabbed her purse and kissed Khalid's cheek on the way out. She'd gotten what she needed too, now she had to decide what to do with it. Ship was her uncle, but he'd broken that loyalty when he skipped out with five hundred kilos of which he was supposed to split with her and Trey. The game was getting darker and darker and Rocsi had to navigate through the black hearted streets at her own speed.

CHAPTER 23

QUAN

I watched from the corner of my cell as Krispy sat at the edge of my bunk sulking like a little bitch. I'd grown to like the nigga and for what reason, I had no idea. He wasn't cut from the same cloth of me and my squad. We were certified street soldiers and he was a coward. I didn't even know Detroit bred niggaz like him.

"Krispy, man, what the fuck is you trippin about?" I asked, showing no sympathy for the shit that he'd gotten himself into. He was a showoff and had finally been charged for being a fraud. I was going to hit him, but someone had made the jump on me, beating me to the lick. 'Shit!' I thought angrily. Everything was set to the beat of my drum, but some fool had been a little swifter.

Rocsi's uncle, Ship, was a grimy muhfucka. Pulling jack moves on niggaz in the game. I'd heard about his team. They'd been terrorizing the streets of the Motor City for a while, but that shit was about to end. Hell yeah! I nodded insidiously, knowing that Drake had kidnapped Chico already. Rocsi had assured me that Chico would be solid. Insisting he'd be a heard break, but Gucci's mans, Tutsi, guaranteed us that he'd loosen him up before nightfall.

"I'ont know, my nigga," Krispy's voice was shaken with fear and I saw worry lines creasing his forehead. He'd taken in millions of street money from different teams throughout the Midwest and niggaz were expecting their supply. Suge and his goons had been keeping a close eye on Krispy also and that worried the hell out of Krispy, but I had his back. He was my meal-ticket and it was a must that I ate.

"You don't know what, nigga?" I was tired of watching him mope. If he was going to do shit like that, he'd have to do it somewhere else because he was fucking up my mood.

"I'ont know about these brick I'm s'pose to produce." He threw his hands into the air, signaling his defeat. 'Coward ass bitch!' I thought.

"Man, you gotta get the fuck on," I demanded. I'd had enough. "You's a real hoe ass nigga. Fuck them taco hoarders, nigga! We can bury them bitches!" The blood boiled in my veins. I wanted to go to war for a pussy muhfucka who wasn't willing to man up for himself. Fuck this shit!

"Quan man, I can't leave here, my nigga." He lifted his head toward the range causing me to look in that direction. Suge was posted still keeping a watchful eye on Krispy. "Quan, I'ont know how Imma pay these boys back or pay them El Salvadoran motherfuckers."

"What the fuck are you talkin 'bout, nigga?!!" I didn't understand where he was coming from. Krispy had me under the impression that he'd paid the connect for the shipment, but he was saying something different now. 'What's up with this fool?' I wondered, hoping he'd stay alive long enough for me to collect on those kilos of cocaine. I'd put too much time with him to let the money slip away without my cut. Not to mention that Drake and the team would be scorching hot if we didn't come up off this nigga.

"I made a half payment with the money I scraped up from my guys around the Midwest, but I still owe up."

"Owe up like what, nigga?" I asked as if I could help him with his problem, knowing I couldn't ante on one bird let alone a thousand.

"Like something I can't pay without moving the rest of that work!" Krispy dropped his head into the palms of his hands. I watched, sickened by the sight of a nigga so cowardly. I'd been in more childhood drama than he'd participated in throughout his entire life – which would be cut short if he didn't come up with a plan to get the hood niggaz their product and the cartel their money. Krispy was caught between the barrels of two guns and both ends were ready to squeeze.

"We gonna come through for you, brah!" I shook my head thinking to myself 'this nigga bout to get fucked in the game!' Drake was about to crack Chico's ass wide open and whatever was in the piñata would be ours to split. Look at this punk. I could tell that he was terrified. His eyes were misty and he looked like a real bitch.

"If you say so, Quan, man…." Krispy sighed before looking back over to me. "What about Khalid? You think he's in on it too?"

"Sheeeit." I shrugged my shoulders not knowing what to say. I knew how money made niggaz act because I was the thirstiest nigga out there. 'Hell muthafuckin yeah, nigga!' I thought, wanting to be straight up with Krispy for a change. I felt sorry for the chump, like he was one of my little sisters or something because he was too soft to be one of my goons. A few squads across the prison yard wanted to get at him, shake him down for a few dollars or something, but I kept them silent for the time-being. I was short to the streets and knew that shit would get hectic for Krispy after I walked. Suge and his clique would definitely be charging him to breathe.

"So, what's up…" he threw his hands into the air, wanting to know what I thought about Khalid possibly being involved in the jack move.

"Brah, sheeit… A nigga might do anything for that type of come up. You reel me?" I asked insinuating that it was possible. Khalid was a homothug, one of those creeps who posed as a gangster, but took wood, so there was no telling what he was capable of. 'Besides, who am I to judge that nigga? I'm at that paper too,' I thought. I shrugged my shoulders because I really didn't give a fuck. We kicked it for a few more hours, until Suge and his goons pulled out. Krispy peeled off shortly after. There was drama on both fronts. My niggaz were at Ship and his team, trying to recover those slabs; I was trapped in here protecting Krispy's coward ass until we filled our plates.

CHAPTER 24

GUCCI

I walked in still thinking about the sex that Pat had put on me. She was a freak and I was feeling her. 'She can be my vet bitch at least,' I thought with a slight chuckle before seeing a nigga tied to a metal workbench. These muhfuckas done smoked the nigga already! I hoped they'd gotten the information we needed before they cooned him. If not, Quan would be pissed. He'd put in months of mole work to sniff this shit out and I didn't want to be part of fucking it up for him.

"Gucci?" I heard drake call for me. His voice was close, but I didn't see him. 'It's some bullshit in the game!' I thought while easing my hand behind me, grabbing my heat that was tucked in the waist of my jeans. Maybe Drake found out about Omar? I was sure that he'd want drama after that. The news report said that the bodies had been burned too bad to identify, but that new forensic shit was bringing the truth out of murder scenes. I crept closer to the table that homeboy was stretched across. He was bleeding pretty bad, but I could hear him breathing. I guess he was lucky and unlucky at the same time, because life wasn't being too good to him.

"Gucci?" Drake called again. This time I followed the sound of his voice and saw him waving me toward the back of the warehouse. Although he was my guy and I trusted him, I was aware that blood was thicker than hood love so I kept my strap out, hanging it to my side. I didn't want to seem suspicious, insinuating that drake was trying some foul shit, but I wasn't about to be caught slipping out of loyalty and respect either. The streets were an ugly place where real goons were blackhearted. There was no doubt that Drake was an official goon.

"Sup, my nigga?" I greeted Drake with a pound, still clutching my steel just in case the sham was up. My eyes canvassed the area, looking for Tutsi because there was no way that he'd sell me out, but he wasn't in sight. 'If Drake done offed my mans……' I thought, hoping the end of my clique wouldn't be in bloodshed. Quan and Drake had been there trapping and robbing when the world was against me, but Tutsi saved my life, coming to my aid in my darkest hour, so I felt compelled to reciprocate. Shit!

"What's up, baby brah?" Drake asked, eyeballing me like he'd read my thoughts. "You look shook, my nigga." He chuckled, giving me a sense of relief. 'Maybe I'm bugging…' I wondered, still keeping a watchful eye on my surroundings.

"Yeah…." I replied. "This shit looks wicked." I swung my head backwards toward the guy sprawled across the metal table. "What's the deal with homey?"

"The nigga been holding out." Drake started walking toward the workbench and I followed him, relieved that my intuition had foiled me because a war with Drake was something that I could live without.

"Roc was right. This nigga's a loyal muthafucka, brah," Drake finished as we stood beside the man's blood stained body. His breathing was heavy from the clots in his nostrils and one of his eyes was closed shut from swelling.

"Y'all put in work on this nigga huh?" I chuckled, knowing that Tutsi took pleasure in fucking him up. Tutsi hated the police. Worse than that, he despised snitches, so the news about Trey would be music to his ears. "Where's my nigga?" I asked wondering where Tutsi had slid off to. We had Hashes manning the courtyard. Things were trapping as usual at the building, so he didn't need to be there.

"Some hoe called him, but he said he'll be back to clean this up," Drake shrugged, letting me know that he didn't have an idea about who the female was. 'I did though, that black muhfucka!' I thought with a chuckle. Tutsi had knocked that broad who we'd been peeking in on and was spending too much time and too much cash on that hoe. This bitch done trapped my mans. I shook my head somewhat jealous because I didn't get to tap that ass first.

"So where we go from here?" I asked, wanting to get the show on the road. Me and Pat had big plans that didn't include sticking niggaz, so I wanted get this shit over with fast. It was time to lay on something knitted with white sand beneath it or something. Even if we came up on the missing cakes, I was still disappearing because the game would be in a murderous uproar. Those Made Men niggaz had an iron reach that stretched across borders. Pat was scared shitless when that Colombian pushed his way into her safe house. 'But the bitch bossed up!' I thought with a chuckle that caused Drake to focus on me.

"What's funny, my nigga?" Drake asked, falling into a chair across from the table holding the cop down.

"None of ya business, nigga." I walked over and took a squat beside him. Although Drake had no idea about us laying Omar down, my conscience wouldn't let me be easy around him. I knew Drake. We'd grown up together running the streets of Detroit, so I knew what he was capable of – especially if you crossed his loved ones.

***

Back when we were trying to get a rep in the streets, instead of some paper, we ran across beef everywhere. The whole hood was under siege when we were around. Quan was a real manipulative nigga. He'd given me the short con game, changing money and shit. Drake was more of a blood-thirsty cat. He'd knife anyone who tested his gangster. And I was a hustler, running the street with whoever was getting money. At that time, nothing mattered but that almighty dollar.

"What's up, Gucci?" Drake pointed to the liquor store, insinuating we go in. I knew what he was implying because I'd been bragging about shortchanging clerks all day. I was twelve and Drake was fourteen. Impressing my peers was a must, that's how I got the name Gucci, and it got worse when a nigga was older than me.

"What?" I asked in reply, although I already knew what was going on. He wanted me to man up about the lies that I'd been telling. 'Shit!' I thought, nervous about trying my hand without Quan around. He was a professional con at an early age, getting schooled by his uncles from Chicago. I didn't know shit about the game. Even when I was with him, it would happen so quick that I'd be tricked too.

"Let's see what up, nigga. You talking all this gangster shit….." He pointed toward the store. "Let's go." Fuck it. I was sure that I could emulate Quan and come up with a few extra dollars.

"Let's roll then," I finally answered and walked across the street. We walked in together and Drake slipped toward the back of the store. I was sure that Drake wanted to be out of the way in case I was busted.

"Agh! Shit!" I heard a scream from the back of the store. Whipping my head in the direction of the scream, I saw Drake standing over an older nigga who hung around our projects. Blood dripped from the blade in Drake's hand and menacing look sunk in his eyes. 'Drake done plugged a nigga!' I thought, unable to speak because my mans was facing some juvenile time. We had to break out.

"Let's bounce, brah!!" I waved to Drake to follow behind me. I wasn't about to leave my nigga. Drake tucked his knife back into his pocket and darted into the direction of the exit. I tailed behind him relieved that I wasn't exposed for being a fraud and shaken by the thought of my guy being pinned behind prison bars.

"What happened, Drake?" I asked, winded from our sprint across Chalmers Street. Drake was still seething, shuffling ahead of me like he didn't hear my question.

"That clucker beat my pops for a couple of dollars before," Drake barked, still marching back towards the projects. 'Huh?' I thought, knowing that his father had been dead for the last four years. This nigga's lying.

"I thought Big Drake was dead?" I asked, although I already knew the answer to my own question. 'Maybe there's a family secret or something…' I reasoned because Big Drake was killed in a drug raid along with some other niggaz from his team. He was a real street soldier too. One that me, Quan and his son, Drake, tried to imitate.

"Right, I was about ten when it happened, but I always remembered his face in case I ever caught him slipping. My dad couldn't get at him, so I manned up and gave the nigga what he had coming." Drake explained to me how the fiend had stiffed his pops with some leaded dice during one of the hood crap games. He'd gotten over on the whole set, but Big Drake was the only one who had picked up on him. Big Drake had confided in his son, telling him that he'd be paying that swindler a visit, but his untimely death prevented him from getting his payback.

That day, Drake showed me what true hood love was. Even in the grave, his father was avenged by him. Drake had a deeper commitment to the loyalty of his family. I respected that about him, which was why the situation with Omar was haunting me.

DRAKE

I sat across from Gucci wondering why he was so jumpy. 'This nigga's changing!' I thought, knowing that he'd taken on some fucked up qualities since he'd been bringing in bird money. He wasn't the same nigga that I'd grown up with and I wanted to know why.

"Man....you been acting strange," I stated, hoping he'd explain to me why. Of course, all friendships were conditional and shit could change between us in an instant, but whatever he was hiding had to come out sooner or later. 'Hopefully sooner,' I thought, knowing when the truth showed up late, it came with drama.

"I'm good, my baby," Gucci tried playing it off, but it was evident to me that something was eating at him. 'This nigga's hiding something,' I thought, nodding at his response although I didn't believe shit he'd said.

"Argh!" Chico grunted and coughed up blood. 'Daaayum!' I thought, staring at his body convulse on the table.

"Shit!" Gucci leaped up and rushed over to him unstrapping his restraints.

"What the fuck is you doing?" I asked, reaching for my strap. 'This nigga is gonna make me smoke him!' I thought, hoping he wasn't trying to make a move on me. "What the fuck is up, brah?!! Homebody's the muthafucking law!" I wanted to make it clear that he was taking the straps off of a nigga who wouldn't have had the same mercy for him.

"He's choking, nigga! Come help me lean him upwards!" Gucci demanded, pulling the last strap off his wrist. 'Shit!' I thought, pulling my hand away from my heat and rushing over to the table. I hadn't thought about it and was ready to jump to conclusions.

"We still gotta bleed this nigga, brah brah!" Gucci spat, leaning him upright, letting the vomit spill from his mouth. He'd been suffocating on his own spit up.

"Puh....please," Chico begged through swollen lips. He'd been beaten to a pulp, and still managed to keep his integrity. 'Hood niggaz need to take lessons!' I thought, knowing how niggaz were selling their teams out for crumbs.

"Y'all got the wrong muchacho. Please, mi familia," Chico begged, letting us know that he had a family.

"Nigga, I know about your wife and son," I snickered. "You should be thanking me for not wrapping them up in this package." After that, Chico fell back onto the table and Gucci strapped him back down. We walked back over to our law chairs and posted.

"Drake? Man....I do have something to tell you. I wanted to wait until Tutsi got back, but this shit is deep, my baby." He nodded, assuring me that he was about to drop a hammer on me.

"What's the deal?" I asked plainly, not wanting him to pull any strings. If there was a problem between us, I wanted it out on the floor.

"The hoe, Pat, who I be copping those thangs from....."

"Yeah, the vet bitch." I was hip to her. 'This nigga bout to jump ship for a hoe?' I wondered, thinking he was pulling the string on his parachute. He'd been implying that he was through with the streets for a few weeks, but I'd taken his talk as him just venting. A hustler's feet didn't get sore and there was no question if Gucci was a hustler, he was the hustle!

"This nigga, Trey, who she be offing work for..."

"Trey?" I asked, cutting him off. 'I keep hearing this nigga's name!' I thought, wanting Gucci to give me Trey's resume.

"Yeah, my nigga. Trey is the nigga's name and he got the bag."

"What bag?" I asked while thinking 'this nigga is fickle as hell.' He'd assured me that his pistol hand was over after this come up and now he was setting up another lick. "I thought you were outta the game, brah?" I knew my niggaz feet were planted in the blacktop of the project walkways! I chuckled, mocking his crafty ways.

"Nah, Drake! He's the nigga with those missing birds!" he explained boldly. I stared at him trying to see a chink in his armor. A glimpse of where he'd shifted gears.

'Gucci's bugging the fuck out!' I thought, upset that he'd be crying wolf while we were on a jack.

"This ain't the time, brah." I was tempted to slap Gucci upside his head with my thumper. He was pushing all the wrong buttons and I was starting to think he was purposely provoking me into a beef with him. What's this nigga's angle?

"Brah, I'm speaking the muhfuckin gospel." He nodded, still trying to convince me that some nigga named Trey was behind the truck jacking. "She almost got smoked by a Colombian muhfucka...." Gucci paused before describing the drama that his broad had gotten herself into. He told the story like he was there. Although it was far-fetched, I believed him because Gucci wasn't that creative. 'Goddamn!' I thought, listening to how she played her connect for thirty kilos of pure cocaine.

"She's a real gangster bitch!" I laughed and gave Gucci a pound. I was glad that he'd gotten the secret off his chest because his distance was spooking the hell out of me. 'Damn, I was ready to blast my mans,' I thought, feeling horrible about thinking so heartless. Gucci and Quan were my hood family, but the streets had turned my heart into a subzero ice box causing me to think too irrational.

"I know, but fuck that bitch! What if the rest of those kilos got GPS on em?" Gucci asked, being his usual self and thinking on his feet. "Damn!" I thought, finally realizing why Gucci's demeanor was so heavy. He was putting this shit together. My mans was thinking about the bigger picture, trying to keep our come up secure and I was criticizing his swag; thinking he was trying to pull some underhanded shit when he was the only nigga on the team who was focused.

"We gotta put some speed on this shit, brah," I said, pulling my cell out and dialing Tutsi's number. "Tutsi?" I greeted him after he'd answered. "We need you to put some speed on getting back." Our conversation was short because Tutsi was already on his way back to the warehouse. He'd picked up some skills during his time in the raid teams that ravished his country and what he'd learned was about to loosen Chico's tight lips.

CHAPTER 25

SHIP

I shrugged my shoulders, folding my tie into a double Windsor know, unfazed by what Rocsi was trying to tell me. She'd violated the team one time too many and I was through with her. 'Scheming ass broad,' I thought, shaking my head while pulling the knot in my tie tighter, knowing that I would have killed her a long time ago if we didn't come from the same bloodline. It was my day. My retirement was settled on both fronts because the game was history for me. I'm done. I wiped my hands, symbolizing me cleaning my hands of everything in my past.

"Ship.....Ship?!!" Rocsi called out, breaking the silence in the room. She stood in front of me, hands on hips, seething about me being so uninvolved in the conversation that she was trying to have with me. She was persistent, though; something that she'd learned from me and wasn't giving up without me hearing her out.

"What?" I asked, calmly replying, wanting to know why she was still in my presence. I didn't know what, but there was something lurking between her and Trey. I guess, in a way, they looked at me different.....like they knew what I had done. 'Maybe Chico had sold me out before his coward ass skipped town?' I wondered, knowing he was feeling some kind of way about Trey and Rocsi's newfound camaraderie. "Hell!' I thought, knowing that a guy would pull out a parachute on his family would definitely fuck over a friend. I couldn't believe how he'd left his wife and son high and dry.

"What?" Rocsi threw her hands into the air, outdone by my nonchalant attitude. "I know you didn't just 'what' me after I told you about Trey being made?" The fury of a scorned woman was in Rocsi's eyes. Animosity was written across her thin brows. She hated me, something that I'd realized a few weeks back.

"I'm done, Roc. If Trey's loose enough to do business with a fool who'd throw him beneath a bus, then that's on him. I'm done with the streets on both fronts." I slid my hands across my throat and mouthed the word 'finished.'

"What about the team, Ship? Alright then....fuck Trey, but what about me? What about cuzz?" Rocsi whined wanting to know where she stood with me. Although I was furious with the way that she'd been acting lately, I couldn't crush someone that shared the same genes as me. 'Damn!' I thought, wishing my heart was a few degrees colder, allowing me to say fuck Rocsi and blow her head off.

"If you're with me, you have to be all the way with me, Rocsi." I fell onto the sofa and slid my feet into the hand-crafted leather wingtips that sat in front of me. Pulling a loop into the strings of my shoes, I looked upwards at Rocsi. "I'll lay you down too, Cuzz." I smirked, trying to convince her of my seriousness. Rocsi was a real hood chick and I wasn't about to play her any less than a boss.

"I'm with you, Ship. We're family and I love you," she smiled, lying through her teeth assuring me of what I'd already gathered: can't even trust family these days.

Rocsi went on rambling about Pops, an older hustler who Trey did a lot of business with. Trey had slid him thirty kilos that we'd jacked the Made Men for when we kidnapped Ace. Trey had charged him, making Pops cash out twenty at twenty thousand a piece, so what Pops had done to him in return wasn't surprising. I'd cracked a few safes during my time on the force making some of the starchest hustlers break down, so hearing that a coward like Pops had rolled over on Trey was expected.

"So what's up with this guy Khalid?" I asked, catching Rocsi off guard. She wasn't expecting me to ask about him. It was plain to me that Rocsi had grown feelings for this guy – a guy that was supposed to be a mark. "How did he become a part of this?" Rocsi shrugged her shoulders, showing me no sign that she was lying. 'So why is he so concerned about what's going on?' I wondered, hoping Rocsi hadn't crossed over trying to establish a team of her own. There was no doubt in my mind that she was scheming, but what she was gaming her way into was a mystery.

"Sheeit, hell if I know," Rocsi replied. Her look was authentic, but I still wasn't convinced that she was telling the truth. Women could be the most deceitful creatures on the earth when their hearts were involved. It was clear that her feelings for Khalid had changed since the bunco began.

"So why would Pops want to sell some information that Khalid didn't need? And how would Khalid know that the truck had been lifted instead of intercepted by the FEDs?" I knew that Khalid had his hands into some heavy hitters nationwide, but none that could tell him about our team except Rocsi. 'No, cuzz!' I thought, feeling apprehensive about continuing our conversation. Cuzz could be trying to set me up. I was certain that the cartel had a hit out for the men who had jacked their cargo, especially if the supply was returned.

"He didn't say." She raised her hands while shrugging again. "And I couldn't tell you how, but he definitely knew about the truck being licked." Rocsi nodded her head. I looked over to her, wishing I'd see something from her past: an image of her innocence. But, it was gone, didn't exist any longer. That image had been replaced by a treacherous streak of deception. I'd treated her like an equal and it had come back to haunt me. That was the problem with women, if you treat them like equals, they'll eventually start to believe they are. Can't even trust my own family.

TREY

I pulled into my driveway, sitting high on thirty inch sploaters. My whole swag was custom, from my paint job to the frost hanging from my earlobes. The four carat solitaire stones were like the Florida skyline – cloudless. It was my guy's day. Ship was retiring from the force and the streets. 'Damn!' I thought, shaking my head, knowing the hustle wouldn't be the same without Ship.

Having hood etiquette is something that I could live without. Of course, I'm an authentic street soldier, but the new code to honor other thieves was unrealistic to me. I'd been robbing dope boys and redistributing their product for years, never caring that I could get caught because my team was ruthless and carried badges to protect their murderous mentalities. Now, Ship was retiring and Chico had disappeared. "Hmmph!' I though, knowing that I'd been left with Rocsi because she wasn't trying to break ties with the game. She was a real gangster bitch.

"This clown must have gotten himself a new toy," I chuckled, seeing a candy painted CBR motorcycle sliding up my street for the third time this week. It was getting cold out, letting me know that he was trying to get his last thrill before the weather really broke. I shook my head and walked into the house.

It was time for me to suit up. I was sure that the honeys would be out celebrating. Ship was notorious for shaking down whorehouses and unlicensed strip clubs so the party would be for the prostitutes, madams and pimps too because they wouldn't be getting stripped for a bribe any longer; at least, not from Ship. *Ring Ring* My cell rung, disturbing me as I got out of the shower.

I smiled, looking at the caller ID. "Pat?" I said after answering. I still had a thing for her, but she wouldn't break. Pops was a general in her eyes and she refused to violate his trust like that. 'Damn, I need me a hoe to hold me down like that,' I thought, waiting to hear what she called me for.

"Yes, this is me," Pat giggled flirtatiously. 'I know this hoe's a freak!' I thought, smiling at the sound of her girlish laughter. Toying had become a part of our conversation when we did business, whether it was a smile or a simple gesture, it was there.

"So what can I do for you, Pat?" I grabbed a towel and walked off toward my bedroom. I wanted to make our conversation quick because the night was falling and I didn't want to be late to Ship's bon voyage. He'd hit the roof if I wasn't there to support him on time.

"I'm trying to gain sixty pounds today," she giggled again, talking in code while asking me to cop thirty more kilos of coke. "Can you feed me today?"

"I can cook, but I already have a date tonight." I wanted her to know that I had the work, but there wasn't a chance that she'd be getting a hold of it as soon as she needed to.

"Oh, I'm not that important any more, Trey? Is it like that?" she asked, using a soft voice with a sexual undertone to it. 'Give up some of that sweet thing and it'll be different,' I thought, feeling my manhood pulsate from the sensuality of her voice. Pat's sway was as exotic as any that I'd ever seen before and she wasn't ashamed to let a man take a peek either. Mmm!

"Nah, baby girl. It ain't even like that. My mans is having a get-together and I can't miss it." Ordinarily there was no way that I'd pass up the kind of money that a thirty cake sell would bring in, but today was different.

"Alright then. I know how it is when a friend needs you," Pat agreed without protest.

"Thanks for being understanding, Pat. I gotcha, though, and I'll make it right by you," I encouraged, hoping she didn't take her money elsewhere because that money would be hard to part with.

I hung up the phone and slid into my Sean John boxer briefs. 'What in the fuck just happened?' I thought, pausing for a second, when it hit me. There was something in the way that Pat had emphasized "I know how it is when a friend needs you," before hanging up that cautioned me. What she'd said wouldn't have been abnormal if it had come from an average type of female, but Pat was a thoroughbred, a sheep that would fight wolves to keep her nigga's crown unshaken. Rocsi was like that for the team at one point, but things had changed. She'd lost faith in us somewhere along the way. Ship's discreet demeanor had caused her to question his loyalty and that wasn't a good thing. Hell nah!

I knew how women got when they felt trapped. They would become slippery, unwilling to be conquered, even if it meant destroying everything around them. Although we'd raised her in the game, Rocsi would take Ship down before she would let him spin circles around her. That's why females are equated as one and the same to felines. They loved being pampered, but aren't susceptible to being tamed. *Ring Ring* My cell rang again, making me laugh because I was sure that it was Pat, calling to persuade me into making the sell to her. 'I know the bitch ain't that understanding,' I thought with a smirk. "Hello?" I answered without looking at the caller ID. If I had, I probably wouldn't have answered.

"What's up, bro?" Ship replied casually. 'Is this muhfucka tryna check on a nigga?' I wondered, heated about him keeping an eye on my timeliness.

"Shit, what's up nigga?" I shot back boldly, letting him know that I wasn't about to accept him prying into whether I was ready or not. 'Fuck this nigga think I'm his hoe??!' I thought; ready to bug out on Ship.

"Same here before Rocsi stopped by babbling about some off the wall shit," Ship chuckled, but it wasn't a joyous chuckle. It was a snicker that I was positive would be followed by some type of conspiracy.

"What type of off the wall shit?" I asked, knowing Ship was about to push a load of game on me. Although I'd known Ship the better half of my life, I still didn't trust him fully and was sure that he'd slipped a few fleece moves in on me during one of our dealings. He was a straight hood nigga, but my nigga, nonetheless.

"Pops has been putting you out there, Trey." As soon as I head Pops' name I shut down. 'That's what I heard in that bitch's voice!' I thought, knowing that my intuition had given me a heads up.

"Putting me out there like what??" I asked, upset and ready to use the four pound that was tucked into my Brooks Brothers slacks.

"He's been talking about what happened with his wife, insinuating you as the reason why. You hear me bro?" Ship reiterated, making sure I understood what he had conferred to me. 'This slimy muthafucka!' I thought, wanting to keep my composure because ship was an easy scare. He'd annihilate everything involved, including me, if he thought there was a chance of him catching heat, so I wanted to avoid that. I listened calmly as he explained to me everything that Rocsi had brought to his knowledge. He had an easiness to his tone, but I knew Ship. He was a cautious guy, and smelled the quick fizzle of a firecracker wick. Maybe it was all of his years on the Detroit Drug Task Force or possibly his hood sense. Whichever it was – he had it.

"Yeah, Ship, I feel you. I'm all over it," I said and hung up, seething about what I'd just heard. I'd told Pops when we first started doing business again "If you play me, though, Imma cut your eyelids off and make you watch me rape and kill Pat's fine ass" and now it was time to live by my words because I'd slid out of check and positioned a mate.

"I'm killing them sorry muthafuckas!" I said sardonically, pushing my arms through the sleeves of my blazer, knowing that what Rocsi had stumbled upon had saved me from whatever Pops and his bitch were trying to implement. I'd shown Pops love, letting him flood the streets while the drought was at an all-time high and this is how he'd repaid me. 'Cold sold a nigga out!' I thought, shaking my head; disgusted with the way the game was being played in the new millennium. Niggaz is fugazi out here! Tryna shiest Trey??!!!! I laughed, not believing a coward like Pops was capable of making a call like that by himself. It had to be the bitch!

CHAPTER 26

THREE DAYS AGO

Tutsi strolled into the warehouse swinging a suitcase, whistling and smiling with a new air of confidence. Gucci and Drake watched him intently, thrown off by his sudden change in personality. A mysterious haughtiness that neither of them had seen in Tutsi before. He was usually subdued; his wide eyes, which sunk into his dark face, were emotionless. His heart was blackened, an apathetic man who was disengaged with society. But, something had changed. Gucci glanced over to Drake before addressing what he'd noticed in Tutsi's swagger.

"What's up bratha?" Gucci mocked Tutsi's tone and chuckled. "Lil mamma must've put that hot box on you." They all laughed; Gucci, Drake and Tutsi.

"No doubt, my brotha," Tutsi flashed his poor dentistry and nodded, agreeing that he'd just come from being laid. It had been a while for Tutsi. He'd usually trick with fiends and other hood chicks that roamed the project corridors, until Gucci caught wind of what he was doing.

***

Gucci climbed into the fire escape window, trying to creep up on Tutsi. He'd been hearing some things from the young hustlers who caught their crack spot residue when the fiends were short. Doug ran up to Gucci, giving him a pound, before letting him know what was going on. "Gucci, ya boy! The African muhfucka....is on some other shit," Doug laughed, telling Gucci about Tutsi paying fiends to perform sex acts with him. Of course, Gucci was all hood and had nailed a few strawberries in his time, but the game had changed and the players had to evolve with it. 'Tutsi's outta his fucking mind!' Gucci thought, rushing off after hearing Doug snitch to him about what his mans was doing in the trap.

213

Now, Gucci crept through the kitchen and into the front room. 'What kind of shit is this?!!' he thought, seeing Tutsi slow grinding a basehead; making love to her like she was his woman or something. "Tutsi?!!" Gucci called out to him, shouting over the slow jams that caressed the room. This muhfucka's making love to a crack addict! Gucci was sure that Tutsi had been terminal illness because the addicts in Detroit were class acts when it came to erotica. Damn! He felt bad, knowing he should have warned his mans about screwing crack customers before he was tricked into the game.

Tutsi's body froze in mid-stroke. He had been caught in the act. 'Shit!' he thought, sure that Gucci would ridicule him for making a poor judgment in women. Alcestis was a junkie and he was a dealer, which should have prevented the two from being together. But, Tutsi's feelings had become involved – he'd fallen in love with her. Deep enough to be having unprotected sex with her, even though she was an addict.

"Pull up outta that bitch!" Gucci yelled, scared for his guy. Scared that Tutsi could have come out Alcestis with a death sentence. 'Dirty, trifling, hoe bitch!!!' he thought, praying for the first time since he'd seen the court room – hoping his guy was safe.

Tutsi pulled his limp member out of his woman, not wanting to infuriate Gucci any further because Gucci had taken him in. Tutsi felt a sense of loyalty to Gucci; a fidelity that couldn't be trumped by living because he'd lay his life down to have his brothas!

Alcestis, the woman who lay bare beneath Tutsi, pulled the sheets across her thin, naked body. Gucci had already taken in a sickening view of her dark, galvanized skin that lay over her skeleton-like frame. Something had eaten her flesh almost to the bones. 'I hope that's crack, bitch!' Gucci thought, vehemently staring at her; praying that Tutsi had been spared from contracting AIDS.

"Listen!" he snarled, staring at Alcestis as he hid her frail body beneath the thin sheet. He wanted to pull his cannon from beneath his shirt and lodge a hot rock between her eyes. "What's your status, basehead ass hoe?!" Spit flew from his mouth while barking questions at her. He wanted to know whether Tutsi's life was in jeopardy or not. He waited, his eyes still shooting daggers, while restraining himself from strangling her.

"I'm clean," Alcestis whined in reply, tears welling in her eyes as Tutsi glanced from Gucci to her. He wanted to console her, but not at the expense of his respect for Gucci. "I swear to you!" she cried. "I don't have anything but a bad crack habit..."

"Get this bitch outta my trap, Tutsi!" Gucci spat, turning and leaving through the same window that he'd come through. Tutsi rushed behind Gucci, watching as he descended the fire escape and walked up to Doug. He reached into his pockets and broke Doug off a few ends, nodding before walking off. "I'll kill him!" Tutsi assured himself, knowing Doug had sold him out to Gucci; it was obvious. That night when Doug had mocked Gucci, disrespecting their grind, Tutsi took advantage for the situation, killing Doug for being a Janus faced coward!

***

Gucci glanced over to the suitcase that Tutsi had carried in with him, sitting it beside the table that Chico lay across. It was an odd looking piece of luggage, something that an older person would carry. Dingy hunter green with cinnamon argyle squares and Gucci wanted to know why his mans was hauling it around.

"What's up with the throwback suitcase, nigga?" Gucci asked Tutsi, causing Drake to look over to the rugged piece of luggage and chuckle

"It has to be durable," Tutsi answered frankly, not joining in on the laughter, "so it won't leak." He snickered in a hushed tone.

"What the fuck is it for?" Drake joined in, wanting to know why the bag had to be so wear resistant. He'd noticed how careful Tutsi had handled the baggage when he had first come into the warehouse, but hadn't bothered to ask until Gucci broke the ice.

"This is his transportation." Tutsi opened the suitcase and Drake laughed.

"Muthafucka....." Drake chuckled before continuing, "I thought you were carrying explosives in that joint!" He stared at the 3M plastic that was neatly folded inside of the luggage. "What the fuck are you gonna do with that shit?"

"This nigga's tripping!" Gucci shot out, watching Tutsi unfold the plastic and line the suitcase with it, knowing his mans was about to do something diabolical to Chico. Tutsi had detailed stories about mass mutilation killings while growing up in Sierra Leone and know they were about to experience what Tutsi had running with the Bloodshed Squad.

"Tutsi...." It had finally hit Drake. 'This son of a bitch is nuts!' he thought, sure that Tutsi was about to butcher Chico. "Man, whatever it is that you're gonna do, let's find out where those birds are first." *Ring Ring* Drake's cell went off and he excused himself to the back of the building, leaving Gucci to watch Tutsi in action.

Gucci sat attentively, secretly intrigued by that he was about to witness. Tutsi looked surgical, pulling rusty scalpels and rib crackers from the pockets of the suitcase. 'Shit!' Gucci thought, wincing at the image of what Chico would be going through shortly.

"The kidneys purify the body....' Tutsi said, glancing over to Gucci, his thick accent emotionless.

"Puh....please, hombre," Chico begged, his voice weak from malnutrition, as he lay naked across the workbench. "I have a son, amigo." His voice a damp whisper, but Tutsi's ears were shut, only concentrating on what he'd come to do.

"If we poison him while removing his filters..." Tutsi snickered evilly, "I wonder what his death would be like?"

Gucci's eyes bulged, sure that Tutsi was a sociopath. 'Dayum!' he thought, understanding why Tutsi had strolled in with an enthusiastic sway. He was pumped about slaughtering this nigga! Gucci was sure that Chico would prefer death of the pain from Tutsi's bestial hand. He saw Chico's mouth move, but his words were faint, too quiet for him to hear. 'What's up?' Gucci wondered, seeing Tutsi lean his ear closer to Chico's mouth, like Chico was whispering something to him.

"What?" Tutsi asked, leaning in so he could hear what Chico had to say. 'Come on with it,' he thought, knowing Chico was about to break.

"They're in the car wash," Chico whispered. "Five hundred of them," he confessed, not wanting to live through the type of pain that having his kidneys removed would cause. He'd lived the life of a soldier, but at least at that moment it all came to an end. Tutsi slit his throat, letting him die a less horrid death after he'd given him the detailed location of the coke.

CHAPTER 27

ROCSI
I straddled Khalid's lap, rubbing my small full breasts against his lips. It was time to produce. I had to put up or shut up, but his hammer wouldn't salute. 'Oh my God!' I thought, grinding against his naked body, him rubbing my ass causing my negligee to rise and fall over my waistline. His actions were telling me that he wanted me, but his reaction to my sexuality was telling something different. This nigga has to be gay. Quan had mentioned Khalid being a homothug during one of our visits. He told me that Krispy, the guy who had given him the drop on the truck being jacked, was Khalid's man.

"I'm telling you, Rocsi....ya mans is a homo," Quan laughed after insisting that Khalid was a down low brother. Now that we were in the midst of fucking, I'm starting to think Quan's assessment might have some weight to it. 'Why else would he be so limp?' I wondered, still trying to bring him out of his shyness.

I'd already called Drake, setting everything up. They were sending Hashes, a young goon who rolled with Gucci, over to help me out. Khalid wasn't falling for me tying him up or anything like that, so we'd just have to manhandle him. 'Maybe slap him upside his head with the heat or something,' I thought, kissing him behind his ear and feeling his nature rise. It must have been his spot because that was the only sign of manhood that I'd received from him. *Bzzzzz Bzzzzz Bzzzzz* My cell vibrated and I was certain that it was Hashes.

"One minute, babe." I kissed Khalid's lips and rushed off to answer the phone. *Bzzzz Bzzzz* The phone shuffled across the table. 'Shit!' I thought, knowing Hashes was too early. Khalid was still bright-eyed and bushy tailed.

"Hello?" I answered and it was Hashes just like I'd thought.

"I'm here," he replied. I looked back towards the room before rushing to the door. 'What the hell!' I thought, covering my mouth so I wouldn't gasp for air, while staring through the peephole at Fatso, sitting outside in Gucci's whip. He was ducked off behind the driver's door with his eyes glued to the front porch. I'd told him to watch for the porch light to come on before sneaking inside, but the plan had changed.

"Somebody's testing a bitch!' I said to myself, sliding my hand into the drawer of a table near the entrance. Ship kept a strap there, in case someone tried to catch him slipping. This was my time to use it. I kept my eyes glued to the peephole, watching him closely, not knowing who was making a move on me. I hope Gucci's grimy ass isn't trying to try me! I dialed Drake's cell, still keeping a watchful eye on Fatso as he slouched deep into Gucci's Monte Carlo.

"Drake?" I said once he answered. "One of Khalid's boys just drove up in Gucci's car!" I was frantic, not knowing what to expect from Drake. He could be in on this shit! I wondered if I should have called Ship, warning him about everything. Maybe this is the cost of scheming against family.

"What?" Drake replied with a question. It was evident that he didn't understand where a bitch was coming from, so I had to make it plain.

"The nigga y'all sent over here is working for Khalid!" I said, looking back toward the bedroom, hoping Khalid didn't get restless and come looking for me.

"Nah, Roc! Hell nah! Is he in the Monte?" Drake asked, still not wanting to believe what I was saying. Either he was playing me real close or he'd been duped too. 'Oh shit!' I thought, knowing that Gucci hustled in the same projects where Doug was killed. He's trying to make Gucci! Khalid had sent Fatso to find out who had smoked Doug and he'd hooked up with Gucci as a result. Maybe Khalid sent Fatso at Gucci?

"Hell yes its Gucci's ride!" I said, still unsure about trusting any of them. 'What if I wouldn't have checked the peephole first?' I wondered, grateful that Ship had made me be so cautious. Under a different circumstance, we would have still been blood, but he'd crossed me, canceling any love that I'd ever had for him. Some things just couldn't be replaced and loyalty was one of them. Once it was gone, it was gone for good. And mines for Ship was a wrap!

"I'm on my way! Don't signal him until I call you and keep the momentum going with Khalid!" I heard angst in Drake's voice, letting me know that he was definitely not in on whatever was going on. "Quan's gonna goose Gucci!' I thought, certain that my man would let hammers knock slugs for my honor. I hung up and strolled back into the bedroom, finding Khalid snoring. 'This guy!' I thought, at that point I'd been assured that he was a homo. What other reason would he pretend to be asleep? 'Fuck it!' I thought, figuring there was no need in waking him from his phony rest. Ship and Trey should be at the party by now. The Task Force was sending him off in style, not knowing what kind of dirt he'd done in their name.

DRAKE

"I can't believe this hoe shit!" I yelled, pissed about what Rocsi had just told me. 'Is this nigga in on it?!!' I wondered, glancing over to Gucci as him and Tutsi checked the chains on the bikes. We were set to roll out in an hour and a half, ready to chop Ship and his mans Trey down, but the layout had changed. The plot had just thickened that Hashes was a mole. What the hell is going on? The whole thing was getting complicated. Unforeseen shit had been leaping out of everywhere, especially what Rocsi had just discovered.

"What's up with you?" Gucci asked, walking over, leaving Tutsi to check the bikes by himself. He looked cool, like he didn't have a care in the world, making me think he had been had too. But I was still unsure, especially knowing the caliber of nigga he was. We'd grown up hustling together, making moves in and out of town slinging crack. Back then, our relationship wasn't as thick because Quan didn't trust Gucci.

***

"I'm telling you, Drake...." Quan shook his head, gesturing that something was wrong. "It's something about Gucc, my nigga," he finished, discreetly taking a peek at Gucci as he lounged on the couch. We were trapping on the west side of town, the 7Mile and Evergreen area, which meant we were out of place. There were some real grimy cats over there. Street soldiers aligned every block of those sticks, serving fiends, trying to make a come up at all costs.

"Yeah, I feel you, but he's harmless to us, my baby," I tried to assure Quan that Gucci was down for the team. I'd had my doubts about him too, but they didn't concern his loyalty to our clique. He was too fly; always cleaning his sneakers and fitted caps, making me wary about him bagging a nigga if the game called for it. But, he eventually proved to be Teflon. Gucci was a certified gangster and I trusted him. However, Quan wasn't fully on board.

"Nah, Drake. That muthafucka's been blowing chronic with the locals. Fucking up the flow of the trap," he exaggerated, because the product was selling at a steady pace, moving a quarter brick in stones a week. Quan was just stubborn, never giving anyone that wasn't hood the benefit of the doubt because he'd been burned as an early adolescent. Some Highland Park cats had chained him to a radiator in one of their drug spots, making him sell their bag without being paid. That had made him defensive against anyone who wasn't with him. *Ding Dong* Quan's head whipped in the direction of the door after hearing the bell ring, knowing it wasn't a hype because they were aware of the drill. All business was done through the milk chute on the side of the house.

Gucci glanced over to me and Quan before walking to the door, peeking through the peephole before opening it. "Sup homey?" he asked, standing between the door of the house and the guy who had rang the bell.

"Where ya mans Quan at, Gucci?" the guy on the other side of the door asked aggressively, sounding like he was looking for trouble. Quan immediately leaped up and rushed to the door.

"Here I am," Quan said, cracking the door open further and taking a stance next to Gucci. At that point, I knew what was up. 'Shit!' I thought, certain that Tez – a hustler out of the hood we were in – had come to check Quan about Pashia, a female that he'd been hammering since we had set up shop around that area. I eased my .40 caliber from beneath the sofa cushion that I was sitting on and crept to the door.

'These niggaz bout to get ignorant,' I thought, hoping the drama wouldn't turn into pistol play, fully prepared if it did. *Click Clack* I discreetly slid one into the chamber, ready to mail lead through the door if the beef was on.

"Hold up, brah...." I heard Gucci's voice change octaves and saw his arm stretched out, holding Quan back. 'I know Gucc ain't about to defend this nigga?!!' I wondered, after noticing the agitation in his tone. I flinched when I saw Gucci reach behind his back, clutching the handle of his heat. I had a choice to make right then – strike pre-emptively or wait until Gucci made move of betrayal.

"Tez, you asking for some shit that start and end with bloodshed," Gucci continued, giving me some sense of relieve because I'd almost made the wrong call and dumped something in him through the door. 'I told Quan we were hood!' I thought, content that Gucci was still riding strong with the team that we were building.

"Whit his..." Tez barked, pointing to Quan in a threatening manner. "If he'ont straighten up! Ya head me brah?!!!" Gucci nodded, releasing a light chuckle, letting Tez know that his intimidation attempt was mediocre at best, but not the least bit effective. BOCCA BOCCA Two shots rant from Gucci's biscuit. It happened too swift for me to react. He'd pulled his strap swinging it toward Tez as he turned to walk away.

"Put some base on him, Drake!" Quan demanded, wiping his pistol off and cementing it to Tez's lifeless hand. He wanted to phony up the scene, making it look like a drug deal robbery before we bounced out.

***

That day had sealed our solidarity, making us closer than ever because the trust was born. Gucci had chosen, letting his four pound salute in honor of his mans. That was how we rolled back then, but times had changed. Big chips were in play and money made the loyalest of comrades pull fast ones on one another. 'I hope my mans ain't tryna snake me!' I thought, shaking my head, trying to ease Gucci's worry.

"I'm good," I said, giving him dap and chuckling. "Man, you know how it is with this gunplay." I sighed, trying to throw him off. I had to slip out to check on Rocsi to see what was up with her, but I didn't want to involve him and Tutsi because Hashes was their mans. For now, I'd keep it on the hush until I found out what the deal really was. 'And if Gucci is in on it!' I thought, positive that I'd have no other choice but to lay my guy down. Betrayal could only be avenged with murder in the streets that I'd grown up running.

"Yeah," Gucci replied, sitting next to me on an old termite invested bench. The stench of Chico's slain body still filled the room. He was Tutsi's responsibility. He'd already dug a hole to lay him in, but we were waiting until nightfall, which would come right before we rolled out.

"Drake, man...." Gucci sighed, letting me know that he was uneasy with what we were about to put down too. My nerves had settled earlier, but Rocsi's telephone call had changed shit up. Now I was apprehensive about the whole gig. 'All this cake mix is driving muthafuckaz crazy!' I thought, wanting to tell Gucci about what was going on. But can I trust him? Is he in on this shit? It was too confusing, so I stood on keeping Hashes' treachery to myself. 'Fuck it! I'm out,' I thought, giving Gucci dap while standing up.

"I gotta stop by the house before we ride out," I said to Gucci, before looking over to Tutsi as he finished inspecting the bikes. "Check the frame on those rockets too, Tutsi." He gave me a thumbs up and I rolled out. I'd wasted enough time small talking with the team. I had to make another move that might cause a war amongst thieves if the honor has been breached.

CHAPTER 28

Rocsi lay beside Khalid, nestling against his warm body; him unaware of what she'd been planning for him. Ship's service revolver was tucked beneath the mattress. Rocsi was awaiting the right time to make her move. She felt the bulge in his crotch rise, a sleep-filled erection because he'd made it known that he wasn't interested in her sexually. Rocsi rubbed her thigh against him. "Mmmmm," Khalid moaned. "Yeah, baby boo," he said in a panted whisper.

'Oh yeah,' Rocsi thought, guessing that Khalid was interested in getting some head. She'd done everything else trying to bring the man out of him. Now all of a sudden, he was ready. 'Maybe he's one of those freaky motherfuckers...?' she wondered, thinking he could be into fetishes, still wanting to give him the benefit of the doubt. Strange as it may sound, Rocsi had grown to like Khalid – not enough to spare him because a mark was a mark, but there was just something in accusing a man of being homosexual that crossed the line. She had to keep him interested, so she ducked beneath the sheets, kissing his naked thighs, causing him to release salacious moans. Moans that usually came from women.

"Oooooooooh....yes, baby boo!" Khalid cooed, his scrotum contracting and his rod stretching as she nibbled her way up to his crown. "Yes, Krispy baby, Yesssss," he moaned.

Rocsi's nibbling stopped, lifting from beneath the thin sheets. 'This nigga's a creep!' she thought, stunned although Quan had already warned her. Khalid's eyes were closed shut. He's still asleep. She spit the taste of his testicles from her mouth, hoping he was clean because she'd tasted his semen when her tongue touched his crown. Although she'd stopped her sexual foreplay, Khalid's moans continued. He was trapped inside of a homoerotic fantasy –

one that included himself and Krispy. *Bzzzz Bzzzz* Rocsi's cell vibrated. She answered quickly, ready to get Khalid's setup over with. She'd already cleaned the barn out, taking all of the cake, leaving nothing but hay inside. Her and Quan were looking at a healthy future together once he was released.

"Hello?" Rocsi answered, knowing it was Drake because she'd blocked calls from everyone else, certain that a phone continuously vibrating would wake Khalid from his lofty night fantasy.

"I'm out front," Drake said, his voice hushed like a stranger was in earshot. "I'm ducked off in the cut, but I can see Hashes from here."

"So what's up?" Rocsi was ready to get it over with, especially after what she had just heard. Knowing that Khalid was into men was sickening to her. She wasn't a homophobe, having a few lesbian friends herself, but knowing that she'd put her lips on a fecal infested pecker was grotesque to her.

"Go ahead. Unlock the side door and flip the light switch. I'll slide in after Hashes."

"What? Ahhhh...hell nah, Drake. What if they smoke a bitch before you slide in?" Rocsi was jittery, thinking Drake might be fucking with the enemy! Rocsi walked to the front of the house, glancing through the window blinds, seeing Hashes still ducked off in the Monte. Her eyes canvassed the block, trying to see if there was something offsetting, but nothing was noticeable.

Fatso leaned upright, seeing the porch light finally turn on; he was ready to move. Gucci had blessed him, making him a major hitter in the streets, so he felt obligated to take care of this for him. 'All's I gotta do is blaze this fool and move the body into the basement,' he thought, remembering what Gucci had asked of him. Khalid had sent Fatso to the Chalmers projects, wanting to find out who had snuffed out his son, Doug, but Fatso had bonded with

Gucci unlike any that he'd ever had, including his business dealings with Khalid. 'Fuck that queer!' he thought, discreetly slipping out of the Monte.

Fatso knew about Khalid's sick sexual practices. Him and everyone else from the Made Men clique were homothugs. Ace was Fatso's cousin, the one who introduced him to the game, but the hood had taken him under. The word on the streets was that Ace had killed a cop before getting shot himself. About three weeks after the drug raid where Ace had smoked a Task Force member, he was found dead in the alley from a graze wound to the cranium. Although Ace was part of a bad stereotype, a guy who had converted into a homosexual while in prison, Fatso still admired his cousin; especially knowing that he'd let his pistol unload against the law. Everything was handled with street justice according to Fatso's principles. His cousin didn't fold when the pressure was on and neither would he.

Fatso crept around the house, peering through each window. He wanted to be precise. He'd watched a record high of homicides become murder trails and that was something that he was trying to avoid. He had always been cautious when doing a job because a lifetime behind prison bars wasn't attractive to a guy who loved the streets.

Drake watched intently as Hashes rolled out of the car, easing the door shut before scrambling toward the side of Ship's house. It was dark and the house sate in a cul-de-sac where there wasn't too much movement. That's why Drake decided to park his bike a few blocks over. He was already leathered out in all black, ready to ride down on Trey and Ship so it was easy for him to move through the dark streets undetected by anyone. He had been doing breaking and enterings since he was a juvenile and knew how to use discretion when it was needed. This was definitely one of those times.

He'd been watching from the street, seeing Rocsi's shadow when she glanced through the mini-blinds and when she unlocked the side door. 'I gotta make this right,' he thought, sure that Quan would kill him if anything happened to Rocsi. She'd been his lifeline throughout his stint, even putting the finishing touches on the caper that hey were on then.

Drake saw Hashes peeking through each window that he passed. 'What the hell is he looking for?' Drake wondered, knowing it was possible Hashes was searching for him. Everyone was on pins and needles, not knowing who to trust, hoping their instincts would warn them trouble was prevalent. "This hoe better not be tryna snake me," Drake whispered, dipping behind his house and toward the driveway that led up the door. He pulled his heat from his waist, checking it, making sure it was locked and loaded because he was going into uncharted territory; not knowing who was the sheisty one. One was already lodged into the chamber and the clip was lined with a full arsenal. 'Let's get at it!' he thought, hearing a loud gasp from Rocsi.

"Aaaah!" Rocsi yelped, standing nude, hands in the air and tits jiggling, while Fatso held his iron on her. Her bare skin shimmered, causing an erection to grow in Fatso's pants.

Fatso had a sanguinary glare in his eyes; bloodthirsty, like he's just slain ten men. 'I'm hitting that!' he thought, seeing Rocsi's flawless body just as he'd imagined. She had disrespected him, calling him a slouch at Chris Webber's ball and he'd given her something that he was usually against – mercy. But he planned to collect his debt later.

"Bitch!" Fatso barked, waving his pistol wildly. "You ain't gone yet? Get the fuck on outta here," he spat, his eyes menacing and he kept the hammer locked on Rocsi. He wasn't sure about her, thinking Khalid could have set the whole thing up, testing his loyalty. But Khalid's facial expression settled Fatso's doubt.

Khalid lay naked, his eyes wide and his flesh trembling. He was in a state of disbelief, not knowing what had taken place, changing the venue of his dream, knowing what was going down couldn't have been real life. Rocsi was standing at the foot of the bed, held hostage at gunpoint by Fatso, her hands still high in the air as she slowly moved across the floor. 'What the hell??!!' Khalid thought, wanting to leap up and slap the pork rids out of Fatso's ass.

"What's up, Fatty?" Khalid asked, leaning upward, hoping he had more clout than the burner that stared him square in the face. He'd witnessed the brutality of Fatso's hands, ordering some of it himself. Therefore, he didn't want to make any false moves that would cost him a limb or his life.

"Lay back down, fag!" Fatso smirked, thinking about how long he'd wanted to call Khalid out on his unnatural sexual tendencies. He'd known for months, ever since he'd caught Toya, the receptionist, with a half foot of strap-on up Khalid's read end. It was a sight that he'd stripped from his thoughts, never wanting to rehash that image. Rocsi's drag made Fatso grow tired and horny. Seeing her stain skin, Brazilian waxed kitten and the perfection of her ass cuff was too much for a masochistic lunatic like Fatso. He swiftly swept over to Rocsi, pulling another magnum from his beltline. WHACK The horrid sound of metal connecting with Rocsi's skull was deafening.

"Bitch!" Fatso barked, eyes glued to Rocsi's nakedness. "Doggie style....all four, hoe!" He held one pistol on Rocsi, watching her and Khalid's every move, as she spun around, obeying his demands while Fatso used his other hand to unzip his jeans.

Rocsi's thoughts were everywhere. Imma kill you, bitch! She crawled further up the bed, arching her back, making sure Fatso's rapist ass got a good view of her pulchritude. Her hand slid on the side of the bed, hearing Fatso breathing heavily as his pants fell to the floor. *Chink* His belt buckle rattled. Khalid watched, fascinated with what he saw fall from Fatso's pants. Even in peril, moments before his death, his sordid fantasies were replacing his fears.

"What do I have to pay?" Khalid begged, trying to spare Rocsi, even though she had done the unthinkable. "Come on Fatty baby. We can work this out."

BLOCCA BLOCCA

The ring of two shots hung in the air. Fatso's body stiffened, his mouth hung wide open and his eyes rolled into the back of his head. It was a look of ecstasy.

BLAH

A single shot flew from his rod, hitting Khalid between the eyes as he fell to his knees, dying.

Drake stood behind him, blocking the entrance of the room. Rocsi's naked body still in the doggie style position, face forward, not wanting to see the pour of blood that gushed out of Khalid's forehead.

"Roc?" Drake called out, her head whipping backwards toward him. "You alright?" he asked, hoping he wasn't too late. He had to hear it from Hashes' mouth that he wasn't part of the scheme before he reacted. He was sure that there had been a breach of trust within their clique, only to find out it was all love.

""Let's put it together and be out!" Drake said, knowing that the time was upon them.

CHAPTER 29

TREY

The club was packed. Women were everywhere. Wall to wall, a party filled with dimes. My mans Ship was moving on, stepping out of the game, taking another perspective on life. His hood status was impeccable in my eyes. He'd scuffled fro crumbs. Robbing and doing hand to hand crack sells until he came up with an exit strategy. 'A muhfuckin plan!' I thought, shaking my head, knowing it was time for me to make a move too.

I'd been in the streets since birth. A second generation hustler. My mother smuggled heroin around in my baby stroller. The lights sparked throughout the club floor. I watched, sure that Ship's exit from the game meant mine wasn't too far away. Hustlers had two styles of death – a life sentence in prison or a chalkline on Broadway street; neither of which I was trying to experience. Knowing that, I had to start my transition. 'It's my time too,' I chuckled, walking over to Ship as he danced with a honey complexioned chick. Look at my guy. I smiled, seeing the happiness in his face as he partied.

"Ship..." I got his attention, pulling him away from the fine hunnie that he was stepping with. He looked over to me, probably thinking I was hating, before excusing himself from the broad.

"Hey, my brother," Ship smiled, giving me a pound. "What's the word?" I'm sure he could tell that something was bothering me. We were like brothers and the streets was the household that we'd grown up in, wilding out at any given time.

"Imma be jumpin up outta here in a minute, my nigga." I took a sip from my champagne glass. Usually, I'd be bumping and grinding against some potential action for the night, but something had dampened my spirit. An emotion that I'd never experienced before, like I was losing something. It was always be and Ship.

When Chico skipped out, I was still around, ready to do whatever for the team. Even when Rocsi was showing her ass, trying to violate the law of the squad, I stood fast with my guy. 'And this nigga is leaving me stranded?' I thought, sure that what he was doing was unfair to the bond that we had created over the years.

"You're leaving?" Ship asked, surprised that I wasn't in the partying spirit. He looked from me, glancing around the club, landing his stare back on me. "With all of these groupies lurking?" he chuckled, trying to provoke a laugh, but I wasn't feeling it.

"Yeah, Imma stop at the barn and drop this load first," I lied because the business I was about to get into involved pistol play alone. 'I'm coming hoe!' I thought, an evil smirk creeping across my face. I had to avenge myself against Pops' dishonorable acts of betrayal. He'd tried to sell my life for a morsel. Mmph! After all I've done for that old muhfucka!

"What's with the smirk?" Ship asked, noticing the way my lips wisped across my face. I could have kept my mouth sealed, being persistent about having a sell to attend to, but Ship would have pinned my deceit. He'd been around me too long not to know my ways.

"I can't live with what Pops did, fam..." I sighed, keeping it one hundred with Ship because I would still need his connects if shit got funky. "So I gotta handle up."

"In Armani?" Ship asked, not questioning why I wanted to react so soon. He'd retired from the streets, but the hood was still embedded in him. He knew that disrespect couldn't go unchecked or it would continue. 'Something that I can't have,' I thought, shaking my head before answering Ship's question

"Nah, my nigga," I chuckled, for the first time feeling better on my way out than I did on my way in. "Imma stop by the apartment and suit up. You know, in case shit gets raggedy." We both laughed, certain that smoking Pops and Pat would be a walk in the park. Pat was the real gangster in their relationship. She had put holes through the Colombian who had made an attempt on her life looking for kilos of coke that my team had stolen. That was a major lick; hitting that truck had changed my life. 'I'm a fucking millionaire!' I thought, certain that I'd done what every hustler in the game aspired to do – get paid!

"Let me walk you out..." Ship chuckled. "You never know...one of these fools might get thirsty and try a jack move. I saw what you've done to the H2." He smiled, giving me a head nod, gesturing his admiration of my style. I'd waited years to ball out like I was able to do now, knowing that money wasn't a setback for me any longer. I could cop whatever I desired and the tricked out H2 was just a start!

"Yeah I did my thing with that joint. Custom sploaters and the whole nine." We walked out, me still holding my champagne, Ship signaling a few patrolmen to follow us.
WHAT THE FUCK??!!!!!!

GUCCI
I blew through the Detroit city streets, letting the cool fall air sweep through my helmet lens breezing across my face. The Vance and Hines pipes on my Hayabusa purred like ferocious jungle kitten. The dark streets ere reminiscent of an 'I Am Legend' scene, the movie in which Will Smith starred alone. The animals were all that was missing because the hypes were out, scouting the deserted streets looking for a soldier to cop stones from. I slid up St. Jean, taking a quick glance at the eleventh precinct before hooking a right on Jefferson.

A few hoopties cluttered the parking curbs aligning the streets, decorating old dilapidated mom and pop shops that head been closed for business since the riots. 'This shit is getting real!' I thought, passing through the desolate streets in a haze. At a hundred miles an hour, everything seemed small. My bag sat snugly nestled inside of my seat net and my tinted visor hid the content of my eyes. I'd blown a Swisher full of Kush, leaving my emotions and body numb to what was about to go down. I was ready for the fall.

"Slow up before we swing the corner," I heard Drake's voice burst through my chatter box. Peeking into my sideview mirror, I saw a set of lights whip behind me. Always ride in two's. I thought about what Quan had told us when he turned us on to riding. Paralleling the lights made drivers think a car was approaching them instead of a motorcycle. Right on time, baby! The lights separated and Drake's CBR blazed up on me. I slowed, letting him pass me and I took his place, paralleling with Tutsi's Ducati.

Tutsi swiftly glanced over to me and nodded, letting me know that everything was set to go. The hit would be made and we would be a distant thought in the fleecing wind. Hustling had become too complicated and less productive, so I was changing lanes.

"You ready, Gucci?" Tutsi asked, his calloused voice spoke into my ear. I nodded, answering without hesitation.

"Hell yeah, my nigga!" I watched as Drake swung the corner, easing his Mac 10 from beneath his jacket, his shoulder strap blew in the wind. Me and Tutsi followed suit, reaching for our tools: mines a calico and his two grenades.

The club hadn't quite let out yet, but niggaz were doing what they did on a Friday night – parking lot pimping to the fullest. Some of the illest whips were out front. Jaguars, Mercedes and an inked up H2 Hummer, which was the truck we were looking for. The H2 was wet as a water moccasin. A custom joint that set high on 30 inch sploaters, those rims that spun and floated at the same time. 'That's it!' I thought, knowing the truck couldn't be mistaken because Drake had staked Trey's crib out before he left, making sure he was driving the Hummer. 'Yeah, clown ass nigga!' I thought, knowing that what Trey was about to get was certified street justice for all of the dirt that he'd done to hustlers. My finger was clutched tight around the trigger as I hit the corner behind Drake, leaning hard, knees low enough to scrape the gravel. Blah..tah..tah..tah!

The sound of Drake's Mac spitting fire was music to my ears. I held the handle bars of my bike stiff and peppered the scene with my calico. Brack..cack..cack..cack... Drake had already riddled Trey Pack's body with slugs, but mines and Tutsi's jobs weren't done. We were the clean up team. Drake hit them both with the gas and we hit them with the flame. The lead flying from my heat melted the windows of police cruisers sitting out front of the club, slumping an officer that sat inside. Ship rolled beside a squad car and burst off a few rounds from his police issued heat, making me laugh.

"I thought they used automatics nowadays!" I joked with the fellas before spraying the area with an arsenal of rounds. I heard two explosions immediately after I passed, assuring me that Tutsi had ended what we'd started – a muthafuckin war! We all zipped off into different directions, leaving Trey dead and Ship wondering who and what had hit them. But most of all – knowing we were about to eat!

DRAKE
'We did it!' I thought arrogantly, pulling the throttle back, letting the exhaust CBR flutter, knowing that this would be it's last ride. The traffic was minimal on the streets. No one walked around except for the crack-fiend zombies. They had died off to a minimum, some resting; their habits laying dormant until they committed their next come up felony, but the game wasn't dead.

"Hmmph!" I grunted, certain the slugs that I'd filled Trey's body with had sent him back to his quintessence. The coldest hit in Detroit history because the prince of the city was a dead man. And it was all from the heat that I'd sprayed!

I pulled into the back yard of our safe house, lifting the garage door and pushing the CBR inside before closing it. I didn't notice any trail marks out front which assured me that I was the first to arrive at the meet up spot. "Sorry baby." I rubbed the side of my bike, knowing that it would never see the road again. We'd been through a lot together, but this was the end of our journey. I flipped the kickstand down and walked over to the toolbox. It was time to strip her down. Skinning the bikes was part of our getaway strategy. It was the only thing to do. 'Ain't no way I'd still feel comfortable on this muthafucka!' I thought, dropping the fiberglass off of the frame. I whipped my head toward the door of the garage, ready to grab my heat before realizing that the fellas had to meet me. That must be Gucc, I assumed because Tutsi was the worst rider of us all. My nerves settling after hearing the sound of gravel popping, know that it was only the sound of one of my guys.

Tutsi was a nigga who Gucci had brought into our fold. Before he came along, it was me, Gucci and Quan. But circumstances made us trust him. Tutsi was a triple black muthafucka with purplish lips. Not from smoking because he wouldn't touch the ganja! He was from Sierra Leone – a wartorn African country, where the bloodthirsty diamond trade had caused the death of a whole civilization.

After the cease fire agreement of 1999, Tutsi was granted citizenship for his work with UNICEF. He'd helped them navigate through the heavily violent terrain of Zimi and other parts of Sierra Leone. What they didn't know is that he'd participated in the mass killings. He'd been reared as a child warrior from an early age, bred to destroy shit. He'd tell us stories about a team back home – the Kill Man No Blood Unit or KMNBU – that he'd been a part of. Describing brutality in a way that only a monster could think of.

Their clique was assigned to raid villages, assassinating the villagers without causing any bloodshed. Entailing graphic shit that was so savage it seemed impossible.

I walked to the door and chuckled. "Ain't this some shit!" I said, lifting the door, letting him push his bike inside. I'd been waiting to see Gucci, ready to gloat about me being the first to reach our meeting spot once again. 'Fuck it!' I thought still chuckling. Tutsi's black ass will do! I glanced over to him, ready to talk shit, but his demeanor was low. I peered throughout the vicinity before closing the garage door. It was evident that something had went wrong and I wanted to make sure we weren't having any unwanted company.

"What the hell happened?!!" I asked, my voice high-pitched with worry because we'd done could end with a death sentence for us. 'Shit!' I thought, sure that whatever it was, it had something to do with Gucci. He was like a brother to me, so I prepared myself for a deep cut.

"Brotha," Tutsi began, his deep hardened voice was solemn. "I saw the law get behind Gucc and his bike went down." He shook his head, thinking the worst had taken place. 'Hell nah!' I thought, hoping Gucci's last breath wasn't blown as he lay across the cold blacktop of the Detroit city streets. 'Hell nah!' I thought, wanting to blame Tutsi for Gucci's fall, but knowing it was no one's fault. At least, not any of us because we had executed the plan to a science.

"Fuck it!" I barked, tapping Tutsi on his shoulder, signaling him to follow me outside. "We goin to get him!" From the corner of my eye, I saw Tutsi glance over to me. Say it, bitch ass nigga! I warranted a cowardly response from him. I still had my four fif tucked handily in my belt and I wouldn't hesitate to use it. Gucci's my mans, but Tutsi was just a nigga I met along the way which made him expendable. Shockingly, though, something that rarely happened with Tutsi took place – he smiled, flashing all thirty-two of the gold rocks lining his gums.

"I was waiting on the call, but it had to come from the head," Tutsi replied, pulling his heat from his back and cocking it. *Click Clack* The sound of metal grinding together filled the yard as we walked toward the Suburban. We were using the truck to flee the city with the bike parts, but the plan had changed.

"I got more heat in the truck," I assured him as we cascaded through the yard. I'd known Tutsi for a while, but at that moment I realized that I'd picked up a new comrade. I had three mans now: Gucci, Quan and Tutsi. If one eat, we all eat. And if one leak, we all leak. Me and my mans, Tutsi, leaped into the Suburban and peeled out of the alleyway. We were on a mission. No man left behind!

I slowed to a cruise, seeing the lights ahead. Five 0 was everywhere. 'Damn!' I thought, unable to see anything through the blaring red and blue flashes. The nightclub had been evacuated and the scene was chaotic. News reporters filled the area, unaware that their lives were in imminent danger because I wasn't leaving without Gucci. Even if that means more gunplay.

"So what's next?" Tutsi asked, obviously ready to go in blazing heat, but I wanted to be sure it was worth it. 'This shit is wild,' I thought, sighing. For the first time, I wondered if Gucci was dead. Tutsi had seen his bike go down, not knowing whether he was killed or captured; only that he'd laid his cycle down.

"Let's park. Bring a strap though, because jail ain't an option tonight." I was serious as terminal cancer because there wasn't a chance that I'd lay down for a pig. I still had my split of the coke that we'd taken from Ship's car wash. Ninety kilos all to the good because I hadn't spent a dime for them. Rocsi had taken Quan's share, and Tutsi had stashed his with Gucci. Five hundred to split, ninety a piece and fifty as a donation to the hood. 'Fuck that shit!' I thought, grabbing a Berretta 9mm and leaping out of the truck. I had to make it back because I'd put in too much work not to enjoy the fruits of my labor.

"Let's split up," Tutsi encouraged, wanting to take different sides of the streets just in case we needed a shot from two angles. There were at least sixty officers out patrolling the streets so it was evident that we were outnumbered.

"Aight, my nigga," I gave Tutsi dap, our eyes never meeting. I stared toward the lights because I didn't want him to see my discouragement. I watched as he jogged across Jefferson. I walked around back near the rear entrance to the General Motors building, about a quarter mile from where Gucci's bike had went down. I trekked up the block, discreetly ducking through the car filled parking lots, nervous, not knowing what to wish for. 'What if Gucc is in a squad car?' I wondered, knowing I'd have to make an attempt to rescue him.

"If one eat, we all eat. If one leak, we all leak," I said to myself, closing in on the taped off area. Blocca Blocca I heard two shots ring out followed by an arsenal. "Ah shit!" I spat, knowing that Tutsi had manned up, taking heat to the law and being killed in the process. I weaved between a few more cars, pulling my strap from beneath my hooded sweater, ready to knock an officer's shield off their chest. 'This some bitch ass shit!' I thought, staring at Gucci's Hayabusa splayed across the pavement in scraps and two body bags close by. I stopped, tossing my thumper into a bush and walking off. It was me against a team of licensed killers. 'I can't win!' I thought, picking up my step as I walked away, knowing that when I was faced with an awful death, I chose a good life.

EPILOGUE

Gucci lay back, lounging in the smoldering summer heat, enjoying the good life. Georgia was nothing like Detroit. All hip and no hop, but he still felt the vibe.

"Hey, babe?" Gucci called, watching as his woman acknowledged him, swinging her hips from side to side as she swayed towards him. 'Mmm mm mmm!" he thought, still captivated by her sexuality. In Gucci's world, there was nothing more alluring than a woman's saunter. It's that walk! He palmed his crotch, making sure she recognized the torture that she was putting him through. Having a fine ass woman prancing around all day, knowing that he could not have her because she was having a burdened pregnancy was rough, especially one as sensual as his. She knows what the fuck she's doing!

"Whatcha need, Gucci?" Pat asked, leaning over to him, making sure he caught a glimpse of her tits. 'I know...I know,' she thought, teasing Gucci with a soft kiss on his bare chest before sitting on his lap, nestling in the lawn chair with him. Pat sighed, looking around their spacious country estate: four bedrooms, three bathrooms and an in-ground swimming pool. Life had looked up for them since they had slipped out of Detroit. That night was chaotic.

Gucci heard the sound of Drake's Mac 10 blah...tah...tah...tah. He clutched his handlebars, leaning hard as he succeeded his mans, slinging a flurry of gunfire that peppered a patrol car. The officer that was inside slumped over behind the steering wheel. He saw Ship roll beside another police cruiser and let off a few rounds. Blah...blah....blah

"I thought they used automatics nowadays!" Gucci joked, laughing while spraying an arsenal of rounds into Ship's direction. He was almost certain that Ship had been hit. Blacoom..Blacoom

Two explosions followed him, letting him know that Tutsi had cleared the rest of the Task Force, so he pulled the throttle back, zipping out of sight about a quarter mile down the road. Skkkrrrrrrrr! The shrieking sound of metal scraping the asphalt was deafening. Gucci slid about thirty feet before leaping into a full sprint. 'I'm outta this muthafucka!' he thought seeing Pat driving up with the trunk already popped. Gucci hopped inside, closing the truck lid once he was in. Pat whipped off at a casual speed.

Pat had already settled her affairs, putting a hot one into Pops' back and laying him in the middle of the road, where Gucci had slid his cycle. They'd framed Pops down to the same leather that Gucci wore, knowing that the law wouldn't have any other leads.

"We eating out here in these streets, baby," Gucci said, slapping Pat across her wide ass. She liked that, how Gucci was rough with her, unlike what Pops had become. Pat was a gangster who, like Gucci, needed someone from the hood to hold her down.

"Look at them, Gucci." Pat pointed over to Tutsi. She felt his swag, evil eyed and trustworthy because he'd been there to polish the scene.

Tutsi had led Drake back tot the scene, making him believe that Gucci had went down. Gucci felt bad about running a mirage on his mans, but the game was changing. Gucci knew he had to worry about himself and Tutsi – the only man that he trusted on earth. Tutsi had saved his life, so he felt obligated.

"Yeah, I still don't trust that hoe," Gucci replied, staring at Tutsi lounging by the pool with Alcestis between his legs. He had come clean to Gucci, telling him about getting her cleaned up, but Gucci was still skeptical. He'd heard his mother always lying about leaving the smack alone, but it never happened – eventually taking her six feet beneath the earth. He'd never forgiven his mother and he'd never trust Alcestis. 'Junkie ass bitch!' He thought, turning back to his pregnant woman. Gucci smiled, wondering why Tutsi was questioning Pat's loyalty, she betrayed her husband but she was still just as down as Rocsi.

Rocsi was swift on her feet, calling Gucci to drop Chico's body off at Ship's pad. She had set the scene down to a science: taking ten kilos from everyone's cut, stashing it in the basement with Chico's battered body. She left Khalid's and Fatso's bodies in the bedroom just as they were. The news reported the killings as a lovers' quarrel, noting that Fatso had sent a hit out on Ship because of his transgressions with Khalid. Chico was later found to be the cop who had opened up the investigation, finding out about his partner, Ship's, crooked cop practices.

Everything had unfolded as planned, Gucci and his team were made men now. Drake was still running things in the Motor City, while Gucci and Tutsi were getting cash in the south. They were making a mint, dropping their bag on a team of young soldiers out of College Park. They barely knew the camp, making it easier to do business with the them because that's all there was – BUSINESS AS USUAL, Pt 2 of We Gon Eat.

SO REAL PUBLISHING, INC

www.ingramcontent.com/pod-product-compliance
Lightning Source LLC
Chambersburg PA
CBHW070601130626
46556CB00001B/240